DEMONS DO IT BETTER

A Hidden Species Novel

LOUISA MASTERS

Demons Do It Better

DEMONS DO IT BETTER

I work for Lucifer. Only, it's not as cool and satanic as it sounds.

The truth is, I'm an admin assistant who applied for a job that sounded kind of interesting and ended up working for the Community of Species Government. I'm the only human in the office, and basically I ride herd on a team of rambunctious shifters and demons.

I also spend a lot of time avoiding Gideon Bailey, the demon I had a one-night stand with right before I took this job. He hates me, and I really want to avoid being murdered. But I've been offered a promotion that will mean working with him, so we're both going to have to get over it.

Plus, people are going missing. Pregnant people. And the word is that someone is dabbling in genetic experimentation. Putting a stop to that is more important than the sexual tension Gideon and I have been ignoring... isn't it?

CAST OF CHARACTERS

Community of Species Government - CSG

Malia - God, Head of State of the Spiritual Plane
Percy Caraway (felid shifter) - the Lucifer: Head of
State of the Physical Plane

Senior Investigation Team:
Sam Tiller (human/felid shifter) - Team Admin
Gideon Bailey (demon)
Elinor Martin (hellhound)
David Carew (sorcerer)
Lily Heath (succubus)
Andrew Turner (vampire)

Alistair Smythe (hellhound) - Sam's best friend
Aidan Byrne (felid shifter) - Shifter Species Leader

CHAPTER ONE

I STARE up at the building. It looks pretty much like every other office building on the street—concrete, steel, and boring. Like the last one I worked in, and the one before that.

But this one promises to be different. The ad said so.

ADMINISTRATOR WANTED: EXCITEMENT
AND ADVENTURE GUARANTEED

It was like a golden ray of sunshine in my gray, boring day. I've been working in administration for a long time, and while jobs in my field are often advertised as "exciting" and "challenging" and "fast-paced," what that actually means is "you'll be doing the same old administrative tasks but at a company that does cool things you'll have nothing to do with" or "you'll be doing the job of two people" or "the people you'll be supporting are assholes/imbeciles/both." I've never seen the word adventure used to advertise for an admin, and I was intrigued.

And bored. Because my current job is for an "exciting" tech development company where I have the "challenge" of supporting a team of asshole marketing consultants who constantly forget to advise me of deadlines, which means I'm always working at a "fast pace." For once I'd like the fast pace to be because things are happening fast, not because some dickwad was too busy telling me to get him a coffee to remember to add that he needs a report by the end of the week.

Just so you know, he never got that coffee. I don't feel bad about it, because he didn't tell me about the report until two hours before he needed it.

So, yeah… ready for a change. And adventure sounds right up my alley. As long as I can do it from my desk or couch. Virtual adventure, that's what I want.

Which is why I'm standing here, staring at a building that's nice and close to home—about eight blocks.

Do I really want adventure? I'm not really an adventurous kind of guy. My name is Sam Tiller. I'm thirty-four years old, five foot six and a quarter, with brown hair and eyes. In my younger days, I was the twinkiest twink that ever did twink, until it became too much effort. I'd much rather order takeout and watch TV in my sweats than squeeze my balls into skinny jeans and get stepped on by some dick in a club who's too busy feeling me up to realize he's crushing my foot.

I do miss getting felt up, though.

Sighing, I stride into the building. It can't hurt to interview, right? I'm not even sure what the company—CSG—does, really. There's a generic website positively buzzing with all the right terminology, but no information on what products or services they deal in. Or with. Or manufacture. Maybe this will be an actual exciting job? Maybe there will be non-douchey people working here who can feel me up.

Outside of working hours, of course. Some lines, I don't cross.

The ride in the elevator feels endless. There are two others in here with me, and I think that's the only thing that keeps me from changing my mind. Because I don't want to be that guy who rode the elevator up and then down again for no real reason that they decide to call security on.

Been there. Not fun. Long story.

By the time the doors open on my floor, I'm ready. I've talked myself into believing this is going to be *amazing. Epic,* even.

So I march out of the elevator.

And freeze.

There are animals here. Huge dogs. Three of them. Just wandering around. Well, not exactly wandering. In fact, they seem to be walking with purpose, crossing the reception area toward a door at the far end. But… they're huge. Like… almost to my armpit. I'm not exactly tall, but still. Is this some kind of wildlife rescue? Even so, why would they have such big dogs in the corporate office?

They disappear through the door, and I shake my head and walk up to the reception desk. The receptionist is looking down as she writes something on a memo pad, and I wait—

What the fuck? Does she have…? Are those *horns* nestled in her hair?

Shit. Am I hallucinating? That's never happened to me before, but—

She looks up and sees me. Surprise flares over her

face. I suck in a deep breath and screw my eyes closed for a second, and when I open them, the horns are gone and the receptionist is smiling.

"Can I help you?" she asks sweetly.

I swallow. "Uh. Yes. I, um, have an appointment. With…" Fuck. What's his name? The dogs and the maybe-imaginary horns have thrown me off my game. What's his *name*? "Harold!"

She taps at her keyboard, then smiles at me again. "He'll be right out. Take a seat."

I cross to where the waiting area is, but don't even get the chance to sit before a big man comes in and says, "I'm Harold. Come on."

I follow him through a door and then through an open-plan office space, trying to keep up. This office is seriously weird. There are more of those huge dogs, and… is that a *tiger* standing by the window? No fucking way. It's got to be a toy of some kind.

Before I can decide if it's a giant stuffed animal or if there is indeed a wild creature in the office, Harold leads me into a small meeting room and closes the door behind me. I've barely planted my ass in a chair before he starts barking questions.

We confirm my experience.

We confirm that I have no problem working for a team rather than a single person. "You won't report to any of them," he grunts. "Officially, I'd be your boss."

"That's great," I volunteer. "It makes it easier for me to push back when their expectations are unrealistic."

He nods, and although his face doesn't change from its grumpy scowl, I get the feeling he's pleased.

Then he starts going over the job. "You'll be the administrator for a team of fifteen. Job specs will be emailed to you through an automated system, and your role will be to allocate the job to a team member based on their skills and ability. You'll act as their liaison if they have any requirements—equipment and personnel requisition and the like. And you'll help them file their reports and report their hours against each job."

This is a job I could do in my sleep. Where's the action? Where's the adventure? I'm so disappointed.

"This is not a nine-to-five, Monday-to-Friday job. You may receive job specs at odd hours or on the weekends. They need to be allocated to a team member immediately, so you'll be essentially on call 24-7. However, outside of that and answering emergency calls, it doesn't matter to us when you work, as long as all tasks are completed in a timely manner. You can set your own hours, as long as you're available to your team when they need you."

Well, that's a bit more unusual for an admin job. Not really exciting, though.

And… what the hell does this company *do*? Like, is it an emergency plumbing service? Or maybe it's an escort agency. I should ask some questions, and maybe things will become clearer.

"That—" I clear my throat. "That sounds fine. The, uh, the ad mentioned adventure. It also didn't say what kind of company this is."

For the first time, he smiles. It's more of a smirk, really. "The adventure is really more about the people you'll be working with. But don't worry, you won't be doing anything illegal. We're a government department."

I blink. "You… are?" Don't government departments usually advertise with logos and complicated recruitment processes?

"Yes. The team you'll be working with are investigators. People report unusual or potentially dangerous events, and your team investigates them and takes action if needed."

Uhhhh….

"What kind of action?" I don't think I want to work with a team of hit men, even if they are government sanctioned.

He laughs. "Not murder. Arrest. Usually that's not necessary. Mostly your team will be investigating false tips or helping people who aren't aware of the funding and programs available to them. You'll be enrolling a lot of people into educational courses."

I'm confused. A potentially dangerous event that results in someone enrolling for night school?

"So, how does it sound?"

"Great," I say honestly. I mean, aside from the whole part where I don't understand what the company does. Still, would that be so different from when I worked for KPMG?

"When could you start?"

What?

"I… You're offering me the job?" Just like that?

"If you want it." He eyes me. "There's just one more thing you'd need to know, but if you're not planning to take the job, I can't tell you."

Yeah… I'm not curious. Are you curious? Why would that make anyone curious?

I swallow hard. "Sir, this job sounds good, and I'm looking for a change, even if it just ends up being more of the same in a different office. But I'm really worried about what you're about to tell me."

He smirks again. "I like you. If you don't freak out, you could go far at CSG."

If I don't freak out…? That doesn't inspire confidence. "Freak out?" I ask, and my voice doesn't even squeak. "Uh, and what does CSG even stand for?"

He braces his elbows on the table and leans forward. I lean forward too, because it feels like I should.

"Are you religious?"

I sit back. If this is some kind of cult— No, wait, he said it's a government agency.

"Not really," I say warily. "I mean, I was technically raised Catholic, but my family was always Christmas-and-Easter kind of Catholic, and the church and I parted ways when I was a teenager anyway." When I realized I was gay, but he doesn't need to know that.

"Good. So you know the doctrine?"

It's my turn to laugh. "Yeah, I know the doctrine. The only decent school in our neighborhood was a Catholic one, so my parents sent me there." It was actually the closest school to us, and they sent me there so I could walk and they didn't have to spend any time driving me. But he doesn't need to know that.

"Not much of it's true."

This is getting super weird. "Yeah, I figured." Is this still part of the job interview, or is he working a personal agenda? Maybe trying to recruit me to his religion?

"When I said earlier that we were a government department, you didn't ask which government."

The breath freezes in my lungs. Fuck. Fuck. Is he a foreign agent? Am I being recruited to betray my country?

Why me?

I mean… seriously. Why me? I'm an admin assistant with no social life.

"I didn't think I had to," I croak, and he smirks again.

"Relax, kid. We're operating here with the full knowledge and permission of the US government. Well… those who need to know, anyway. You wouldn't be doing anything illegal."

Why doesn't that make me feel better?

My head is starting to spin. This is… I should have known an "adventurous" admin job was an oxymoron. This has to be some sort of practical joke. Maybe one of those weird reality TV shows?

I stand. "Thanks for seeing me today, but I think I'll be going now."

Harold opens his mouth to say something, but I'm already turning toward the door. Two long steps and I wrench it open, my gaze skimming across the open-plan office as I step out and half turn to close the door—

Fuck.

Me.

I freeze. Literally. I can't move. I can't even look away. My gaze is locked on the man standing about fifteen feet away—where one of those big dogs was just a second ago.

I'm not insane. I'm not. I'm not hallucinating. I'm not.

But… where did the dog go? And where did the man come from?

A hand clamps firmly on my shoulder, and Harold steers me back into the meeting room and sits me down. He leans on the table and looks me in the eye.

"We're not human. Species you might call paranormal are real. We have our own government—the Community of Species Government. CSG. And the investigative team you'd be part of works to find people who don't know they're not human and help them assimilate with our society."

I blink. My jaw is still dropped. I'm pretty sure I look unevolved right now, but... did I just see a dog turn into a man?

"What?" Crap, can Harold turn into a dog?

He sighs and sits down. "Are you okay? Do you need a glass of water?"

I screw my eyes shut and take a deep breath. When I open them again, I'm... calm. Calmer than I've been for a long time.

"Explain this to me. What's the connection to religion?" Because he wouldn't have fumbled around with that if it wasn't important.

He smiles, a real one this time, looking pleased that I've put those two facts together. "God is real," he declares, "but he's not some omnipotent being, and not much of that crap in the bible is true."

"Okay." I wait.

"One thing you humans got right is that god is a title, not a name. It's even true that there's only one god... at a time. God is the head of state of the spiritual plane. The current god is named Malia."

Wow. God is a woman. *Take that and choke on it, you patriarchal fucks.*

"Is it... an elected or hereditary position?" I ask faintly, and he nods at me approvingly.

"Neither. It's... so, magic is real, right?"

"Uh... right." Holy fuck.

"God is a magically selected position. We've been studying the process for a long time, but we're still not sure how. It just seems that the person best suited to the role at a particular time is invested with the power."

Wait…

"So there's no set term of… godhood?" I'm fascinated despite myself.

Harold shakes his head. "Nope. We've had our current god for about fifteen hundred years, but there have been gods who only served for a few years. The longest-serving god was— I'm getting off-topic. If you really want to know this, there are some resources I can point you to."

I nod. I mean, what else can I do?

"So, god is the head of state of the spiritual plane."

He said that before. What does it mean? "Like… an afterlife?"

He shrugs. "Yes and no. It's a noncorporeal dimension. If you're a being that doesn't need a physical body, you don't have to die to go there."

Can of worms, open. I keep my mouth shut to hold in the million questions that want to burst out.

"But most species can't go unless they've shed their physical bodies, so yeah, afterlife works. Or pre-life, since that's where you'd be before you applied for another stint in a physical body."

"So reincarnation is real."

He rolls his eyes. "Of course. An eternal soul is too valuable to waste on a single physical life, and then… what? Sitting around admiring oneself? I don't know about you, but I'd be bored in a heartbeat. This is my ninth stint on the physical plane. I only last for so long before I start wanting the physical stuff again—food.

Sex. Even taking a dump can feel real good, you know what I mean?"

I nod. Because I do. And also because I don't know what else to do. Reincarnated because you miss… shitting? Sure. Why not.

I feel like we might be getting off track again.

"So why don't humans know about any of this?" I mean… surely there should be rumors?

Harold huffs. "Hold on, I'll get to that. Right, so god in charge of spiritual plane. Now, magic never intended for the *physical* plane to be split up and governed like this. It invests a leader here, too."

I turn that over in my mind. "A god of earth?"

"Not quite. God is the title given to the leader of the spiritual plane. The leader of the physical plane is called—"

It clicks. "The devil?"

"Close. Lucifer. The 'devil' is a human construct. The current lucifer is a real easygoing guy, likes to rollerblade and do jigsaw puzzles. Now, about eighty-seven hundred years ago or so, there was this human clan leader here on Earth. I forget where exactly. Anyway, this little upstart clan leader broke a treaty or something, and the lucifer at the time was forced to sanction him. He didn't like that, and being a dickweasel of the highest order, he started some rumors about how the lucifer had been sent to Earth in disgrace, barred from the spiritual plane. Some other folks who were kind of power hungry and didn't like that the lucifer wouldn't let them invade their neighbors jumped all over it, and it snowballed from there. Within a hundred years, humanity was convinced that the lucifer was an evil being whose purpose was to tempt them into giving up their souls. What would anyone even do with their souls? It's not like a physical body can use more than one, and slavery is impossible on the spiritual plane, so…"

Is it just me, or has Harold gotten really chatty? What happened to the gruff guy who barely looked at me during the interview?

"So the devil doesn't want our souls," I manage, and he looks at me like I'm stupid.

"There is no devil. But yeah, souls not wanted. Anyway, things got kind of ugly then with the species wars."

I'm so glad I'm sitting down. "The species wars."

He nods. "Basically, humans against everyone else. It didn't start out that way. There were some sub-groups within other species that thought overthrowing the lucifer would be a great way to further their own gain." He stops, seems to think about it. "Only the humans really believed that the lucifer was 'the devil.' None of the other species fell for that crap. I wonder why?"

Is he… expecting me to answer him? Because I don't know.

He shakes his head. "Anyway, the species wars started out kind of like an all-out brawl, but then the humans started bringing their religions into it and declaring that all other species were abominations and tools of 'the devil,' so after a hundred or so years, it was just humans against the rest of us as we struggled to survive."

Fuck me. Sometimes I'm really ashamed of humanity.

"I feel like I'm missing something. Didn't you outnumber us—I mean, humans? If all the species banded together. So why aren't things the way they're… supposed to be?"

His smile is sad. "Actually, humans outnumbered us. As a rule, every other high-intelligence species lives longer than humans, but as a balance, we find it harder to conceive, and thus our numbers are fewer."

Yeah. That sounds about right.

"Things were getting dire, but in the end, magic itself provided the solution. One day, everything went dark, darker than the darkest night, and when the light came back, a new lucifer had been invested and humans had forgotten us."

"*Forgotten?*"

He shrugs. "I wasn't there. This is just what I've been told. Our history shows that all our species were granted a small amount of inner magic that day, even those who'd never had it before, to help us hide in plain sight. But it didn't seem that the humans were even look-ing. And to this day, there have been thousands of times when the truth could have come out—during archaeo-logical excavation, for one—but somehow never does."

"That's why her horns disappeared!" I realize. Yeah, the idea of *all of history* being a lie we just never noticed is huge, but I'm mostly relieved to know I wasn't hallu-cinating.

"Whose?"

I explain, and he nods. "Yeah. This is generally a safe place for us, so we tend to let the glamor go. I forgot to tell everyone there would be a human visiting."

Which raises an important question. "Uh, Harold… why me? I mean… why hire a human? This isn't exactly a job that only I can do. And if you hired someone else, you wouldn't have to explain all this to me."

His gaze slides away.

Uh-oh.

"Harold?"

"Look." He chuckles nervously. "It's not a big deal. I just thought hiring a human might make for a nice change."

Can anyone else smell the bullshit? Because it sure is thick.

I don't say anything, just stare at him, and eventually he gives in.

"So, this is where the adventure comes in. The team you'd be assigned to… they're good people. They're just… well, they're mostly hellhounds. We generally try not to assign too many hellhounds to the same team, because they can be a bit much in groups. Rambunctious. I'm not sure how this lot all ended up together, but now we can't separate them."

"*Rambunctious?* Like toddlers?" I ask incredulously. "What do you mean, you can't separate them?" I remind myself again that I actually saw a dog turn into a man, that this isn't a joke. It's not.

"They won't allow it." He grins suddenly. "I should say *we* won't allow it."

Huh? Oh.

"You're a hellhound? Hey, if the devil isn't real, then hell isn't either. So why that name?"

He rolls his eyes. "Humans were using it as a slur back during the wars, calling us the minions of the devil and all that crap that meant nothing to anyone but them. The species leader at the time had a twisted sense of humor, so she officially changed our subspecies name to mess with them."

What.

The.

Fuck.

"She… changed your species name… because she thought it was funny? And it stuck?"

"Sure." He shrugs. "It *is* kind of funny, you gotta admit."

I don't want to tell him that I don't get the joke. I am, however, beginning to understand why hellhounds might be referred to as rambunctious.

I swallow hard. I wanted a change. A challenge. But dealing with colleagues who seemingly have driven off all my predecessors?

"I'm hoping that by hiring a human, I can convince them to be on their best behavior," Harold rushes on. "And I think you can handle them."

"What did they do to drive away everyone else?" Knowledge is power, right?

"Nothing bad," he hastens to assure me. "Mostly they just got too clingy. Most of the administrators before you had families who objected to always having a hellhound pop in. We tried hiring a few single people, but as a species, hellhounds tend to be overprotective and nosy, so two of them quit when their dating lives took a turn for the worse, and the third couldn't handle their constant need for attention and reassurance."

Hellhounds sound a lot like golden retrievers.

I rub my face and think about it. I really need a change. And, canine colleagues aside, this job is perfect for me. But I don't know….

"What happens if they drive me nuts too and I want to quit?"

Harold shrugs. "You quit. And I seriously consider killing the lot of them for putting me through another round of recruitment, especially since I have no idea what I could possibly do next."

Great. I'm the scrapings at the bottom of the barrel.

"No, I mean… I'm human. And now I know about"—I wave my hand—"all of you."

"Oh. Well, you tell me… what would happen if you tried to tell people?"

Realization hits.

"Exactly. Nobody would believe you except a bunch of nutjob conspiracy theorists. You could take video of your team members shifting, and you'd just be accused of doctoring it."

"So you'd just let me quit."

"Yeah. I'd be pissed, because I had to get special permission to even interview you to begin with, but if you wanted to quit, that's up to you."

I bite my lip.

He studies me.

I nod. "I'm in."

CHAPTER TWO

"I'M *IN*?" I groan. "What the hell was I thinking?" The bartender casts me a wary look. I don't blame her—I've been sitting here muttering into my drink for the past half hour.

I got halfway home—so not far at all—before it really sank in that I've just signed on to work for an interspecies government body and I began to freak out. I'm actually really proud that I kept it together that long. I was perfectly calm when Harold gave me a two-line overview of each species—two subspecies of shifters, vampires, demons, succubae and incubi, and sorcerers —and then directed me to a series of web archives where I can do more research so I won't make any huge social blunders.

I was even calm when he gave me such tips as "don't wear heavy cologne around shifters" and "don't ask a demon their middle name." Things got a little shaky with "never rub your throat around a vampire unless you're inviting a bite," but I pulled it together for "if an incubus or succubus invites you for a hookup, set ground rules from the outset, because once you start, you'll forget everything else." That last one was even kind of intriguing.

So I don't know why the panic suddenly hit on the way home. It seemed like the best solution would be to sit down and have a drink to calm my nerves, and fortunately, this bar was only steps away. I've been here before—it's nice and close to my place, as I said, so it's a good place to meet up with Grindr dates while I decide if they're safe to take home or not—but I wouldn't call myself a regular.

The dilemma I'm facing now is whether or not to call Harold and say thanks, but no thanks. I feel stupid even considering it, because isn't this what I wanted? A change from my everyday boring existence? The job itself is something I can do with my eyes closed and my hands tied behind my back (metaphorically), and the money Harold offered is amazing—so much better than my current job. Plus, it would be a new environment, with lots of exciting and interesting things to learn and see.

On the other hand, I'd be working in an office with *vampires* and *hellhounds*. Let's not even get into the whole demon thing. If the devil's not real, demons can't be his minions, but it's still a word that conjures up some negative images for this poor human. And Harold's warning about the hellhounds on my team being "rambunctious" is worrying me more and more.

I sigh and thunk my head down on the bar a few times. Maybe shaking up my brain will help me make a deci—

My forehead hits flesh.

I jerk back so suddenly that I fall backward off my barstool. Arms windmilling, I wonder how much it's going to hurt when I hit the ground, but in the next second, someone grabs me by the shirt and hauls me back onto the stool.

I collapse onto the bar, panting a little from the adrenaline rush.

"Sorry. I didn't mean to scare you."

Straightening, I turn my head to look at the man beside me—my rescuer and also the reason I needed rescuing.

I have to look up a long way. This guy is *big*. I mean… a lot of people are tall compared to me, but the stranger beside me is inches over six feet and *built*. Wide shoulders. Broad chest. And muscle everywhere. He's a fucking tank.

I tear my eyes away from that impressive torso to take in the rest of him, which is just as impressive. His face is beautifully symmetrical and his skin a gorgeous bronze. Deep-set dark eyes. Blue-black hair that's just long enough for me to tell it's silky-looking. I'd say this guy should be in magazines, but honestly, I'm not sure whether I should cringe away or not—he saved me from falling, but either he's pissed off or he has the worst case of resting bitch face I've ever seen. He's all scowly and glowery, and paired with his size and physique, it makes him one motherfucking scary bastard.

"Uh, it's fine."

"I just didn't think you should do permanent damage to that pretty face."

Ding. Was that my gaydar pinging? I check him out again. He's still ginormous, and yep, still scary as fuck, but there's something in his dark eyes and the way he's leaning against the bar beside me, body language completely open, that makes me think he's not actually preparing to murder me.

And in that case…

"That's so sweet of you," I murmur, turning toward him and smiling. A distraction could be just what I need right now. Something to clear the mind. Invigorate the body. "Can I buy you a drink as a thank-you?"

His mouth quirks into an almost-smile, and I get a glimpse of how breathtakingly good-looking he'd be if not for the resting bitch face. Don't get me wrong—he's superhot even with the glower. In fact, something about it adds to his sexiness. But it does distract from the fact that his features are chiseled-statue perfection.

"No, but only because I was on my way over to buy you one when you decided to start beating yourself up." There's a hint of a question in his tone, along with a very faint lilt that makes me think either English isn't his first language or he was raised by non-English-speaking parents. I wave a hand.

"Work problems." It's true enough, and he doesn't need to hear the whole weird story. "Let's order, and we can decide who gets to pay later."

He slides onto the stool beside me, and the bartender is instantly there. I mean, the place isn't crowded, what with it being three o'clock on a workday afternoon, but she certainly wasn't that quick off the mark when it was just me. He ignores her flirting, though, which makes me feel a lot better. Maybe I shoot her a smug little smirk as she walks away to get our drinks. Don't judge me for being petty.

"I'm Sam," I say, offering him my hand. He encloses

it in his giant, warm one, shaking once before sliding away slowly, his fingers stroking over my palm.

Wowza.

"Gideon," he replies.

"Well, Gideon, what brings you here on a workday? Are you considering a change of career too?"

He shakes his head. "No. They'll have to pry my cold, dead corpse away from my job. But sometimes it screws with my head and I need a break to think."

"Sure." That makes sense, even if the way he phrased it came out kind of... weird. Like, serial killer weird. "Uh... there've been a lot of times I just had to get away from my colleagues before I did something I'd regret."

He snorts, tipping his head at the bartender as she brings our drinks. "Unfortunately, I think I'm the 'colleague' in this scenario. My teammates told me to take a break and get out of the office before they were forced to murder me and dance on my grave."

A laugh bursts out of me. "Were those their words, or are you paraphrasing?"

He holds up a hand as though taking an oath. "Direct quote. So I decided a walk would do us all good, and then I saw the bar, so..." He shrugs.

I lift my glass toward his. "Well, it's a lucky coincidence for me." We clink glasses, drink, and the conversation turns to me ("I got offered a job, but I'm having second thoughts"), his sister ("She quit her last job because they wouldn't buy hazelnut creamer for the break room. I still don't know why she couldn't bring her own"), music, the fact that he rarely watches TV, and whether or not it's actually bad luck to cross paths with a black cat. He's got this blunt, grumpy kind of charm that sucks me in—like, I can tell he's got very little patience and that when I'm waxing on about how fantastic *Game of Thrones* is, he really wants to tell me I'm wrong and possibly an idiot for devoting so much enthusiasm to a fictional world, but he just lets me prattle along, not quite smiling but not looking as scary as I'd bet he can.

And as we talk, we touch. It's casual. It's totally G-rated. A hand on his. A pat to my arm. I grip his knee as I lean forward to explain that black cats are *different*. He clasps my shoulders as he tells me no, they aren't. And suddenly, we're in each other's space and I no longer give a shit about cats, black or otherwise, or about the half-empty drinks on the bar—our third? Fourth?

Gideon's dark eyes are locked on my face, intense, all hint of a smile gone. His huge hands are still on my shoulders, the heat burning through my shirt, and I want so badly to feel them elsewhere, directly against my skin.

"My place is just a couple blocks from here," I whisper. I don't really want to wait that long, but honestly, I want more from him than a few minutes in a bathroom stall. I want to get my hands and mouth all over his body.

He smiles now, but it's not a happy smile. It's intense and lustful and makes a shiver go down my spine.

"Let's go."

He puts money on the bar and whisks me off my stool and toward the door before I can protest. "Thanks," I murmur as we step out onto the street, deciding to just accept gracefully. "Uh, it's this way." The workday is coming to a close—shit, I hadn't realized we'd been talking so long—and the sidewalk is more crowded than earlier. Gideon sticks close, his big hand on my back and his long length pressed mostly to my side. It's astonishing how much easier that makes it —normally, I'd have to weave through a crowd like this, but people seem to just step aside for him.

Yet another reason I'd like to be tall. Too bad I'm not likely to get any taller.

I peer up at him. "Do you work out a lot? Or are you just naturally ripped like that?" In other words, how much of a chance is there that I can attain a similar physique? I may not be able to get taller, but I could bulk up.

I ignore the laughter in the back of my head.

Gideon's blank stare makes me shake my head. "Never mind." We turn off the main thoroughfare onto a slightly quieter street. "It's just up ahead."

"Both."

I tip my head back again. "What?"

"It's both. I work out, but all the men in my family are built the same way."

Oh. I muster up a smile, trying not to think about a room full of buff, burly, insanely hot men who look like Gideon. "That's nice."

That's nice? Ugh, could I have said anything more stupid? I hurry ahead and unlock the front door to the building. Gideon's there in the next second, holding it open and ushering me in.

"Move faster," he says in a low rumble that goes right to my dick.

I do.

In fact, I don't think I've ever taken the stairs this fast before, not even the time I had food poisoning and was racing home to get to the bathroom. Gideon keeps pace easily, a hot presence egging me to go faster. I skid to a stop outside my apartment door and drop my keys.

"Fuck!"

Gideon swoops down and snatches them up. "Which one?"

"Uhhhh…" I grab it, and just moments later, we're tumbling through the door, slamming it shut, and then I'm being pushed up against it, Gideon hoisting me up with his hands on my ass and devouring me with his hot mouth.

For a second—okay, longer than that. A *lot* longer—I let myself get lost in the kiss. Lips, hands, hot, wet, tingly, hard… nothing else matters but grinding up against him and feeling him up through his clothes.

Clothes.

Fuck that. I want skin.

I break away from his mouth, just far enough to say, "Get your shirt off."

"Whatever you want," he promises, bending his head to suck my neck in a way that has my nerve endings firing and my eyes rolling back. "You too."

"Bedroom," I gasp with the last remnant of sanity. "Supplies."

His head comes up and turns away from me as he looks around. I whimper and grab his face, pulling him back for another deep, wet kiss. My legs are wrapped around his hips, and his cock jerks against mine.

"Bedroom," he says in a growly voice. "Or I do you right here against the door and fuck the consequences."

I'm not sure how, but I can tell he doesn't really mean that. Still, there's no point torturing us both. "That way. Down the hall." I wave blindly in the right direction, bracing myself to let him go long enough for us to get there.

The next thing I know, I'm moving quickly toward my bedroom. Ever been carried to bed for a good dicking? It's H-O-T. Especially when the guy carries you without any strain. I mean, I know he's huge and I'm not, but I'm still a full-grown adult. It shouldn't be effortless for him, right?

Who the fuck cares?

I tumble back onto my bed, pulling him down with me—not that I have to pull hard. This is so much better. He can use his hands now, his big, hot, strong hands….

I push him back and sit up, grabbing his shirt and yanking at the buttons. He helps, and soon both our shirts are off, then our pants and briefs, and we're naked, rubbing against each other while our hands explore. His skin is hot everywhere, almost too hot, and velvet smooth except for the hair on his chest. He's ridiculously perfect all over, like something from a men's health magazine, only pornier because of that dark body hair and hard nipples and veiny, beautiful arms. Muscles ripple in reaction to my touch, and it makes me feel incredibly powerful to know that I have this effect on him.

His dick presses against my thigh, and whoa, it's thick—thicker than any I've seen before. My hole twitches at the thought of taking it, but it's not a bad twitch. I wrap my fingers around it, and Gideon groans, the sound wrenched from his lungs.

"Please say you bottom," he breathes, one huge hand on my left ass cheek, a long, blunt-tipped finger tracing my crease.

I shiver. "Yesss."

That smile is back, the one that wouldn't be out of place on the face of a ravaging marauder. I don't know why it's such a turn-on. "Lube?"

I force myself to move away from him and scramble through my nightstand drawer for lube and condoms. I'm on PrEP, but I don't know what he—

"We don't need that," he says, tossing the condom back onto the nightstand. I guess he's on PrEP too.

He opens the lube and squeezes some out onto his thick fingers, and I lie back and bend my knees, planting my feet flat on the mattress and spreading them wide. I don't normally like fucking strangers face-to-face, but I really want to watch him when he finally lets go.

The first touch of those fingers to my hole comes moments later. He's meticulous about preparing me, stretching me gently and thoroughly. Just taking his fingers is an effort at first—it's been a while for me, and I may have mentioned a few dozen times that he's big all over. The look of concentration on his face is ridiculously endearing, and I'm just about to tell him so when he pegs my prostate and my whole body jerks.

"Ahhhh." Oh fuck, it's been waaaaay too long. It just does not feel the same doing that to myself. "I'm ready," I gasp. I want him *now*.

He hesitates.

"Now, Gideon. Fuck me!"

His fingers withdraw, my legs are flipped over his shoulders, and ohhhhhhh…

My eyes roll back in my head and I clench my teeth. The thick slide of him entering me is both incredible and uncomfortable. He must be used to that reaction, though, because he waits, all the way in me but unmoving until my muscles relax and I look up at him.

He's watching me, that resting bitch mask back in place.

"Okay?" Strain is clear in his voice.

"Amazing," I whisper. "Go. Fuck me."

He does. It's hard and fast and sweaty. I can hear myself shouting, but fucked if I know what I'm saying. All that matters is Gideon in me, on me, his body under my hands, pumping into me until every muscle in my body goes tight and my brain shuts down.

I slowly ease back to full awareness with the sensation of a hot, heavy band over my stomach. I'm lying sideways across my bed, and there's a long, warm presence beside me—Gideon. That's probably his arm over me. I should be thankful that he had the presence of mind not to collapse on top of me, because as nice as it can be to be fucked into the mattress by a big, strong body, it's less nice when that same body passes out and traps you in place.

A wicked smile teases my lips as I remember Gideon fucking me into the mattress. That man has serious skills —I wonder if he'd be up for another round?

My stomach growls, and I lift my head to look at the clock on the nightstand. Another round after we eat, maybe. I really hadn't realized how late it was—great sex clearly makes me lose all track of time.

"What are you doing?" Gideon mutters as I begin easing out from under his arm.

"Refueling for round two," I tell him, then wince. "Uh, first I'm going to clean up." I'm all sticky from coming, and it's starting to go crusty and gross.

He rolls onto his back as I get up, putting his hands behind his head and watching me. His legs are hanging over the side of the bed in a way that should look stupid, but he's just dead sexy instead. "What are we eating?" he asks, and I pull my brain away from its inspection of his eight-pack and mentally assess the contents of my kitchen.

"Takeout. Unless you want to wait for me to turn limp vegetables into soup." It wouldn't even be real soup, just veggies boiled until they got mushy. Before I discovered the wonders of recipes, I invented my own. None of them were any good.

"Takeout it is. I'll order it while you wash up." He sits up, muscles rippling in a way that makes the blood rush to my head—both of them—and looks around. "Where's my phone?"

"Uh… clothes. Floor," I manage, then make a dash for the bathroom before I ask if I can lick his abs. I'm sure he wouldn't mind, but there's no way we'll get around to eating food if we start that again.

When I come out of the bathroom after a quick wash, the bedroom is empty, but I hear Gideon's voice from the living room. He's on the phone when I get there, and looks up as I come in.

"Perfect timing. What's your address?" I give it to him, and he passes it on and then ends the call. "We're having Chinese."

"Sounds good to me," I say, walking past him toward the counter that separates the kitchen from the rest of the room. "Something to drink?"

"Water's fine."

I get him one and one for myself, and then watch as he wanders around the room while sipping. He's put pants on but hasn't bothered with a shirt, and it's absolutely no hardship to just enjoy the view in silence.

"This is a nice place," he says finally, standing by the glass slider that leads out onto my tiny balcony.

"Thanks. I, uh, couldn't really afford it on my salary, but I had an... inheritance that helped me buy it." Fucking hell, did I really need to say that? Talk about oversharing. The guy's here for a fuck, not my life story.

"What is it you do?" he asks politely. "You said you were having work problems, right?"

Well, we have to fill the time while we wait for the food somehow. I sigh. "Not problems, really. More that I'm just bored and really sick of the people at my current job. I'm an admin assistant. I had an interview today for another job, and now I've got no idea what to do."

He comes to lean against the counter, putting all that bronze skin nice and close. My fingers itch to explore. "Did the interview go badly?" He's scowling now, and while I think it's supposed to be a sympathetic and concerned expression, it's actually much closer to down-right terrifying... or would be, if I wasn't overcome by lust.

"No," I admit, "it went well. Kind of." Weird, but not bad. "They offered me the job. But it's... a completely different kind of working environment, and I'm not sure if I want it."

His face relaxes back to its usual resting bitch state, with only the softness around his eyes and a slight lip tilt to tell me that he's amused. "That sounds like cold feet, Sam. You said you're not happy with your current job. That you're bored. A completely different environment would be a change from that."

"Yeah. I'm just... uh... nervous, I guess." I can't tell him why. He'd think I'm insane. Honestly, I'm not sure that I'm *not* insane. Maybe I hallucinated everything that happened today?

He shrugs. "Change makes most people nervous. You've got to weigh up if it's worth it."

"Good point," I mutter, thinking about it. It's not like I'll be locked into this decision for life. I can always quit if I end up hating the job. And in the meantime, it would get me out of my current cesspool of a workplace and, let's face it, it sounds like it could be fun. Like something out of a movie or book. I mean… I'd be working with *hellhounds* and *vampires*. That's totally cool. "I guess I'll take it. Anything has to be better than where I am now."

"Why's that?" His eyebrow quirks up, and I find myself telling him about some of the more annoying things my colleagues have put me through. Dinner arrives, and we eat perched on the stools at the counter as Gideon matches my stories with some of his own— a colleague who refused to change his "lucky" socks and made the whole office smell vile; two coworkers who were hooking up and thought nobody knew, despite the fact that they would sneak off to a supply closet at the same time every afternoon and loudly proclaim their lust for each other. I'm still laughing at that one when I put down the empty carton of fried rice.

"You done?" he asks, and once again I get a glimpse of that not-smile that I find so damn sexy.

"All fueled up and ready to go."

———

MONDAY MORNING, I don't bother stopping to stare at the façade of the building. I don't need to. I'm not nervous *at all*. I'm going to make this job my bitch.

Having sex with Gideon was the best thing I could have done for my confidence. It blew away all the cobwebs in my brain—and other places—and has left me feeling empowered. Never again will I go that long without having sex with another person. Gideon left after a round of mutual blowjobs that had me on an endorphin high until the next morning. I'm going to remember him fondly for a long time, and not just because he gave me plenty of material for my spank bank.

So yeah, new job, I'm ready! Vampires, hellhounds, and demons, brace yourselves, because here I come!

I blow through the lobby, and what do you know, there's an elevator just waiting for me when I get there. That's a good sign, right? Yeah! I squeeze in with about a dozen other people, and for once, my head doesn't end up stuck in someone's armpit. This is the best Monday morning ever, and another sign that taking this job was the right thing to do.

I get some curious looks when I get off the elevator. Presumably the others who get off at this floor can tell I'm human and are wondering what the fuck I'm doing at CSG, even though Harold told me there are *some* humans in their community. I just smile at them confidently and make my way toward the reception desk. I'm only halfway there when Harold comes in and calls out to me.

"Good, you're on time. This way. We'll get your ID first, and then you can settle at your desk and meet the team."

The morning passes in a whirlwind of activity. I'm quite the curiosity in the office—it seems that, despite many human partners and parents existing within the community, I'm the first and only human to have gotten a job at CSG. There are stares, whispers, giggles, and from one charming fellow, a hiss.

"Did he just hiss at me?" I ask Harold. We've just left the security office, where a lovely assistant told me she'd never taken such a terrible ID photo. Didn't I want to use some glamor to smooth out the fine lines and brighten my skin?

Working here is going to be tough on the ego. Also, I take *excellent* care of my skin, fuck her very much, and it's just as bright and dewy as a twenty-five-year-old's.

If the lighting is right.

"Don't mind him," Harold declares cheerfully. "A hiss is just like a hello around here. Uh, but maybe don't go wandering around alone until people have had time to get to know you."

Great. I have no idea what species that guy was, but the chatty photographer, between insulting me, told me she was a felid shifter. Shifter, I get, but I'm kind of stuck on felid. Is that like feline?

I ask Harold.

"Sure, yep. Felids shift into cats. I told you that hell-hound wasn't our original subspecies name, right? We used to be canid shifters, but hellhound sounds way better, don't you think?"

"Uh, yeah. Of course." Never argue with a crazy man. Although it does have a certain ring to it. "So, is it like an overarching designation with several different… I don't know what word to use. Breed? Different breeds of hellhound or felid shifter?" I spent some time online on the sites that he recommended, but they mostly assume basic knowledge like this, and I really don't want to say the wrong thing and offend someone.

He stops and looks at me like I'm missing a few brain cells, so yeah, this would be the kind of thing that everyone just knows… except me. "Nah. You're thinking that we shift into a species that exists in the animal world, aren't you? It's not like some stupid werewolf thing. We're a completely different species to any existing animal species."

"Ohhhh." I nod. There goes my hope that I can research some wildlife sites and learn to understand my colleagues better. "Uh, what about… I mean, the other day, there was a tiger in the office?"

He starts moving again, leading the way toward where I'll be working. "That's Tony. Pretty lifelike, isn't he? He's the mascot for the accounting department."

The…

You know what, I'm just going to go with it. I mean, what kind of accounting department *wouldn't* have a real-looking, life-size toy tiger as a mascot?

"He's great," I manage, but Harold's laugh tells me I'm not as convincing as I'd hoped.

"Don't worry," he assures me. "You're gonna fit in great."

Yeah.

We turn a corner into another open-plan office area. Only about half the desks are occupied. There are people moving around and clustered in conversation, but even so, I'd say the office isn't full. Maybe some are doing fieldwork?

Harold leads me over to a group of desks. There are three rows of five, and about eight people are scattered throughout them. Most of them are huge. Like… way bigger than me. Even the women. One thing I did manage to ascertain from the internet is that the biggest species are hellhounds and demons, who are on average bigger than humans. Vampires, incubi and succubae, and felid shifters tend to match humans for average size. It's just my luck that my team is mostly made up of gigantic hellhounds and I'm on the lower end of average size for a human.

"Listen up," Harold barks. Not literally. "I've already told you more times than anybody wanted me to that this is your last chance. If you can't keep this admin, you won't like the steps I'll be forced to take. This is Sam. Yes, he's human. You will treat him with respect. He has a lot of experience that's going to make all your lives easier, so maybe don't be dickbags."

He turns to me and gestures to the desk we're standing beside. "This is your desk. Here are your initial log-in credentials." He reaches into his pocket and pulls out a crumpled envelope. I take it, pleased that my hand isn't shaking. Did the guy in the next row just *lick his lips and rub his stomach*? "I'll leave you to get settled in." He claps me on the back, shoots a warning look around the group, then saunters away, leaving me alone with *them*.

I smile as brightly as I can manage. I'm not going to let a bunch of adult toddlers intimidate me. After all, Harold said most of my predecessors left because the team was too needy.

"Does anyone have anything urgent they need me to do?" I ask. Someone's coming to walk me through the systems in an hour or so, but I could probably wing it. I plan to spend the time poking around and familiarizing myself with the intranet and apps anyway.

The guy who licked his lips gets up, stalks over, and leans in close to sniff me. "Looks like they brought us fresh meat." The way he says it is menacing.

I laugh.

Nobody else does.

"Uh…" I try to tone down my grin. "That was a joke, right? Good one. Definitely made me laugh." I mean, come on. Fresh meat?

Sure enough, the menacing expression fades, and the guy's lips tip up in a slow smile. "Pretty tough for a human."

"If you say so. Who are you?" I gently push him aside and seat myself at my desk, turning on my computer.

"Jim. Uh, if you have some time, I need research on old cases."

"Sure. You're going to have to show me how to access them, though."

He pulls up a chair as the rest of the team gets back to work. I'll make the rounds and meet them all in a little while and introduce them to my preferred process. It's good for them to see me being useful before I make any demands.

Jim shows me how to access old cases and run a search through them, then returns to his desk and sends me a list of what he's looking for. It's pretty easy work and a great way to settle in. I'm nearly done, and it's coming close to the time when one of the other admins is due to show me how things work, when a hush falls over the area.

I look up and see most of the people around me staring back toward the main hallway. So, of course I twist around in my seat to see what's so interesting.

My mouth drops open.

Standing in the entry from the hall, talking to another man, is Gideon.

Yep. My Gideon. The one I had an insanely hot one-night stand with just days ago. The one who basically convinced me to take this job. Did he know? I honestly can't remember if I said anything that would have given it away. I was trying to be circumspect, because who'd believe me if I started talking about going to work for nonhuman species?

Aside from a member of one of those species, of course. Because nestled in his gorgeous blue-black hair is a pair of horns.

They weren't there the other day, but even as I think it, I'm bombarded with little flashes of memory. Me, reaching up to sink my hands in his hair… and Gideon pinning my wrists to the bed. Me, grabbing his head to haul his mouth closer… and Gideon pulling back and changing our positions. I guess whatever magic is used to hide horns from sight won't stand up to touch.

Also, I fucked a demon, which is not something I ever thought I'd say. Just thinking about it sends adrenaline surging through me, and my cock twitches.

I half stand, not sure whether to go over and say hello or not. The movement attracts his attention, and he glances over at me, does a double take, and then sears me with the most frightening glare I've ever seen in my life.

I sit back down.

Gideon's resting bitch face is something I found incredibly attractive. It hid a charming, slightly blunt but mostly sweet, sexy man who, to use a cliché, rocked my world. This look, on the other hand… there's no underlying softness there. No warmth in the eyes. No micro-scopic quirk of the lips.

He clearly is not glad to see me.

I turn back around in my swivel chair, not really sure what I should do. Going to say hello is obviously not an option, but… what? Am I supposed to ignore him? Pretend we've never met? Am I going to need to see him every day? Fuck, is he on my team?

Jim rolls his chair over. "Relax. He's not gonna hurt you. Asshole is just his primary setting."

Oh, great. Other people have witnessed this moment.

"Uh…" I clear my throat. "Who, uh, who is he?" *Please don't say he's on the team, pleasepleaseplease.*

"Gideon Bailey. He's on the lucifer's senior investiga-tive team. You won't see him a lot, or anyone from that team—they work on the next floor up. He's only here now because Alistair is referring a case over to them."

"Oh. Uh, so it's not just me?" Only I could have hooked up with the office asshole and not even known it.

Jim shrugs. "Well, he's never really been shy about his opinion of humans, but he genuinely is a dick most of the time, so probably not."

Holy fuck. I hooked up with someone who doesn't like humans? How is this my life? I mean, he had to know I was human, right? Everyone else seems to.

Maybe I should find a way to talk to him. Just clear the air and make sure there aren't going to be any issues in the office. Although, not gonna lie, part of me is utterly disappointed that there's no chance we can hook up again.

I peer over my shoulder. His gaze slices into me with laser intensity, and no, nope, no fucking way does he want to talk to me. Ever. I've gotten some nasty looks in my life, but this one takes the cake, smashes it to pieces, and sweeps the remnants into the trash.

With one last contemptuous stare, he turns on his heel and walks away.

Leaving me feeling like the shit he scraped off his shoe.

CHAPTER THREE

FIVE YEARS LATER

Mostly, I love my job. It's fantastic.

Except when it sucks balls.

And not the good way, either—there's no enjoyment to be had from this kind of ball sucking. Unless you're the ginormous hellhound currently "hiding" under my dining table. He probably likes sucking his own balls.

Ugh, now I need brain bleach. I do *not* want to think about my best friend that way.

"I swear to almighty fuck, if you don't get out from under there and out of my house, I'm going to drag you to a human vet, have you castrated, and poison you with your own fucking balls!" It's an empty threat, of course, since he'd just have to shift before we got to the vet to avoid having his nuts hacked off, but I'm hoping it's suitably scary to make him come out… and get out. The worst damn thing about shifters is that the only lock they can't open is the one on their smartphones.

Seriously. Back before facial recognition, I watched a

shifter stroll through a dozen doors with heavy-duty locks on them like they weren't even there, and then spend twenty minutes trying to unlock his phone to send a text saying he was in… and fail.

I laughed a lot that day.

Not like now.

Now, I'm stuck dealing with a fucking shifter who has no understanding of boundaries. I just wanted *one night* to myself. One.

"Don't make me warn you again, Alistair," I growl, although it's a pretty pitiful effort compared to what he can do. It seems to do the trick, though, and he finally slinks out from under the table and looks up at me with a pleading puppy-dog gaze. Because, yes, hellhounds can be just as adorable as any other dog. Any dog that's nearly four feet high and looks like it's stepped out of your nightmares to eat you, that is.

I harden my heart and shake my head. "Shift and get out."

The hound whines, and then there's a… I have no idea what to call it, despite having watched it happen for years. It's not a flash of light, because there's no bright-ness. It's some sort of distortion of light, though. Anyway, a moment later, there's a six-foot-five, broad-shouldered, incredibly buff man wearing chinos and a polo shirt standing where the hound was.

Until I met Alistair, I had no idea hellhounds were so into Abercrombie and Ralph Lauren. I mean… who woulda thunk it? If someone had asked me what the human version of a hellhound would wear, I would have imagined a biker vibe. Chains and leather, yeah?

No. I made the mistake of mentioning that to Alistair once and got a diatribe on stereotyping and how hurtful it can be.

"Time to go," I declare, pointing toward the front door.

Alistair sighs and hangs his head.

"Now."

He pouts. "But, Sam——"

"No. No, no, no. Nope."

"But I'm having a terrible day and I haven't told you about it."

"For the millionth time, I *am not your therapist.*" Alistair has this idea that because I'm human, I can give advice from a different perspective. It caught on at the office, and I've somehow become their unofficial agony aunt. Hence the appearance of hellhounds, demons, and incubi on my doorstep at all times of the day and night.

He huffs, turns in the direction of the door, takes six steps, and flops down on the couch.

"I've met the most amazing man in the universe," he declares. I look around. Have I actually been talking to myself? You heard me tell him to leave, right?

"I don't care. Go home." I don't move from where I'm standing. If I give an inch, he'll take it as permission to continue.

"He's handsome, kind, intelligent, and he has the hottest little body…."

Of course, I don't actually need to give an inch for Alistair to take that mile.

"…asked me to go home with him, and I was halfway to the door, but then his boyfriend turned up and had a hissy fit. Which is why I'm here with blue balls instead of fucking the perfect man." He heaves another sigh. "Why are you humans so emotionally delicate?"

I blink. I wish I could tell you this is an unusual question, but sadly, it's not.

"Humans aren't emotionally delicate. The poor guy was about to get cheated on. What the fuck is wrong with you?"

Alistair rolls his eyes. "He just kept yelling and whining—"

"Shut up," I interrupt. "He was allowed to be upset. His boyfriend was about to cheat on him. You're ridiculously possessive; you should understand not wanting to be cheated on." I've seen him get pissy over someone borrowing a pen, for fuck's sake.

"That's not something I can ever understand. I will never be cheated on," he declares. "After all, who wouldn't do everything in their power to keep me in their life?"

"I wouldn't. In fact, why don't you leave now so I can prove it?"

He laughs. "Thanks, Sam. You always know how to make me feel better." He puts his feet on the coffee table. "What's for dinner?"

I give in and go collapse on the couch beside him. "You're not leaving, are you?"

"Nope." He turns his head and smiles at me. "If I can't have sex, you're the next best option."

Great. I grimace. "Pizza?" I can't be bothered cooking.

"Sure. I'll order it." He pulls out his phone and hands it to me, and I can't help but chuckle.

"Why don't you just use the facial recognition? I've been meaning to ask that for ages." I take the iPhone and input the code he tells me. Honestly, I have no idea how it is that shifters can't do this. It's the weirdest fucking thing. Code or fingerprint—neither will work for them. Yet they can easily use the same features to access apps once the phone has been unlocked. Luckily, the advent of facial recognition seems to have leveled the field.

"I've got it set up," he says glumly, taking it back and bringing up the app for a local pizza place. "But I don't want to use it unless it's absolutely necessary. Just in case it realizes what I'm doing and evolves to shut me out."

I open my mouth to tell him how utterly ridiculous that sounds, but then close it. Who knows? Maybe he's right. After all, it makes no sense that even if he puts in the correct code, it won't unlock.

Either way, I can't be fucked arguing about it. Instead, I turn on the TV and wonder how I got stuck having dinner with a hellhound when all I wanted was some quiet time alone.

Surprisingly—or not, really. He knows me well by now—Alistair isn't too much of a nuisance. We only argue about what to watch a few times, he doesn't snap or threaten to claw me when I reach for a second slice of pizza—although he looks a bit grim when I snag a third—and he leaves fairly early. Aside from the whole letting himself in despite the locked door and then thinking he can escape my wrath by shifting and hiding under the table, he's an okay friend.

Who am I kidding? He's the best friend I've ever had.

I lock the door, which won't stop Alistair or any of my other shifter colleagues from getting in, then put a chair in front of it, which should make enough noise if someone comes in that I'll at least wake up. You have no idea how disturbing it is to get up in the morning to find a hellhound making pancakes in the kitchen while an incubus surfs through all your cable channels and complains about the lack of options.

Fuck, I'm so glad I took that job.

I wasn't, at first. Even after that first day and the almost-confrontation with Gideon that left me feeling like garbage, I had to go through some hazing.

Have you ever found a giant stuffed dog in your shower? Or a dozen stuffed puppies in your dishwasher? Has anyone ever programmed your Google Home assistant to howl every time you asked it to do something?

Those were just a few of the welcome-to-the-team gifts from my hellhound colleagues.

Honestly, if Harold had told me before I took the job that shifters could get through locks without even trying and that they would try to get me to sign legal papers for them to adopt me, I probably would have said "no thanks" and kept looking for a different job. By the time I realized how... *intense* they really were, I was already comfortably settled. And really, it's nice to be wanted. I've been on my own for a long time. I kind of like being able to complain about how clingy my guys are.

About two years after I started working with CSG, Harold and his boss, Geoffrey, asked me to move to an emergency response team. I'm quick to action jobs, efficient, and can deal with even the most annoying agents (there's an unofficial medal amongst the admin staff. I've won it three years out of the last five). The emergency response teams are basically the first responders of the community. I politely declined. It's a higher-paid job and generally considered more prestigious, but my team kicked up a fuss that just wasn't worth dealing with.

The thing is—and this is why I wanted a night to myself—Harold and Geoffrey have asked me for a meeting tomorrow. I meet with Harold all the time and Geoffrey occasionally, but the only time I've met with both together was when they offered me that job. So... maybe they're going to offer me another one. And this time, I might be interested.

Don't get me wrong—I love my team. I'm really attached to them. But five years in the same job, even if it is interesting and exciting, is more than I've ever done before, and I'm ready for a change. There's going to be a vacancy in one of the emergency response teams starting in two weeks, and the faster pace would be a fun change.

So I wanted tonight to think it over and decide if I want to take the job—that is, if they offer it to me. I might be jumping the gun a little.

Either way, I won't know until tomorrow.

COME MIDMORNING, I'm still not sure what I want to do. Feeling a little unsettled, I leave the nearly empty team area and make my way back to the meeting room that's been allocated for my meeting with Harold and Geoffrey.

Only they're not there. Instead, the table is surrounded by six people, one of whom I've spent years avoiding.

"Oh." I freeze in the doorway. "Sorry. I-I must have

the wrong room." I glance at the number on the door again. 3.6. That's what was in the calendar invite.

"Sam Tiller?" the plain, slight man at the far end of the table asks.

"Uh… yes. Sorry, have we met?" Fuck fuck fuck. He knows my name, and he looks kind of familiar, but I'm not sure…

Except I am, because Gideon plus five other people can only mean one thing.

"Not yet." He stands and comes around the table, holding out his hand. Closer, I can see that he's a shifter, and based on his size, I'm going to guess felid. I shake his hand. "I'm Percy Caraway."

Yep. "The lucifer?" Unlike human leaders, the lucifer doesn't appear on TV. There are no photoshoots, and public appearances are rare. He's an administrator, and since he doesn't need popular support for reelection, he doesn't waste time glad-handing or promoting his image. So I've only ever seen a couple of pictures of him.

He smiles, and it's a genial, friendly smile. He's only an inch or so taller than me and has the kind of face that's nice enough to look at but is completely forgettable. "Yes. Come in and sit down." He gestures toward the table, where there are still a couple of empty chairs and one of the other people—I'm guessing a succubus, but she could be a vampire. They both have strong charisma, and unless fangs are on show, it's hard for me to tell—is getting up. She steps past me to close the door, winking.

I sit nervously. Fuck. A meeting with the lucifer? This can't be good. Maybe he never knew he had a human working (indirectly) for him and wants to fire me himself? But why would he bring his senior investigative team along for that? As bodyguards?

No, that's dumb. Five bodyguards to protect him from me is waaay beyond overkill. I've long acknowledged the fact that should there be a zombie apocalypse, I will be one of the first to die.

Zombies aren't real, by the way. Just in case you were wondering.

The lucifer smiles again. "I know this is very belated, but welcome to our community. It can't have been easy for you to get used to all of us after not knowing we existed for most of your life."

I try to smile but only manage a grimace. "Everybody was very… friendly."

One of the others laughs. "So we heard. You're a brave man, taking on a team of mostly hellhounds."

"I resemble that remark," the only other woman in the room, a hellhound (obviously) says, but she's grinning as she turns to me. "Alistair is a cousin of mine. I admire the heck out of you for being able to work with him this long."

"He's not so bad," I find myself defending. "He just needs boundaries." So he can ignore them. Alistair has mentioned this cousin, Elinor, a few times. He talks about his family all the time and seems to have a million far-flung relatives.

She snorts, and that more than anything tells me she definitely knows him personally.

"Regardless," the lucifer says, "there must have been some culture shock involved, and from all accounts you handled it like a champion. We appreciate all the work you've done to keep the community safe."

I smile uncertainly. Is this a compliment or the lead-in to a brush-off? "Thank you."

"Let me introduce you to these others." He turns to the woman on his left, Alistair's cousin. "This is Elinor Martin. David Carew, Lily Heath, Andrew Turner, and Gideon Bailey."

I force another smile and nod to acknowledge the introductions. I know who they are, of course, by name and reputation. I'm a champion lurker on the community social media sites and forums, and the lucifer's senior investigative team is a popular topic of conversation. Their job is to identify, investigate, and prevent anything that may possibly expose the community to humanity on a large scale or that might endanger the community. Technically, the lucifer heads the team himself and they report only to him, although of course he's not involved in actively investigating. They're living legends online—everybody wants to either be them or fuck them. In one forum, it's both.

I'm not here to judge.

I've actually had dealings with this team before. Kind of. In the loosest definition. Some information came up while one of my people was on an investigation that I thought warranted attention, and after asking around, I booted it to their admin. She came back to me with some questions, which I answered, and that was the whole thing. I doubt anyone would even really remember it unless they were reading case files. I certainly don't think it made me stand out as someone they need to talk to—which is the way I want it. After that little almost-scene with Gideon on my first day, I've gone out of my way to stay out of *his* way. I'm not sure what his problem is, but I don't need that kind of drama in my life.

I am, however, really fucking terrified that I, a human who knows about the community, have been called in for a meeting with the highly deadly team responsible for protecting the community from humans. Forget being fired; now I'm worried about being dead.

"It's, uh… nice to meet you all." I studiously avoid Gideon's gaze.

David, who's a sorcerer, laughs outright. "The sheer terror in your expression is making a liar of you," he… teases? Am I being teased by a man who can wrench my insides out of my body with a thought? His grin seems to indicate yes.

So I push down my fear. "I'm just, uh, a little intimidated, I guess."

"No need," Elinor says cheerfully. "We're actually here to tell you how great you are."

What?

Obviously seeing my confusion, the lucifer takes back the reins of the conversation. "We'd like for you to consider a change in job, Sam. The team needs administrative support, and we'd like to discuss the possibility of you filling the role."

Fuck me sideways.

With a cactus.

"Oh." I sound utterly inane, but I literally cannot think what to say. *C'mon, Sammy, brain on!* "That's very flattering. Thank you. Um… don't take this the wrong way, but I would have thought there are plenty of other great admins who—" Aren't human and haven't fucked Gideon. "—uh, who might suit better." I can think of three off the top of my head.

Silver hottie Andrew, who's a super old vampire but looks like he should be modeling for *GQ*, tilts his head and says in a voice that gives me tingles, "Are you not interested in the job?"

While part of me goes all melty and wants to snuggle on his lap and give him anything he asks for, the part that knows better snaps, "Stop that. That's not okay." Vampire charisma is a potent thing, and the fact that I can still think at all means he wasn't putting any real effort into it, but I still won't be coerced.

A satisfied smirk spreads across his face, and he elbows Gideon. "See. I told you he'd be a good choice, even if he is human." He turns back to me. "So, are you really not interested in the job?"

Am I? It's really a huge ego boost that they're even considering me. This is a top-level job. But… I'd have to work with Gideon. Who's been wearing his usual glower since I walked in.

"Maybe," I say cautiously. "It sounds interesting, but I'd want to know a bit more. Including why you'd consider me when there are other candidates." I don't want to say it surprises me that they'd pick a human over a member of the community, because that would be like calling them speciesist, but it's a valid consideration. My job skill set isn't that special, and as far as I'm aware, I am the *only* human currently employed by CSG.

That's not to say I'm the only human who knows about the community. There's been a certain amount of interspecies fraternizing, to put it politely, over the millennia, and if those relationships become serious, the human is invited into the community and treated as one of its own. I *am* actually unique in that I know about the community but don't have an emotional attachment to a "natural" member. Nor am I a human in a position of government power. I've met a few people over the past few years who consider me an oddity and a liability because I'm just ordinary but also have full knowledge of one of the biggest secrets ever conceived.

The lucifer shrugs. "You're excellent at your job, which means considering you is necessary, and you've proven your commitment to CSG over the years. I also feel that having a human on the team will offer a new perspective. A lot of the situations this team handles involve humans. Your opinions and input could be valuable."

There are some nods around the table. Lily winks again. At a guess, I'd say three of the five of them are on board with me joining the team. One—Andrew—seems neutral-ish but willing to be convinced.

Gideon's face is like stone.

That scares the shit out of me.

Of all members of the team, the least is known about him. He's a demon. He's a top investigator. Currently single—well, he was the last I heard, maybe about a month ago—and tends to date highly intelligent, sophisticated high achievers. His family is some big to-do amongst demons. He's scary as fuck.

And he's hot as hell.

Like, really.

Who knew it was possible to be so scared I might crap myself but also be turned on, all by the same person?

A person glowering at me.

A person who was once so sweet to me. Who fucked

me into the mattress and made me feel sexy and intelligent and intriguing.

I swallow.

"Uh, is this a decision the team has made as a whole?" I ask weakly, not looking away from Gideon. I can't; I'm afraid to. If I take my eyes off him, he might… attack?

I'm such an idiot.

I squeeze my eyes shut, and when I open them, make sure I'm looking somewhere else—specifically at Andrew elbowing Gideon again.

The lucifer clears his throat. "We voted on potential candidates," he says, and there's a thread of amusement there as he looks from me to Gideon and back. "Not everyone voted the same way, but nobody used their veto."

I must look confused, because Lily explains. "We each have the ability to veto an option when we put things to a vote. But we have to be able to justify the veto with evidence, or we lose the right next time."

I nod. Okay. So Gideon just hates me personally but doesn't have any professional reason not to want me on the team. Maybe he's antihuman. I wouldn't blame him if he was—his job is to protect the community from humans, so he's probably uncovered some nasty shit. Plus, having humanity designate his whole species as minions of evil probably doesn't help. And there's the whole thing that happened during the species wars where humans began "summoning" demons—forcing teleportation, basically—and enslaving them, and now no demon will ever share their full name. But then why hook up with me?

"We wouldn't be interviewing you if everyone on the

team wasn't willing to work with you," Elinor assures me.

There's an awkward silence.

"Why don't we talk about the job?" David suggests, and I grasp that idea gratefully.

Over the next half hour, they lay out the exact specs of what they do and how I would need to support them. I've got to admit, it's a peach of a job. Interesting, fast-paced, well-paid.... There's potential for travel too.

Honestly, there are just three things holding me back. First, I would need to leave my current team. They're a huge pain in my ass, but they're mine, and they've become family.

Second, this is a high-profile team. While the previous administrator didn't get as much attention as the investigators, there were still eyes on her. There was information about her life online, and people talked about her in the context of the team. Do I really want that? Especially since I *am* human? Will that factor add to people's interest? Will it piss them off?

And third… the scowling asshole sitting across the table.

"So what do you think?" the lucifer asks, and I look up to see six pairs of eyes fixed on me.

"I'm very interested," I admit. "I… Could I have some time to think about it? And… have you considered what the community reaction might be to having a human on the team?" I didn't really want to ask that, since it makes the community sound antihuman, but it's a valid concern.

To my surprise, Elinor crows triumphantly and holds her hand out to Andrew. "Pay up, bloodsucker! I told you he'd consider all aspects."

Andrew grumbles as he digs a twenty out of his wallet, but there's a tiny smile playing around his lips. They seem to have great team chemistry. Well, I'm not sure about Gideon, since he hasn't spoken yet. At all. Not once. Not a single comment the entire time the others were telling me about the job.

"We have considered it," David says. "There's the possibility that there will be some backlash, but we think the fact that you've worked here for so many years will weigh in your favor."

"We might have a PR rep do some careful spin, though," Lily admits, and I push down the wave of anxiety that causes. A PR rep? "Spinning" details of my life? Do I really want that?

"Tell you what," Andrew says, propping his forearms on the table and leaning forward. "We blindsided you with this, so you probably want to think about it. Plus, you don't know us, and we only know you from your employment profile. Why don't we all go out for lunch?" He glances at the lucifer. "Not you, Percy, sorry. You have that lunch with the save the vapid debutantes society or whatever."

The lucifer winces. "It's the Young Women of Society association," he corrects in a pained tone.

Lily snorts. "Not a single member is under the age of one hundred and fifty, because their aims and purpose haven't changed in about that many years. Go along now, sir, and flatter the wealthy women so they'll donate money to good causes."

As the others chuckle, the lucifer turns to me and says, "Do you see what I have to put up with?" There's a twinkle in his eye, though, that makes me think this kind of banter is normal—and that he agrees with Lily and Andrew about the… whatever they're called.

He gets up and comes around the table, and I scramble to my feet as he offers his hand. "It's been good to meet you. Lunch is on us. Spend some time getting to know these vagrants."

"Uh, thank you. It's an honor to meet you."

He saunters from the room, and I turn back to the table to find the others have all stood and are watching me with expressions ranging from sunny smiles to a dark glower—bet you can't guess who that is.

"Are you ready?" David asks.

I guess I'm going to lunch.

CHAPTER FOUR

I'm HALFWAY through my meal when I start feeling a bit… funny.

We're in the private dining room of a community restaurant, one that's apparently a regular haunt for the team. The food is definitely good, and this private room means we can talk freely without fear of being over-heard by other humans. We also get a special menu—I can tell, because I'm sure the public menu doesn't have blood-garnished dishes on it. Humans don't go in for that like vampires do.

There were some curious and odd looks when I entered the restaurant with the rest of them, and our server did a double take when he first saw me. I guess if I join the team, that's something that's going to happen for a while.

Anyway, as my head spins a little, I drop out of the conversation. I didn't eat breakfast this morning, so I probably have low blood sugar. Best to get some more food in me as quickly as possible.

I listen to the others, letting their words ebb and flow

around me. They're a fun bunch. Alistair and a few others on my current team have this same joke-y banter-y vibe, and the rest of my team balances that, but it's a bigger unit with more turnover, so it's not quite as tight-knit as what I'm seeing here. It could be good to be part of a small, close team.

We've talked a bit about their process for work, too, and I think I could fit in well with it. Plus, I do feel like it's kind of fitting that a human should be part of the team helping to protect the community from other humans.

Fit in. Fitting.

My high school English teachers would have been appalled if they'd heard me use fit in and fitting so close together.

Although… fit in and fitting are close together. It's fitting that they fit in the same thought.

I giggle.

Conversation falters.

"Sam?" David looks at me. "Are you okay?"

I nod enthusiastically, then look down at my plate. My food is nearly all gone. "There are only *two bites* left!" I announce, then giggle again.

This time I can't stop.

"What's wrong with him?" Andrew asks as Lily gets up and comes around the table. I wave a hand dismissively.

"Ow!" David jerks away, rubbing his eye where I've just smacked him.

"So sorry!" I sing. "Is this room getting smaller? Is this like some kind of weird take on *Alice in Wonderland*? I ate the food and now the room shrinks and everyone gets super close?" I drop my voice to a whisper and lean in. "I like you guys, but I don't think I want to get that close to you."

Elinor leans over and studies the remnants of my meal. "Sam, what did you order?"

I wave my hand again, and she pulls back sharply. "It was delicious! Do you think they have more? Or should I hold out for dessert? Are the desserts here good? I looooooooove sweets! I could just bathe in chocolate caramel sauce!"

"Fuck me," Andrew breathes, a delighted grin breaking across his face. "He's drunk!"

I stop my search for a menu so I can check out the desserts and think about that. I don't drink much normally, but I have been drunk a few times in my life. I think back to how it felt and then compare it to how I feel now.

Yep. I'm utterly trashed.

But… how? I've only had water.

"Did you order the spicy stew or the regular one?" Elinor demands, studying a menu that she's made appear magically. Where did it come from?

"I didn't know shifters had teleportation abilities," I tell her, awed. "I thought it was only demons, and they can only teleport things they're touching."

"We don't," she says dryly. "It is only demons. Focus, Sam. Which stew did you order?"

"Spicy, because I love spicy food. One time, Jim who's on my team brought me this meat that was soooooooo good. He said the seasoning was a secret demon recipe and I'd have to marry a demon to find out what it was."

"You can buy demon spice mix from any community grocer," David says, sounding like he's trying not to laugh. I wonder what's funny? "I'll give you a link to an online store that has it, too."

I gasp. "He *lied* to me? Why? *Why* would he *lie* to me?" I fumble in my pocket for my phone. "I'm going to call him right now and find out why he would lie about this, why he would destroy my hopes and dreams!"

"Your hopes and dreams of eating spicy food?" Lily asks dryly. "I think you should give me that." She plucks the phone from my hand.

I pout. "But, Lily, I *need* to know why he would lie to me."

"Maybe he wanted to marry you," Andrew suggests. "He was hoping you would fall in love with him because of his spice mix." He frowns. "That sounds like it should be dirty, but it isn't."

I consider that for a moment, then shake my head. "No, he's married already. And straight." I flop back dramatically in my chair, then have to grab the table to keep it from falling backward. "I can't believe he *lied*!"

"The spicy stew is simmered in shifter brew, isn't it?" a new voice asks.

A deep voice.

Rough.

Gravelly.

It sends metaphorical shivers down my spine.

I turn slowly toward Gideon, who's come to stand beside Elinor and scowl at the menu.

"You can speak!"

Everyone looks at me.

It's one of those moments of complete dumbstruck silence, all attention on me, that would normally freak me the fuck out and have my anxiety rearing its ugly head. Fortunately, drunk me doesn't give a shit, and I just widen my eyes. "He can speak! You all heard him, right? Or am I having an auditory hallucination?"

Andrew blinks. "How can you be drunk and still be able to say 'auditory hallucination'?" he demands.

"Hush," Lily tells him. "Sam, why would you think Gideon couldn't speak?"

I lean forward and beckon for her to do the same.

She does.

So does everyone else. Even Gideon.

"Because. He. *Hasn't.*" I sit back triumphantly. Then frown. "Did he say my stew was simmered in shifter brew?"

I've abstained from shifter brew ever since the first time I tried it and a few sips left me feeling tipsy. Shifter metabolism is higher than human, so brew hits humans harder—or so Alistair explained to me afterward. That's why brew even exists—shifters wanted alcohol that they could actually get drunk on without having to down ridiculous amounts in a short space of time.

Since I don't drink much normally anyway, I never saw the point in drinking something that would get me wasted faster.

I still don't.

But if the dish I ordered is simmered in brew… Yeah. That would explain it. Alistair and I once calculated shifter-to-human metabolism ratios (what? He was drunk, and I was bored. The internet was down), and the way I remember it, they metabolize about twelve times faster than humans (which is why they eat so damn much and often). Even other members of the community metabolize about five to seven times faster than humans. We're basically the slowpokes of the physical plane.

So if they cooked my stew with maybe half a glass of brew, I've basically just had the equivalent of a whole bottle of wine.

And before you start humansplaining the effect of the cooking process on alcohol, let me just tell you that brew doesn't work the same way. The alcohol content is infused by way of sorcery.

"I'm fucked," I announce.

Elinor laughs so hard I worry she's going to hurt herself.

"This was *not* our intention in taking you out for lunch," David assures me. "Maybe we'd better get some coffee in here. And more food. Something carby to soak up the brew." He picks up a roll from the breadbasket. "Eat some of this."

I take it and put it on the table. "I'd rather have cake. Is there cake? I like cake. Also, dude, you sound kind of panicky. Why are you panicky? It's just a little drunk. It'll go away." I frown. "Not looking forward to the hangover, though. Hey!" I beam up at him. "You do sorcery, right? Can't you just—" I fling out my arms and wiggle my fingers.

Everyone stares at me.

Maybe they don't get it.

I try explaining. "Can't you just sorcerize my drunk away?"

"Oh, fuck me," Gideon mutters.

I wink at him, but my eyes don't seem to be working properly, so it ends up being a blink. I quickly turn it into a triple blink so it doesn't look stupid. I'm just batting my eyes at him. I'm so good at thinking on my feet. "Just say when, cutie," I purr.

Gideon takes a big step back, a startled look on his

face. Elinor pulls out her phone. "Could you do that again?" she asks in a choked voice. "I think Alistair will want to see it."

"No video," David insists. "Uh, Sam, my sorcery doesn't work that way. I wouldn't want to permanently fuck up your metabolism or anything, so you're just going to have to deal with the hangover. Sorry."

I pout. "Boo. Is there at least cake?"

"This is gold. It's better than gold." Andrew's grinning so broadly, his fangs are on clear display. I tilt my head, staring. I've never looked so closely at a vampire's fangs before. I'm not that close to any of the vampires on my team, so it seemed rude to look.

The room seems to slide, and I realize that instead of tilting my head, I tilted my whole body, and now I'm falling off the chair.

"Whoops!" I crash to the floor, where I lie blinking, then scowl up at the faces looking down at me. "Why didn't any of you catch me?"

"We're sorry," Andrew declares, offering me a hand. "Here, you sit back in the chair, and I'll go get you some cake. And do you want company being drunk? It's no fun being the only drunk person in a room that has David in it."

"Be nice to my friend David," I tell him solemnly. "His sorcery doesn't work."

"What?" David asks while Elinor appears to choke.

"It's okay," I assure him, leaning in and lowering my voice. "I appreciate you even if you're unable to access your power. You're *powerless*. Power. Less. Power*less*. And your society would judge you for that, making you an outcast, unable to ever be seen or treated as an equal, contributing member of the community. Don't worry." I wink. "It'll be our secret. And how lucky are you, that your teammates—friends!—support you and cover for you so you can keep this secret and continue the work you love so much!" Tears prick my eyes. They're all such good people.

I sweep my arms wide, smacking David in the chest. He grunts. "All of you, so kind and generous. I will aid you in this most noble venture. We will protect David and his secret and ensure that the evil specter of societal expectation is unable to cast him down. We will dedicate our lives to this task, and when at last we all breathe our final breaths, we will know that our existence has not been in vain, for we will have allowed a brave and special man to live the life he deserved."

Silence. I look around, but they all seem to have been stunned by my eloquence and generosity of spirit. I smile at them all—my new comrades, with whom I will dedicate my life to such noble purpose.

I frown. What was it, again?

"I… what?" David asks.

David! Yes, David is the noble purpose.

"I don't even know," Andrew says.

"You should have let me record," Elinor scolds. "Then we could have played it back and maybe worked it out."

"Sam," Lily says patiently. "David's sorcery works perfectly well. It's just not the kind of sorcery that can get rid of the alcohol in your bloodstream. You'd need a different kind of sorcerer for that."

I frown. "You mean… we don't have to dedicate our lives to supporting David in all things?" I sound super disappointed, even to me, and so I hasten to add, "Yay!

So great! Because we want all the good things for you, David. Hooray!"

David coughs. "Uh, thanks, Sam. I appreciate that. And also your willingness to devote your life to me. That wasn't at all weird and disturbing."

I beam at him, because obviously he *gets me* and we're going to be the absolute best of friends. Then what Lily said sinks in a little further.

"Wait… you mean not all sorcerers can do the same things?"

Glances are exchanged. "Did nobody teach you about this?"

I shrug. "Like, not officially. I read a lot online, and my teammates mostly answer questions. But I didn't want to ask anything that might seem rude, so…" I shrug again. It's such a nice motion. It feels so good, loosens up my shoulders, so I keep doing it.

A large pair of hands clamp on my shoulders, holding them down. "Andrew, get him some coffee and cake and anything the kitchen staff can recommend to sober him up faster." The dark, gravelly voice even *sounds* demonic, or at least the way I expected demons to sound before I realized they were just some random species and not the minions of evil. The first demon I met—well, *knowingly* met—was the then-receptionist at CSG, a really sweet young woman with a gentle, lilting voice. It was kind of a letdown.

I tip my head waaaaaaay back until it smacks into Gideon's chest and I'm staring up at the underside of his chin. Nobody should look sexy from this angle, damn it.

"Hey, Gid?"

Lily stops speaking midword and gasps. I tilt my head so I can see her. "Are you okay, Lil?"

Her mouth works, but no words come out.

"She's fine," Elinor assures me. "A bit of dust stuck in her throat. Uh, Sam, Gideon prefers not to have his name shortened. So… don't call him Gid. Ever. But maybe especially when he has his hands on you."

I cackle. "Oooh, I'd like him to have his hands *all over* me."

His hands are gone so fast, I don't have time to correct the angle I was leaning at, and the chair topples. Once again, I am sprawled on the floor, looking up at the faces of my new teammates.

Because I have to join this team. They need me.

"You need me," I declare.

Andrew comes back in just in time to hear me. "Do we? I'm inclined to agree, but please, tell us why. Also, why are you on the floor?"

"Gid let me go and I fell. I have to train him so he's always there to catch me."

Andrew blinks. "You call him Gid? I'm not surprised he let you fall."

Groaning, I roll onto my side and then get up on my knees. "Does that mean you don't want me to call you Andy?"

His eyes widen in what could be horror, but I prefer to think is awed delight that someone is finally willing to bond with him this way. They should all have nicknames, really. It's how we'll show the world our affection for each other.

He swallows hard and looks at the others. I don't know what he sees, but when he comes over and holds out a hand to help me up, he says, "Can we negotiate on that?"

I dust off my knees and think about it. "Negotiate how?"

"I bring you cake, and you call me Andrew."

Ooooh.

"How much cake?" My gaze wanders to the door he came in through. "Weren't you supposed to be getting me cake? Where is it? If I can't depend on you to bring it now, how do I know you'll be able to keep up your end of the deal later?"

"It's coming; the kitchen's plating it up. And it could be cake daily. Every day. Whatever cake you like."

Now, *that's* an offer!

"Let me discuss it with my advisors," I say grandly, then turn to David and yank him closer by his shirtfront. He's not ready for it, and our heads collide.

"Owwwww!" I howl. "What the fuck? Dave, how could you?"

He rubs his forehead. "That was all on you, buddy. Was there something you wanted before you tried to permanently lower our intelligence?"

Rubbing my head where it feels like it came into contact with a brick, I pout. "It huuuuurts. Someone make it better." I glare pointedly at the only sorcerer in the group, but he shakes his head.

"Sorry. My sorcery doesn't work that way, remember? I can't even fix my own headache right now."

"Your sorcery sucks." What's the point of having sorcery if you can't use it to get rid of a headache?

"Before we get distracted again," Gideon interjects, "let's determine a game plan. There's cake coming, right?" He looks at Andrew, who nods.

"Cake, coffee, and something the chef guarantees

will help him sober up but that I wasn't allowed to ask any questions about."

My eyes go wide. "What? Are you trying to *poison* me? I thought we were besties! We were going to band together against the whole community! How could you forsake me like this?" Two fat tears trickle down my cheeks.

"Oh, hell," Elinor mutters. "Alistair never mentioned this."

"Alistair probably never got him this damn drunk," Lily counters.

"Sure he did!" I chirp, suddenly more cheerful. "But not on brew. We went out for my birthday a couple years ago and he bought me a few shots of absinthe. I don't even remember the rest of the night, but it must have been a great party, because I woke up with glitter all over me!"

"Glitter." Gideon's tone is flat. "You measure how good a night out is by the amount of *glitter*."

I blink. "Of course." Somewhere in the cloudy recesses of my mind, part of me is shouting about what a fucking pain it was to get rid of all that glitter and how the absinthe hangover lasted for days, but I blithely ignore it. Because glitter is awesome!

"We should go find some glitter!"

The door to the dining room opens, and our server wheels in a trolley covered in plates of cake, coffee cups, and a tall glass filled with a gently steaming glowing purple liquid.

"Ooohhh...." I forget the glitter when I see the glowing purple drink. "What's *that*?"

"Your cure," Andrew informs me. "I don't know that you'll want to drink it, though." He eyes it doubtfully.

"Are you kidding?! It's purple and *glows*! The only thing that could make it better would be glitter!"

Our server shoots me a disbelieving glance. "I guess I could try to find some…"

"No!" Gideon insists. Man, he's bossy. I forgot how bossy he is. I didn't mind it so much when we were in bed. "No glitter. What's in that thing?"

The server shrugs. "No idea. It's the chef's secret recipe."

"Have you ever seen him drink it?"

Oooh. That's a very important thing to ask. Good thing Gideon's watching my back! I settle into a chair to watch avidly as Gideon prepares to protect me from my doom.

"Carry on," I say grandly with a sweep of the arm. "I am now prepared to witness your brave intercession between me and my doom."

All eyes are on me.

"Seriously," Andrew asks, "*how* does he manage to say these words while this drunk? Shouldn't there be a rule or something?"

What a great idea! I nod eagerly. "There is!" I declare. "It's called Sam's Amazing Not-Sober Rule. No, wait. That name sucks. The name is still in development. But the rule is, when you're drunk, you always sound super smart!"

"Only to yourself," David says dryly as he helps our server pass around cake and coffee. The cake looks amazing—some kind of triple-layer chocolate and vanilla thing with a ton of frosting and decorated with marshmallows. How could anyone go wrong with that?

I busy myself shoveling in the first forkful, and holy fuck, it's so amazingly good. Two more forkfuls follow rapidly, and it's not long until I'm scraping the plate clean.

Someone shoves a cup of coffee under my nose —*rude*—and I take a long sip. It's the perfect cap to the meal.

Or so I think.

No sooner has my coffee been removed than the purple drink appears. It's still glowing, still steaming, but the glass isn't hot.

"Go ahead and drink it," Gideon orders. "The chef said it's safe for humans."

"Yay!" I snatch up the glass and bring it to my mouth. The liquid smells like candy and flowers with a slightly spicy undertone. It smells *delicious*. I take that first cautious sip, realize it tastes just as good as it smells, and gulp the rest down.

About halfway through, my head spins and my eyelids droop. They're so heavy.

"What's this stuff supposed to do, anyway?" someone asks.

Gideon's gruff voice replies, "Knock him—"

CHAPTER FIVE

I WAKE GRADUALLY, drifting up from the warm arms of sleep with the slow, rested feeling of having gotten a full night's sleep with only delightful dreams. The bird that lives in the tree outside my bedroom window is singing away happily, and I smile drowsily at the sound. How nice it is to wake up so lazily, with nothing to do and nothing to—

Hold on.

What the fuck?

I open my eyes. I'm in my bed, in my own bedroom, but the window blinds are open, which they shouldn't be. I always close them before I go to sleep, because the window looks out on a busy-ish road and the thought of people being able to watch me while I sleep is yech.

And I can hear someone moving around in the other room.

With my shifter colleagues, that's not exactly unusual, but they don't usually come into my bedroom and open the blinds while I'm sleeping.

Also, why can I not remember coming home and going to bed?

What did I *do* yesterday?

I had that meeting… that turned out to be a job interview with the lucifer himself. Talk about freaky. Then I went to lunc—

Oh. Yeah, now it's coming back. Lunch, where I somehow managed to order the one thing on the menu that got me drunk as a skunk. I skim through the memories, wincing several times. There goes my reputation as a professional… and any chance I had of joining the team. Fuck, did I actually call my formidable ex-fuck Gideon, who barely spoke and clearly didn't want me there, "cutie"? And shorten his name to Gid? And tell them all that we would rally to keep David's "secret"? What the hell is wrong with me?

Although, it is interesting to learn that not all sorcerers can do the same things. Previously, I'd just assumed it had something to do with level of sorcery strength, rather than actual ability. Maybe I'd better do some in-depth research—and stop being afraid to ask questions. Fear of being rude has apparently hobbled me, and that's not okay.

But before I can get stuck into any of that, I need to find out who's in my kitchen, send an apology to the lucifer and his team, and then find out if I still have a job. Because if word of what happened gets around, it may be in jeopardy.

On the plus side, whatever the fuck that purple thing was, it *worked*. I not only don't have a hangover, I feel generally amazing. That shit needs to be bottled and sold.

I throw back the covers—and shriek.

I'm naked.

Why the fuck am I naked?

Well, okay… I'm not *actually* naked. I'm still wearing my boxer briefs. I guess whoever brought me home took my clothes off before putting me to bed. I just wish I wasn't wearing the briefs covered in little cartoon devils saying "You know you want to…" They were an impulse buy, an "inside" joke just for me. Nobody was ever meant to see them.

And isn't that just an indictment of my sex life.

"It's okay," I mutter. "This is not that big a deal." The voices in the other room went briefly silent when I made that manly sound of surprise, but they're speaking softly again now.

I get up, grab a pair of sweatpants and a T-shirt from the clothes chair, and yank them on. There's no point glancing in the mirror—I know what I'll see. Every day of my life has started with my hair standing straight up. It doesn't matter what I do before I go to bed or what position I sleep in—heck, I've tried all sorts of products, even. I'm the only person I know who ever styled their hair to go to bed. It's all to no avail. I wake up with my hair standing on end.

Heading out of the bedroom—not going to bother showering and brushing my teeth until after I've kicked out the invaders—hey… speaking of brushing teeth, that drink really is amazing. My mouth doesn't taste like three-day-old gym socks, and my breath is pretty decent! I've gotta go back and talk to that chef. If he hasn't patented that recipe, I want in on the ground floor.

I make it to the kitchen and freeze. I was expecting to see Alistair and another of my team members. People who regularly waltz in through the door as though the locks don't exist and help themselves to the contents of my fridge and pantry.

Instead, it's Andrew and Gideon.

I don't think I'm ready to deal with them, so I take a slooooow, sneaky step back—

"Do you honestly think we don't know you're there?" Andrew demands without turning around. "Vampire and demon, remember?"

Sighing, I change course and drag myself over to sit at the breakfast bar. "Why are you here?" Then what he said clicks. "How did you get in?" Neither of them are shifters.

Andrew holds up my keys. "How do you think we got in? We took these out of your pocket when we dragged you home."

"Right, but…" *why are you still here?* I leave it unsaid. Especially since they would have suffered last night— the guest bed is just a double, and they're both big men.

Then I stop fretting about why they're here and take in what they're doing. "Are you reorganizing my kitchen?" I mean… what the fuck?

Gideon pulls his head out of the pantry and glowers at me. "It's a disgrace. How can anyone live like this?" He goes back to stacking canned goods alphabetically, and I turn my bewildered gaze on Andrew, who shrugs and rolls his eyes.

"It makes him feel better. He's done it to all our homes. And his system works really well." He frowns. "What's with your hair?"

"It's always this way in the morning," I mumble. I literally don't know what else to say. Gideon Bailey, uber-demon, able to intimidate with a single glare, taciturn, grumpy… and super organized? Driven to rearrange other people's homes?

What am I even supposed to do with that? It does make him seem a little more like the guy I met in the bar, though.

I watch for a few more moments as Gideon orders Andrew to hand him things and the centuries-old vampire does it, and then I mutter, "I'm going to shower," and head toward the bathroom.

Where I find that Gideon has already worked his magic. "Hey!" I shout. "How am I supposed to find— Never mind." Because yes, he's moved everything around, but it's all now located very conveniently for each task. Not that I'll tell him that.

I run through my morning bathroom activities in record time, because it occurs to me that now I'm out of bed, Gideon might want to rearrange the bedroom, and there are some things in there I'd rather he not find, thank you very much. And it's just as well I hurried, because I emerge from the bathroom to literally run into him as he walks toward the bedroom.

"Whoa!" I grab him in a tackle-hug. Since he's twice the size of me, it won't actually stop him if he's determined, but it's a physical stop sign of sorts. It also lets me press up against him, and I almost whimper. "Where are you off to?"

He gives me an are-you-stupid look that's so good, I actually feel a little stupid. "I need to rearrange your closet."

"You really don't." The closet's safe enough, but if he goes poking around in the nightstand… things could get embarrassing. I forcibly turn him back the way he came and give him a little push to get him started.

He doesn't move.

And by that, I mean he doesn't even *sway* with the pressure of my push. Like, I know demons have more strength than humans, but really.

I shove a little harder.

Still nothing. He looks over his shoulder at me, and is that amusement I see in his eyes? Way down deep, because heaven forbid Gideon Bailey have a non-dour facial expression, but I still see it. The jerk's laughing at me.

I'll show him.

I get behind him, brace myself, and shove with all my might. I'm still straining to move him when Andrew's voice says, "What are you two doing?"

Gideon shifts his weight, my hand slips, and I crash face-first into his back. "Umph."

"I'm not sure," Gideon answers. "I was going to rearrange his closet, but he wanted me to stand here instead."

Fuck my life.

I pull my face away from his spine, glare at his back, and then declare, "Well, it was great meeting you guys. Best of luck finding an administrator. Bye-bye now!"

Silence.

Gideon turns around slowly to stare at me incredulously. "Bye-bye now?"

"What do you mean, best of luck finding a new admin?" Andrew adds. "You're our new admin. You can't just quit before you've even officially started. Not after we gave you such an amazing welcome party!"

He's talking about the drunken (on my part) lunch, right? I really hope so. If not, there's some big gaps in my memory.

From the living room comes the sound of the front door opening, and both my supposed new teammates turn in that direction, suddenly no longer an anal-retentive cupboard organizer and self-proclaimed funny man. Now, they both look scary as fuck.

"Does anyone have a key?" Andrew whispers.

"No," I whisper back, "but that's never stopped a shifter before. Or you, apparently." Taking them unawares, I shove between them and stride up the little hallway into the living room. "Oh, it's you."

Alistair is standing in front of the open fridge, staring at the contents. "What happened here? It's like one of those Tupperware ads, only without the Tupperware. Fuck, is the vegetable bin arranged alphabetically?" He shuts the fridge door and turns, a grim look on his face. "I've heard about this. They got to you, didn't they? They're trying to steal you! I never should have told Elinor how good you are!" He stomps his foot. "I won't have it! You're our human. They can go find their own." Crossing his arms, he glares at me. It's softened somewhat by his pout.

I don't even know where to start. It seems like he's come to the right conclusion, but how? And—oh, crap.

"It's only Alistair," I call somewhat frantically, in case the two highly trained operatives in my hallway are planning some kind of takedown.

"Who…? Are *they* still here?" Alistair hisses. In the next second, he's pushed past me and is crossing toward the hallway, from where Andrew is emerging. I only have a second to wonder where Gideon is before the confrontation is upon us.

"How dare you try and steal my human!" Alistair shouts, hands on hips. "And you tell that creepy demon to get a job at a fucking supermarket if he wants to organize canned goods! I had everything right where I wanted it!"

Andrew sneers. "If you can't manage to keep him, he's fair game. We need an admin, and he's the best, and since *we're* the best, he's ours."

Alistair growls. It's a full-on hellhound growl, and the sound sends chills down my spine. Andrew hisses in response, baring his fangs, which suddenly seem longer.

This could turn ugly.

At the same time, it's so fucking stupid.

"Guys," I say firmly, bravely—or perhaps stupidly— worming my way between them and pushing them apart. To be honest, I get the feeling they only move out of courtesy, because they each take a single step back and then stop. They're both taller than me and continue to glare at each other over the top of my head. I'm really not much of a barrier here. "This is stupid," I insist. "Both of you step back—now!"

Yeah… nothing.

"Step back now or I'll quit CSG and get a job working at a perfume factory!" It's the worst threat I can think of, since most species have an excellent sense of smell and the human habit of wearing too much scent is a nightmare for them.

Sure enough, they both give me horror-filled looks and move back.

"Okay," I say, trying to maintain the upper hand now that I have it. "Let's all go sit down and discuss this. Andrew, you sit in that chair." I point to the armchair across the room. "Alistair, you sit on the couch—at this end."

Neither of them move.

"Now!"

Once they're finally seated, I pace in front of them, alongside the coffee table. "First of all," I begin, "I am not anyone's human but my own. I belong only to myself. If you think of me as a toy or novelty possession, that hurts me deeply and our friendship is over." I direct that comment and a pointed look at Alistair, who hangs his head.

"Exactly," Andrew chimes in with a smirk. I turn the look on him.

"Neither am I a tract of land to be conquered and owned by whoever has the greatest prowess," I say. "I am *not* 'fair game.'"

To his credit, he's immediately shamefaced.

"I don't understand what the hell is going on," I admit. "Alistair, you should be happy for me. This would essentially be a promotion and a pay raise." The lucifer told me about the pay and benefits package, and it's *very* attractive. "And it's not like I'd be moving across the country. We'll still see each other all the time."

His face sets stubbornly. "I found you first. Now you're going to have my stupid cousin and her dumb friends here all the time. They're *already* here, and that weird demon is alphabetizing your house!"

Oh, *fuck*—Gideon! I spin in the direction of the hall, but Gideon is already emerging, his hand aloft, waving the virulently pink dildo I bought a year ago. "Do you want these arranged by color or size or species?"

I close my eyes. My cheeks are so hot, they could combust at any moment.

"Sam?"

I open my eyes. Alistair and Andrew have matching expressions of delighted shock on their stupid faces, but

Gideon's usual resting bitch expression is accented by a sexy little smirk. "Color or species?"

"Just—" I squeak, then swallow hard. "Uh, just leave them, please. I'll, uh, think about how I want them organized." I can't fucking believe he wants to organize my dildos.

He shrugs. "Okay. If you decide you want them arranged by frequency of use, that's fine too." Then, shocking me so much I lose the power of speech, he *winks* and adds, "I noticed the grip on the demon one is starting to get worn. You might need to replace it. Though, you should know that there's no substitute for the real thing." His gaze locks with mine for a long, breath-stealing moment before he turns around and saunters back down the hallway.

My legs give out and I collapse to the floor.

Fuck me.

Also, what the fuck is with him? He treats me like dirt and ignores me for five years, then winks and makes innuendoes like nothing happened?

I don't think I could possibly be more embarrassed.

"So, Sam… you never mentioned you were collecting interspecies dildos. Wanted a warmup before trying the real thing?"

I was wrong.

"Which is your favorite?" Andrew adds. "Vampire, right? Everyone loves vampire dick. It's the spines."

"Please," Alistair scoffs. "You're embarrassing yourself. Shifter cock is clearly superior."

"Please stop talking," I manage. The last thing I want is for them to start a full-on debate about which species' dick is the best. Because, yes, there are differences. While all species living on Earth in the physical

plane are humanoid (or in the case of shifters, sometimes humanoid), there are some slight differences in
physiology. The most obvious are things like demon
horns and vampire fangs, but as I discovered while
trawling the community social media, there are also
penis variations.

As Andrew said, vampires have spines. They're actually more like stiff hairs, quite flexible and not at all
damaging to delicate tissue. Their purpose is to stimu-
late ovulation in female vampires, which works differently to humans, I'm told. Honestly, I didn't pay a lot of
attention to that part. It's not something that concerns
me. Anyway, shifters have retractable barbs, much like
some of their animal counterparts. In real life, the barbs
are controlled by ejaculation. For the dildo, though,
there's a button to retract them—something I should
have checked for *before* using it. That was a very scary
ten minutes.

Demons are very similar to humans, but don't have a
defined head. They tend to be thicker all the way from
base to tip, too, wide enough to streeeetch their partners.

Incubi are probably the most interestingly shaped—
their dicks have a "waist," kind of like a bee or wasp. It
makes fucking stimulating, to say the least.

Anyway, it's not like I went out of my way to collect
those dildos. After discovering there were anatomical
differences and watching a lot of porn to try and spot
them, I found an online community adult store and
bought a set of dildos appropriately called World of
Wangs, which promised to be a collection of anatomi-
cally correct dildos featuring every species on the physical plane. Based on the human dildo in the set, I'd have
to say they did a decent job sticking true to life. And

after my scientific curiosity was satisfied, I set about using each one to satisfy something else.

And yes, the demon one is my favorite. What can I say? I have a size kink.

But I don't want to explain any of this to the two idiots currently in my living room, smirking at me.

"Sam?" Gideon shouts from the bedroom. "Do you want to keep this World of Wangs box?"

I'm going to kill him.

"World of Wangs?" Alistair sounds like he's choking. "*World of Wangs?*"

"Meeting you is the best thing that ever happened to me," Andrew assures me sincerely, pulling out his phone. "I need a picture of that box."

That snaps me out of my state of semifrozen horror. "Oh no, you don't. Time to go. Shoo. Out!"

He crosses his arms and stands his ground. "Not until you promise to start work with us on Monday."

"Nooooooo!" Alistair howls (literally). "Not *Monday*! If you absolutely have to leave us, I can come to terms with it, but we need notice!"

"Harold already has someone lined up to be your new admin," Andrew tells him heartlessly, and Alistair snorts.

"Not *that* kind of notice. We need time to prepare *emotionally*."

What.

Just. What.

"Time to prepare emotionally?" I parrot.

He nods.

I shake my head. "Compromise," I suggest, because I have a feeling it's the only way I'll get rid of them both. "Your new admin will start on Monday but I'll split the week between the two teams so I can give them a proper handover and you can… prepare emotionally."

Neither of them looks entirely happy, but they reluctantly agree.

"Great! Now, time to go!"

I shoo them, both protesting, toward the door and finally get them out. I shut the door in their faces, engage all the locks and the chain (not that it would do any good if Alistair decided to come back in) and finally lean back against the door in relief.

They're gone. I have some peace to assimilate everything that's happened over the past twenty-four hours.

Gideon walks into the room, and I squeal. It's not an embarrassing sound at all. Really.

Fuck. I forgot he was still here.

"I'm done in the bedroom, for now anyway. Do you have a storage locker or anything?" He looks around, as though it will magically transport itself from four floors down in the garage to my living room.

"No," I lie. There's nothing in there except my Christmas decorations, a couple of suitcases, and some odds and ends I don't want to keep but feel bad getting rid of because they were gifts. "Uh, so, is, uh…." I don't want to be nosy and rude, but if this is a condition that's going to bleed into how he works, I need to know so I can adjust accordingly. "Are you, um, do you have a medical diagnosis or do you just prefer things organized?"

His lips twitch into that tiny smile I remember so well, and I swear, my heart freezes in my chest. It just stops beating. Dark, broody, I'm-going-to-rip-your-arms-off Gideon is superhot, but this Gideon? He blows out the meter.

"I just prefer things organized. It's not a compulsion. It helps me think to be doing something relatively mindless with my hands, so I started rearranging my stuff. Alphabetical, reverse alphabetical, by color, size, shape… I got so sick of just doing my own stuff that I went to Andrew's place and did his. Now it's just habit if I'm not doing anything else."

Well, that's not the weirdest thing I've heard since starting work at CSG. My mind catches on something he said.

"It helps you think? Like, about work?"

He nods, the smile disappearing. "Yes. Well, you're awake, your brain seems to be functioning, and I've done all I can here."

I'm still trying to catch up with the sudden change of subject when he unlocks the door.

"Wait… you're leaving?" I blurt stupidly. For fuck's sake, the man just undid the chain and three locks; what else would he be doing?

He looks over his shoulder at me. "Is your brain not functioning? I find it difficult to tell with humans."

Dickhead.

"Don't you think we should talk? Since we're going to be working together—and I'm sure you're going to be a delight to work with."

He leans against the doorframe and glowers at me. I refuse to be intimidated and glare right back.

"Talk about what?"

Really? *Really?*

"How about the fact that this isn't the first time you've been in my apartment? Or the fact that you're such a rude asshole that you fucked me and then ignored my existence?"

He rolls his eyes, and I swear my blood pressure skyrockets. "What did you want from me? You didn't really think a *relationship* was going to come from picking up a stranger in a bar, did you?"

"Of course not! But would it have been too much to ask that you didn't act like I'm someone else's used condom that you just found in your soup?"

He blinks, then shakes his head. "I didn't—"

"Oh yes, you absolutely fucking did," I assert. "And anytime in the past five years that we've even been in the same general area, you did the same thing. I couldn't even glance in your direction without you acting like— like... like I'd spat in your drink." I can't think of a better analogy on the fly like this. "People have even mentioned it to me!" Well, one person. "Is it because I'm human? Or are you just a complete douche to everyone you hook up with?"

The glower is back. "I am *not* speciesist."

"Are you sure? Because word in the office is that you've never had a good thing to say about a human."

The glare intensifies. "I'm fucking allowed to get pissed off at the humans I have to deal with in my job. Most of them are trying to expose our community and put our safety at risk. But that doesn't mean I hate humanity. I don't talk about my personal life at work, and the only humans I have contact with through work suck, so people at the office probably have a biased perspective. Why would I have picked you up if I hated your species?"

I shrug. "How am I supposed to know? The second you were done fucking me, I became public enemy number one to you."

He opens his mouth to respond—angrily, if his

expression is any indicator—then closes it. "Fine," he finally snaps. "Maybe I reacted badly to seeing you in the office. That's only because I wasn't expecting you to be there. Nobody reacts well to having a one-nighter suddenly show up at their workplace—and I thought there could never be even a chance of it happening, because you're human!"

I sneer. "And it's taken you *five years* to get over your shock?"

"No," he growls, and I'm ashamed to say that the sound sends a shockwave of lust through me. "But what the fuck was I supposed to say to you? It just seemed easier to…" He trails off, looking uncomfortable—looking suddenly more approachable.

I nod. "Right." I take a deep breath and rub my forehead. "Look, I guess it doesn't matter. If you don't actually hate me and don't have a problem working with me, then we should just… forget it all ever happened." It's hard to get the words out. I'm still pissed that he treated me that way. I'm hurt, too. And there's a secret part of me that regrets we can never hook up again.

But hanging on to all that crap is just going to make work difficult, and I love working for CSG. I'm excited about my new role. I'm not ready to walk away from the community.

So I need to let the past go.

Gideon looks like he wants to say something, but just nods. "I don't have a problem working with you," he asserts. "I think you're going to be an asset to the team. I just… really wanted to avoid this conversation."

Is he serious?

I start to laugh. I laugh so hard, I can't stop. It's not that funny, but I still can't stop laughing.

"Sam?" Gideon's watching me with this half-amused, half-concerned cast to his usual resting bitch expression.

I wave a hand. "Just go. I'll see you Monday." Gasping in a deep breath, I get the laughter under control.

He gives me a strange, almost wistful look, then leaves.

I look around my suddenly empty apartment and wonder how this can possibly be my life.

CHAPTER SIX

My new job doesn't end up starting on Monday morning. I only get halfway through Sunday before getting a phone call from Lily.

"Can you come in to the office? I need to virtually sit in on an interview some of our investigators are doing in another state, and I need someone to take backup notes."

Um... "Why don't you just record it? I mean, I can come in, but surely a recording would be better."

She sighs. "I've tried that, but even with top-of-the-line phones, a recording of a teleconference is usually pretty crap quality."

I take a minute to puzzle through that. "Lily, are you using your phone to record video meetings on the teleconference system?"

"Yeah. Why?" She sounds puzzled.

I bite back a groan. "There's a recording function on the system. Are the others doing that too?" For fuck's sake, how can they possibly not know how to use the equipment properly?

"There's a recording function? Really? Since when?"

"I'll come in," I tell her.

So I spend Sunday afternoon showing her how the recording function works and then sitting in on the meeting anyway, since it's a good learning experience for me. With the team having so few members and not being able to be everywhere at once, they rely pretty heavily on investigators on the ground in other states to do legwork for them. It's actually really fascinating, and I go home excited about my new job.

Which brings me to Monday.

I arrive bright and early at the office and go straight to my old team to start the handover process to the new administrator. I'm the first one there, which is great. I get most of the handover notes written up before the first person even arrives.

It's Jim, the six-foot-three hulking demon who *lied* to me about the availability of demon spice, something I plan to discuss with him in great depth—except before I can open my mouth, he bursts into tears.

Tears.

And not delicate, elegant, trickle-down-your-cheeks tears. Oh, no. These are great, gasping, snotty sobs.

I don't know what to do.

"Jim? Are you… Is everything okay? Do you… need a tissue?"

Before he can pull himself together enough to reply, three more of our team members (a hellhound, a felid, and an incubus) come in. They see me and start to cry.

Uhhhh-huh.

Something smells fishy.

I grab the box of tissues from my desk, thrust it at

my nearest teammate, then pull out my phone and call Alistair.

"Sammy, hey!"

"Fuck you, you dick. What have you done?"

"That's not nice, Sam," he says in a hurt voice. "I thought we were friends."

"Oh, we are friends." Somehow, I make it sound like a threat. Because I'm awesome and have skills. "That's how I know you're responsible for the *festival of fucking tears* in the office."

"What?" He sounds genuinely confused, and I pause for a second. Maybe he doesn't have anything to do with it?

Two more of our teammates walk in, look at me, and burst into tears. "Oh, Saaaaaaaaam!" one wails.

"Alistair, I don't know what you've done, but you'd better get here now!" I hiss.

"I'm in the elevator. Less than five minutes. I swear, I didn't do anything!" The line goes dead, and sure enough, just a few minutes later, Alistair races in, skidding to a stop. He takes in our bawling teammates and winces, looking somewhat guilty.

"Okay, so, it's possible that something I said was misunderstood," he admits. He looks around and swallows hard. "Really, really misunderstood."

I sigh. "What?"

He hangs his head and mumbles something.

"Gruel would tear UFOs in half?" No way did I hear that right.

Huffing a laugh, he looks me in the eye and says, "You're not allowed to hurt me if I tell you."

I bite my lip. "I feel as though I should just hurt you anyway."

The big, scary hellhound who stands eight inches taller than me and weighs half again as much as I do takes a huge step back. I'd be proud of myself, but I'm too busy trying to deal with the situation.

"Whatever you said to cause this, just fix it." I don't have time for crying investigators. The new admin is due to arrive any second, and I want to start handing over so I can get to grips with my new job.

Alistair takes a deep breath, then raises his hands and shouts, "Hey, need your attention—for Sam's sake."

A hush falls. There's still the occasional sob, a nose being blown, but everyone's attention turns to me and Alistair. There are lots of big sad eyes.

That makes me nervous. What the hell did he tell them?

"So, the message I sent you yesterday might have been… misleading," Alistair begins. "When I said that this cruel world is tearing Sam from us forever, I didn't mean that he was… permanently leaving this world. He's not dying."

"He's not?"

"Really?"

"Oh, what a relief!"

I'm swarmed by hugs and spend a few minutes patting backs and reassuring everyone I'm okay. Have you ever been group-hugged by people who are all bigger than you? It's an overwhelming experience.

When everyone is finally settled and calm, Jim turns to Alistair and asks, "So… what did you mean?"

"Yeah," someone else chimes in. "You better not have put us through this for a *joke*, Alistair."

He holds up his hands, palms out. "No joke. Sam really is being taken from us—by the lucifer. He's going to be the admin for the senior investigative team."

"Nooo!" someone howls. Somebody else bursts into tears again. I'm seized in another hug, this one with the kind of firm grip that tells me I'm not getting away anytime soon.

"Alistair!" I hiss.

He shrugs. "I just told them the truth. It's not my fault they don't like it."

"You can't leeeeeave uuuuuussss!" Jim whines. "You're our human! They can find their own!"

I feel as though, once I get this settled, I should talk to HR about some sensitivity training. There are way too many people who seem to think of humans as toys.

For now, though, I have to—

"What is going on in here?" The strident female voice cuts through the noise in a way I will never be able to achieve. For the second time this morning, the room falls silent.

An older woman—definitely a shifter, and I'm going to guess hellhound from the way Alistair immediately drops his gaze—is standing just inside the door. She's dressed in a power suit and pearls, her hair and makeup immaculate, and her gaze is so confronting that it wouldn't surprise me if she declared she was planning world domination.

"Aunt Vivienne?" Alistair mumbles. "What are you doing here?"

She sweeps in and plants her laptop bag on the nearest desk, which happens to be mine. "I," she declares, "am the new administrator for this team."

I grin. *Oh, Harold, you naughty boy.* I'll have to buy him a present.

Alistair turns sheet white. A quick glance around shows all the other hellhounds reacting similarly.

"B-But—"

"No buts. Mark, if you don't let go of that poor boy right now, I'll—" She doesn't even need to finish the sentence, Mark lets me go so fast I stumble a little, then regain my footing and step forward with a welcoming smile.

"Hi, I'm Sam, the old admin. It's so nice to meet you."

She casts a disparaging glance around at the rest of the team. "I'm sure it is. I've heard about you. You've done good work here, and I won't let them hold you back." She extends a hand for me to shake. "Vivienne Sanford. I'm Alistair's great-aunt—and Elinor's too, so if she gives you trouble, just let me know."

I love this woman!

"Thank you, that's a very kind offer. Can I get you some coffee?"

She shakes her head. "I'm all set, thank you. As soon as these hooligans get on with what they're supposed to be doing, we can get started."

The hooligans scatter.

———

SIX WEEKS LATER, I'm firmly ensconced in my new job and absolutely loving it. Honestly, it's the perfect fit for me. There were some initial teething problems with leaving my old team and then teaching my new team-mates how I like things done, but those didn't take us long to overcome, and now it feels as though I've been here forever. In a good way.

I'm even making new friends. Lily is amazing, and I feel more comfortable with her than with almost anyone else—except maybe Alistair. But I can talk to Lily about things I wouldn't with Alistair. I've never really had a woman friend before, and it's made me realize that I need to be more open to new experiences. I'm nearly forty, and unlike my colleagues, that means my life is almost half done.

So my social life is opening up some, since between Lily and Alistair, I get out a few times a week, and I have an incredibly interesting job working with intelligent, capable people.

It's just my love life that sucks. Which is ironic, because lately, my sex drive has been picking up.

The door slams open, making me jump and nearly knock over my coffee. Gideon storms in, throws his phone toward his desk—which is, as always, meticulously tidy—then stomps around the room in a circle.

I watch him. I'm not sure how to treat him, to be honest. He rearranged my whole house and fondled my dildos, but at the office, we're kind of awkwardly distant. We said we'd just forget the past happened, but it's still hanging over us.

Should I ask him what's wrong? Offer him coffee? Ignore him? Keep staring at him until he notices?

Decisions, decisions....

"Call the others in," he snarls, turning so suddenly that I jump *again*. I'm really not this nervy a person, I swear. "I need a meeting."

I pick up my coffee and take a sip, then casually put the cup down and point to where his phone lies haphazardly near the edge of his desk. "There's your phone. Although Lily may not answer; she's doing interviews."

My job covers a lot, and making calls as part of a case-load is included in that. Calling in team members because Gideon's in a foul mood and occupied by pacing is not.

He glares for a minute, then growls and stalks over to retrieve his phone. "Could you book a meeting room… please?" His tone implies that it's the very least I can do.

"Of course," I say placidly, clicking into the meeting room calendars to find an available one. If he wants a meeting room, he's got a presentation of sorts in mind; an informal chat could be held here in our shared office. I block out the room for the whole afternoon so he can take his time, and then I dash downstairs to the café in the building's lobby to grab some snacks and sodas. There's coffee in the break room if anyone wants that.

When I get back, Gideon's not alone. David and Elinor smile at me, but Mr. Grumpy scowls. "Where did you go?"

I hold up the paper bags full of pastries and cakes. "Supplies. Are Lily and Andrew coming?"

"I'm right here," Andrew says, strolling in. "Hello, Sam. You're looking well. Rather glowing, in fact. Have you been using the magic elixir known as the tears of your teammates?"

It would be so easy to dislike Andrew if he wasn't so charming. Ever since he found out about my old team's reaction to me leaving, he's been teasing me about it. "Once again, if I find out you had anything to do with that, you will regret it," I threaten. "It's bad enough I had to hear you and Alistair bickering like children *again* the other day."

"What's this?" Elinor perches on the edge of

Gideon's desk. He shoves her off. She flips him the bird and comes to sit on the edge of my desk instead. "My idiot cousin and this idiot vampire were fighting?"

"Like men," Andrew interjects. "Not children. Things almost got dangerous."

Elinor raises a brow. I shake my head.

"It was like two toddlers having tantrums," I tell her.

Lily comes in before Andrew can protest, and Gideon shoots up from his desk chair. "Finally! Come on. What room, Sam?"

I tell him, and he leads the way. This must be important—it's barely been forty-five minutes since he came storming in, and he's acting like we've kept him waiting for hours. I'm not actually sure if he wants me at the meeting, but hey, I'm a member of this team, right? If he wants me to leave, he can say so.

To my face.

In front of everyone else.

That won't be embarrassing.

Too late to second-guess. I take a seat at the table and wait while Gideon casts from his laptop to the TV on the wall.

"Okay," he begins, pulling out a chair and sitting on the back, feet on the seat. That's a recipe for disaster, right? He's going to fall. If I was doing that, I would have fallen just trying to balance there. I squint, trying to judge the distance between the chair and wall. If he topples backward, is he going to fall relatively harmlessly to the floor, or smash into the wall and give himself a head injury? I've done first aid courses, both human and community, so I try to remember what the best action would be in a situation like that.

"I've got seventeen cases that have been referred by

investigators over the past week. In all seventeen cases, the system logged greater than 95 percent similarity to other open cases across the world, flagged our team, and sent notification to the investigators. They've all handed over their files—some more willingly than others." The way his eyes narrow tells me what he thinks of that, and I pity the investigators who thought they could keep anything from him. "In every case, we have a missing couple, half human, half community. The community members seem to be randomly selected—we've got four demons, three incubi and two succubae, two hellhounds, two felids, two sorcerers, and two vampires. Each couple has either no family or none in the immediate area. Each couple disappeared from their home overnight, as far as can be determined. None of their homes showed any signs of a struggle or forced entry. In most cases, the disappearance was reported by a work colleague of one or other of the couple. Three were reported by neighbors, and one by a cleaning service. In all cases, the couple is expecting a child within the next four to six months."

"Uh-oh," David murmurs.

"Some kind of breeding program?" I've never heard Andrew sound so grim.

"It looks like it. I've put out a global alert to see if there are any other cases that might not have been flagged by the system for whatever reason."

Gideon brings up a world map that has seventeen (I assume—I don't actually count them) red dots on it, and they start talking about locations, but I'm still stuck on "breeding program."

"Excuse me," I say. "I'm sorry to interrupt. Could

you please explain for me what you meant by breeding program?"

They all look at me.

"What don't you understand?" Gideon asks impatiently. "It's a program to breed babies."

"Yes, I got that, thanks," I tell him with only a hint of sarcasm. "What I'm not clear on is to what end? Is this a baby factory to provide children to couples who want to adopt? Or for child slavery?"

"It could be either," Lily says. "It's hard to know at this stage. But it's not really likely."

"There would be no need to take the father as well if that was the case," David explains. "They'd actually add to the risk factor for the kidnappers. And the babies wouldn't all have a human parent."

"Okay." That makes sense. "So the end game is likely to be… what?" The churning feeling in my gut is a pretty big indicator that I already have an inkling.

"Genetic modification," Gideon says, and the words are as heavy as boulders.

Sometimes I hate being right.

"So," I start, trying to get my head around it, "this is likely humans trying to… what? Give humans greater abilities?" It sounds like a bad movie. And I don't know a lot about genetic modification, but I'm not sure if it's possible. When a member of the community and a human procreate (it *is* possible, though even more difficult than for the community in general, and they already have a low fertility rate), the baby is never human. The other species always breeds true—and I don't just mean that the child inherits those traits. There is no human genetic matter at all. All the research I've read seems to indicate that it's a result of magic—that since community population is so much lower than human, it's magic's way of ensuring the other species aren't bred out of existence.

Elinor shrugs. "It's possible. That happened about eighty years ago, so it's probably due to happen again. But more often, we find it's a group within the community."

My jaw drops. "*Why?*"

"Humans aren't the only ones with dreams of world domination," Andrew says. "There are factions within the community that claim humans shouldn't be permitted to overrun the physical plane this way. That they should be held to the same laws and standards as the rest of us—the way they are when they get to the spiritual plane."

I try to connect that to genetic modification. "Oh. It's numbers. They want to increase community fertility."

"Which doesn't sound terrible, right? That's why they have a solid support base, even if it's small. But the reason humans have greater fertility is because they have shorter lives. It makes sense that if your lifespan is ten to fifteen times shorter than other species, it should be ten to fifteen times easier for you to conceive than them."

"True. Okay." I grab one of the small notepads from the center of the table and begin mapping it out for myself. "So when humans initially got delusions of grandeur all those years ago, they outnumbered the community and were basically slaughtering everyone. Right? Then magic stepped in to prevent that and wiped the human memory of other high-intelligence species. But if there hadn't been more of humanity than everyone else put together, things would have gone differently. I mean, the community has, overall, greater strength and speed, can see in the dark, has claws, fangs, teleportation, the ability to mesmerize… and sorcery. Humans have the ability to get pregnant faster and more frequently. It's not like now, either—the only weapons they would have had were, what, sticks, stones, and knives? When was the first sword invented? Never mind." I make a note to look it up, though, just out of curiosity. "This faction—"

"And magic," David interrupts.

I blink, thrown off my train of thought. "What? You mean sorcery. I said that." One of the first things I learned after joining CSG was the difference between magic—the existential stuff that oversees everything— and sorcery, which is inner power wielded by sorcerers.

"No, I mean, humans had their rudimentary weapons, the ability to procreate faster, and magic."

My jaw drops.

A moment later, Lily says, "Sam? Are you okay?"

"Humans had *magic*?" It comes out all raspy, so I clear my throat.

"Have," David corrects. "Not inner power like what I have, or like the glamor magic the other species use to disguise themselves. But all humans have the ability to manipulate existential magic."

"Really?" I breathe. "So I could… use magic? Why has nobody mentioned this before? Wait, does this mean the Wiccans are right?"

He shrugs. "They don't use it as fully as they could because they've tied it up in religion, but basically yes. Humans need spells and instruments to do anything substantial—crystals, herbs, that kind of thing—but the basic ability is there."

"I'm sorry to interrupt this very important discussion, but do you think we could get back to the kidnapped couples?" Gideon asks sarcastically. His phone chimes, and he glances at it. "Of which there may now be twenty-one. Fuck, I need to make some calls and check." He strides out, already putting his phone to his ear.

"Just quickly," I say to David, "can you teach me magic? I mean, I know it's different to what you use—"

"Yes. Well, I can try." He grins at me.

My face stretches so much with my answering grin that I'm sure it must look scary. "Thanks! Now, back to what I was saying…" I glance down at the notepad to remind myself. "Okay, so this faction figures if they can improve fertility, that would dramatically change the odds in a head-to-head situation and the community wouldn't have to live in secret?"

"That's the best-case scenario. More likely is that they attempt to force humans back into our society. Worst-case is the annihilation of all humans on the physical plane. Either of those scenarios would involve having our current system of government overturned." Elinor speaks matter-of-factly, though her face is grim.

Fuck.

"What about the magic?" I ask desperately. "It stepped in before when things were going wrong. Wouldn't it interfere to prevent the destruction of the government it created?"

Andrew sighs and rubs his forehead. He suddenly looks older. "We don't know. We just… We hope so, but the only way to find out is…"

Yeah. He doesn't need to finish that sentence.

"Okay. Okay. So… this is a long-term plan, right? I

mean, I figure they're interested in babies with one human parent because they figure there's a better chance of being able to… I don't know. Activate human genes? How does it even work? And even if they successfully modify these babies once they're born—"

David shakes his head. "The last time we stopped something like this, the experimentation was happening in-utero. I assume the same this time—that's probably why all the women are only in the second trimester."

I push that thought aside. "So even if they can successfully make a modification to increase fertility, these children won't be reproducing for decades. And then what? It's not like two dozen people can single-handedly close the population gap. I just don't under-stand what they're trying to do."

"Neither do we," Lily says. "We may find more information as we go along. At this stage, we have to assume that the coordinated kidnapping of so many couples with such similar profiles is in support of an act of terrorism against the community, whatever that may turn out to be."

"Of course." Definitely we need to help those people and stop the monsters who think experimenting on people without their consent is okay. "Um, I'm guessing Gideon will give us all the case info when he gets back, but can you give me the file locations for previous cases like this? I'd like to familiarize myself so I know what to expect."

Lily smiles indulgently at me. "You're such a nerd. Our lives were so much bleaker without you." She grabs my notepad, flips the page, and begins neatly writing directory numbers. "We keep copies of all case files of this type in a particular sub-directory for easy cross-checking."

"And you called me a nerd." Mentally, I begin compiling a list of things I might have to do, depending on how Gideon decides to handle this. "What are your cases like at the moment? Is there anything that can't be put on hold or handed over to another team?"

There's a general sense of reluctance and a series of pulled faces, grimaces, and huffs. "None of us like handing over cases," Elinor says, leaning back and putting her feet on the table. "I should be able to wrap up my current one with a couple hours' work, and then someone else can handle the arrest and processing."

"I'll have to hand mine over," Andrew grumbles. "If Gideon needs us all on this, which looks likely, I won't have the capacity to do what's needed within the time crunch. It's not too sensitive, though, so as long as the investigator who gets it isn't an idiot, it'll be okay."

I make a note. "Do you have a preference for who to give it to?" He nods. "All right, we'll talk about that when we know what Gideon needs. David? Lily?"

"I'm in the same boat as Andrew." Lily's smile is gone now. She clearly doesn't like the idea of having to give up cases, but she knows where the greater responsibility is.

"I made my arrests this morning," David says. "I just need to file the reports."

"Smug prick," Lily mutters, and he flips her the bird.

"Behave," I chide, making notes. "David, you're on deck to provide immediate support to Gideon. Andrew and Lily, let me know who you want to pass your cases to, and I'll arrange the handover immediately. Elinor, wind up your case today and I'll tee someone up to handle the arrest. By the time the three of you have done that, I'll have the information you need to support Gideon. Sound good?"

"Thank fuck you're here," Andrew breathes. "I don't suppose I could get you to manage my personal life as well?"

"Not a chance," I assure him. "Will Gideon handle advising the lucifer, or do I need to?"

"Oh, Percy already knows. It's part of the magic of his office. But Gideon will give a full report as soon as we decide what course of action to take." Elinor puts her feet on the floor and sits up straight as the door opens and Gideon comes back in.

His face is even grimmer than usual. "We've officially got twenty-five couples missing," he states. "Waiting for confirmation on three more right now. I think we can expect more. I've asked Percy to authorize a message to all health care providers, asking them to contact any of their patients who fit the profile and have them check in with us." He looks at me. "Can you coordinate the check-ins and then ensure local enforcers are allocated to provide protection?"

"Yes." Fuck. How am I going to do that? I'll just have to work it out.

"The closest kidnapping was in a town about an hour away—I'm heading out there now to see if I can find out anything more."

"David is clear to go with you if you want another set of eyes," I tell him. "Or…" I glance at the map on the screen. There's another dot not too far away. "Or I can arrange for him to fly out to another site. I know it's not practical to visit every scene, but if you manage a few, you might find some commonalities that help." I might be new to this team, but I haven't worked with investigators for the past five years without learning some things.

He nods, and for just a second, I see something that looks like approval in his gaze. It disappears fast. "Okay with you, David?"

"Good to go," David replies.

"Then I'll get you to drive out to the closer site, and I'll take a couple of the farther ones, since I don't need a plane. Can we all meet back here later tonight? The case files are on the system if you've got time to review them before then. And then we'll get a plan in place."

I get up and go to his laptop, ignoring his indignant exclamation as I examine the map more closely. David will need at least two hours round-trip transit time, plus time on scene. "Let's make it around seven thirty," I decide. "I'll have food here in case you don't have time to eat. Any preferences?"

"Whatever's easiest," Lily says. "Thanks, Sam."

"No problem. Let's get this done."

It's after seven that night, and not only am I still at the office, it looks like I'll be here for hours more.

Today has not been what I expected.

But fuck, this job is amazing.

I felt valuable as admin to my old team. I was helping them help people. Most of the cases they're assigned turn out to be members of the community who slipped through the cracks—often the very rare children of one-night stands who don't have a clue that they're not human, but also those without families and young adults who've chosen to leave community-only enclaves and are struggling to cope with hiding from humans. My job was interesting, well-paid, and rewarding.

This job, though… this is next-level. After I requisitioned a car to take David out to the second scene, giving him time to read the case files on the way, and found investigators for Lily and Andrew to hand over their cases to, I hooked into the system, borrowed an intern from another department, and began fielding responses from couples who'd been contacted by their health care providers. Some elected to go stay with family elsewhere, and we made arrangements for them to check in with local enforcers and me daily, but most weren't able to do that, so I organized with their local enforcement departments for them to have protection. If the kidnappings continue, we may have to relocate these couples—and there are hundreds of them now— to another location where they can be better protected. Maybe an enforcement base? I've already started looking into it.

Sadly, I've been advised by seven medical centers that they were unable to contact a client that fit the profile, and when I requested enforcers follow up, they found the couples missing. I added them to the list, had investigators go out to those scenes, and notified Gideon.

A couple hours ago, around the time David called to say he was on his way back but stuck in traffic, I put Andrew and Lily to work liaising with the investigators at each scene and inputting the information into a database that will let us map it out easily. They're set up in the meeting room—which I ended up blocking out in the schedule for the next week—beginning the analysis.

Elinor joined them half an hour ago. And I've been digging into past case files.

It's horrifying.

I know people—of any species—can be monsters, but it's still hard to come to terms with it. Yet I've just read case after case where people were experimented on, often cruelly and painfully, without consent, all so… what? To further the agenda of a radical sect? How is that right?

In most of the cases, the cults involved were identified. But based on the way they set themselves up, it was impossible for everyone associated to be arrested and incarcerated. It's impossible to even identify everyone associated. So it's probably one of these same groups again, which at least gives us a starting point.

I'm making notes on which would be the most likely based on their previous actions when a voice *right next to my ear* says, "What are you doing?"

I squeal and jerk so sharply that my ergonomic chair rolls away from the desk.

"Fuck. Me," I gasp, clutching my chest as I whirl to glare at Gideon. "What the *fuck*? You don't sneak up on people when they're reading about nutjobs who like to kidnap!"

He leans against the desk and crosses his arms. If it was anybody else, they'd probably tease me, but he just looks a little less grim than usual. "I didn't sneak," he says. "I came in, dumped my keys, asked you where the others were, and then when you didn't answer, I came over to see what had you so enthralled."

Oh.

That might be possible. I tuned myself to hear computer alerts and the phone and blocked everything else out—it works really well in an open-plan office to maximize focus, but it does make it annoying for people trying to get my attention.

"Sorry," I say grudgingly, dropping my hand to my lap and scooting back to the desk. "I was reading related case files and got kind of caught up. Uh, David's on his way back, and the others are in the meeting room doing some data mapping. The intern just went home. I'm waiting for the food to be delivered."

That dark gaze studies me. "What are we having?"

I fidget, feeling self-conscious about the way he's looking at me. This man has fondled my dildo collection. *And* he noticed that the grip on the demon dildo is getting kind of worn. "A mix of stuff. Pizza, curry, burritos, rice and veg. I'm not that familiar with what you all like yet."

He just nods, still staring down at me. I resist the urge to squirm or get up. Let's face it, he'd still be looking down at me, even leaning against the desk like he is.

"Thanks for letting me know about the new cases," he says suddenly. "Hopefully the number will begin to slow now."

"Yeah. Uh, I was thinking, if it doesn't, would we possibly want to consider moving the at-risk couples, putting them somewhere we can protect them better?"

At first he looks surprised, then thoughtful. "There are a lot of them," he points out. "So far we've identified nearly seven hundred. Not all of them are targets, but we don't know yet who is. Where would we put them? And find people to protect them?"

"I'm still working on that," I admit. "I just hate the idea of them all being so exposed."

"We'll do what we can to protect them," Gideon says. He stands, reaches out his super-long tall person arm, and snags the chair from Andrew's desk, pulling it over. I'm so jealous. I mean, it's only three steps, but for once, I'd like to be a person who can just reach out for what I want instead of having to take the steps—or use a stepladder.

Gideon sits, and I realize how very, very close he is. Like… our knees are almost touching. If I was to shift just a little bit….

I swallow hard. "What are you doing?"

"Show me what you're reading. I assume you're trying to pull data so we can narrow down who's doing this?"

He's. So. Close.

This is dumb. I don't even like him. I don't even *know* him, really. And he's been a grumpy ass.

I swallow hard. Hormones suck.

"Uh, um, yeah. Here—I'm up to this one from Argentina forty-four years ago."

He leans in closer to the screen, and *our knees touch*. Electricity zings through me. He doesn't seem to notice, the bastard, except to shift his knee away.

I hate him.

I want him.

That's so humiliating to admit to myself.

"I remember this," he's saying. "It was right after I was promoted to the team."

That reminds me again of the difference in our longevity. "How old are you?" I blurt, and then slap a hand across my mouth in horror. Heat burns in my cheeks as he turns to look at me. His face is an expressionless mask.

"Excuse me?"

"Nothing! I said nothing. Sorry. Um. You were saying about the case?" Fuck fuck fuck! Talk about being unprofessional. And it's not even important—I already have a vague idea thanks to the internet.

I try not to sweat under his gaze, and finally he turns back to the screen. Only supreme force of will keeps me from slumping in relief.

I manage to keep it together while he skims through the file I've been reading and adds some observations to my notes. I try really hard not to let my hormones dictate my thoughts and actions during that time, but I can't help admiring the long line of his neck. I understand why vampires like to bite that spot right *there*—it looks delicious.

"Hey, guys. What are you doing?"

"David!" I leap to my feet, once again sending my chair skidding. "Hey! You're here! We're just waiting on the food."

"It's coming," he says, draping his jacket over the edge of his desk. "I passed the delivery guy in reception. I offered to take it from him, but he said you promised a fifty-dollar tip and he wasn't giving it to anyone but you."

Gideon swivels to look up at me. "You promised a fifty-dollar tip? Why?"

I shrug. "Sometimes when the guys on my old team stay late, they 'redistribute' any food deliveries they can intercept. I told our delivery guy that he got the tip if the food was brought directly to me."

"Sneaky," David admires. "And it probably explains why Elinor's cousin Alistair was hovering around reception looking all gloomy."

I narrow my eyes, instantly distracted. Alistair's been quiet all day, which means he's probably bursting to cause some kind of ruckus.

But before I march out to reception to retrieve our dinner, the delivery guy bursts in, looking like he's fleeing the hounds of hell—which turns out to be literally true, as two hellhounds follow him in.

"Save me!" His high-pitched squeal fills the room as he races toward us and promptly hides behind Gideon, who got up when the shifters came in. "Some dudes in reception wanted the food and I wouldn't give it to them so they set their dogs on me!"

I sigh heavily, and the two hellhounds drop their heads in shame. "Sit," I command, as though they were just dogs, and since they're now stuck in the deception they created, they do. The one on the left—Alistair—lies down and puts his front paws over his eyes.

"I'm Sam Tiller," I tell the delivery guy, who has somehow managed to wrap himself around Gideon. Sneaky bastard. "You can let go of him. They won't hurt you."

He eyes them warily. "Are you sure?"

I roll my eyes. "Yes, I'm sure. They never would have hurt you. They just wanted to scare you into giving up the food."

"Well… okay." He reluctantly unwinds himself from Gideon, who's smirking, the ass, and takes off his backpack. I check each dish as he removes it from the bag, then pay him and add the tip. I'm kind of tempted to reduce it after the way he threw himself at Gideon, but he did earn it.

He hesitates. "Will the dogs follow me out?"

Resisting the urge to laugh, because it's entirely

likely that they would, just to mess with him, I say, "I'll keep them in here. I need to give them a talking-to, anyway."

Both shifters whine, but the delivery guy seems satisfied by that and leaves. I shut the door just in case we get loud, then turn on the hellhounds now trying to hide under one of the desks.

"Stop that! Out!" They both whine. "I mean it. Both of you get out here and shift. Now!"

They reluctantly comply, and seconds later, I'm facing two sheepish men who tower over me. "You do realize that we're dealing with a crisis here? People's lives are at risk, and we'll be working late. I need to feed my team so they can be efficient. You know this, because I used to do it *for you*. Remember?"

They mumble a response, but I shake my head.

"Whatever you just said is not good enough. I don't have time to waste making the *human* delivery guy feel better and making sure he didn't see something he shouldn't have. Get out of here, and I'd better not see you fucking with my office again."

"But," Alistair begins.

I raise a brow. "Do I need to call Vivienne?"

"No!" they reply simultaneously, matching looks of horror on their faces. I file that away in my memory for future reference.

"We'll go now," Alistair adds. "Please call if you need any help with the case," he directs in David and Gideon's direction. "I'll see you soon?" he asks me hopefully.

I nod, because he's my best friend and although I'll never tell him, I find him kind of adorable sometimes.

They leave, and I begin gathering up the food to carry it to the meeting room.

"I'll take that." David swoops the containers from my arms. "After your heroic feats, it's the least I can do." He winks, and then he's out the door, leaving me with my arms half-extended and blinking like a fool.

Gideon takes three long steps until he's right in my space, leans down, and with a smirk that makes me want to rip his clothes off, whispers, "That was fucking hot. Competence is a real turn-on." Then he follows David out, whistling.

I… what?

CHAPTER SEVEN

A week later, we're all frustrated and annoyed.

We've made progress—we really have. Of all the at-risk couples we identified, none have been taken. The protections we've put in place are working. But they can't continue indefinitely, and unfortunately, there have been other couples taken that we hadn't yet identified. The number of couples kidnapped is now up to forty-one.

We're leaning heavily on other teams to help with other cases, because of course, the other bad guys planning to expose the community don't take time off when we're busy. That means everyone's attention except Gideon's is divided—they're all nominally managing those cases, even if most of the legwork is being done by others.

And speaking of Gideon.... *big sigh* He's a dilemma wrapped in a conundrum, all packaged in a sexy scowl. Sometimes I feel as though there's something between us, but then he'll be an asshole, and I'll wonder if I'm becoming delusional.

Like, most of this past week I've basically been glued to his side. I'm coordinating all the data collection and mining, plus all the reports from the teams on site, and making sure Gideon has anything he might need to figure this shit out. He and I make an incredible team— we're in sync more than I've ever been with anyone I've worked with. I can mostly tell what he's going to want to see or know next, and he always gives me exactly the information I need to help him—I don't need to ask for more or go hunting to figure it out. He's taken me with him to several of the scenes when he went looking for clues, and he's always super patient about my questions (and also when I threw up after being teleported the first time. That was super fun). And this one time, when one of the investigators asked me to step back (politely), Gideon insisted I stay right where I was. "He's more valuable to me right now than you could ever be," he said, which made me wince but also feel good.

Then there was the time we both reached for the same file at the same time. Our hands touched. We were suddenly standing so close. When I turned my head, I could feel his breath on my face. His gaze locked with mine. He leaned in. I was *so* sure he was going to kiss me, and I was ready for it. Eager, even.

Too bad Elinor walked in right then and ruined the moment.

Which brings me to the times when he ignores me completely.

So… yeah. It doesn't help that I seem to be caught in some kind of hormonal vortex. The last few months, it's been like I'm twenty years younger. Don't get me wrong, I've always had a healthy appreciation for sex— as in, gimme gimme gimme—but once I hit my mid-twenties, it settled down from thinking about it every hour to something that allowed me to actually get other stuff done. Lately, though, it's become somewhat of a priority again, which is kind of weird. I mean, at my age, isn't sexual appetite supposed to be slowing down, not heating up? It's especially annoying because I haven't dated much since I started working in the community, so sex has been limited to random hookups and self-care. And these past few weeks or so have been ridiculous. I only have to take a breath and I'm getting hard. Reminds me of when I was thirteen.

Andrew growls and throws the stress ball he's been squeezing to death against the wall. It actually cracks the plaster, which I wouldn't have thought possible even with vampire strength. "This is fucking stupid," he snaps. "No matter how many times we look at this, it's not going to change. The Coalition for Community Advancement is the most likely and obvious candidate for this whole disaster, but their movements don't indicate any involvement, and we've interrogated as many of them as we can find to no avail. So who the fuck is doing this?"

Lily rubs her palms over her face and leans back in her chair. "I can't think," she admits. "My brain is mush."

Gideon sighs and drops the pen he's been tapping onto the table. "Same. Okay, we need a break. A real break—no checking other cases."

David gets up. "Come on, Sam. Let's teach you how to use magic."

My eyes get really wide, and I battle between excitement and terror. "What? Now? Are you sure?"

"That's a great idea," Elinor enthuses. She looks

around. "Maybe not in here, though. We've got a lot of work here, and if something goes to shit…."

"The break room," Andrew suggests. "There shouldn't be anybody still here at this time anyway."

"Wait, what do you mean, if something goes to shit?" The terror starts to take over. Who do I think I am, trying to use magic? I mean, come on.

"Relax," Lily soothes, grabbing my arm and towing me toward the door. "It's going to be fine."

I resist her pull, dragging my feet. "Then why would you say something might go to shit?"

"It's normal," David assures me, taking my other arm and helping Lily pull me out of the room. "Like when babies are learning to walk and they fall. You know it's going to happen. There's really nothing you can do to prevent it, but you make sure there are no sharp corners or stuff like that."

I turn that over in my mind. There's something wrong with that analogy, but I just can't put my finger on what. I mull it over as my teammates drag me into the break room. Part of me is super excited about the possibility of using magic.

"Okay." David pulls out his phone and begins tapping the screen. "I contacted a friend of mine who's married to a human magic practitioner—"

I snort-chuckle.

All eyes turn to me. "What?" Andrew asks, and I shrug.

"Human magic practitioner. I just… can't believe I'm about to do this. Sometimes I still can't believe you all are *real*. Like… how is this my life? I literally can't talk to any of my old friends about half the stuff going on or introduce them to my new friends, because they'd think I'm a crackpot. Which is how most of human society thinks of 'human magic practitioners,'" I make air quotes, "and now I find out that they were actually right all along and that humans *can* do magic!" I give a weird all-over shudder, and Andrew laughs.

"You're living the dream," he says. "Now pay attention. We've still got a lot to do tonight."

I turn back to David, who smiles and goes on, "Anyway, I got some simple spells that you should be able to do without any real problem and without needing equipment. He said these are great ones to start with because they'll build your 'magic muscles' and your confidence, and you can practice them anytime without worrying about hurting anyone."

"That sounds good." I try to inject a positive note in my voice. The excitement waned a bit with the realization that I could actually hurt someone. But… magic. How great would that be? My humanity has set me apart from my colleagues for the past five years. That won't change, but I'll have a point of commonality with them—a return to how I would have been if my long-ago ancestors hadn't been either brainless sheep or degenerate fuckwits. "Okay. Let's do this!"

Judging by Lily's snicker, the rah-rah tone might have been overkill.

"The first step is to develop acceptance that magic is actually possible. I don't think you have a problem there, do you?" David looks up from his phone, and I snort.

"Nope. Magic is real. Believe me, I know." I've seen sorcerers do some pretty spectacular stuff over the years… and some really mundane stuff, like switching off lights without getting up off their lazy asses.

"Great. So this spell is going to create a ball of light.

Phil said it could be as small as a pinprick the first time, so a dim room is best."

Wordlessly, Gideon, who's leaning against the wall by the door with arms crossed and scowl in place, reaches over and turns off the overhead lights. We're left mostly in the dark, with light coming in from the hallway and from David's phone screen.

"You need to focus on the energy running through your body. The heart pumps blood everywhere. Tune in to the sensation of your own inner energy flowing to your extremities and then back again, an endless cycle of life and power."

Wow, that's kind of…. Okay. I can do this. It does kind of make sense. I take a deep breath, close my eyes, and concentrate on the idea of my blood flowing through my body, carrying life energy with it. Soon I feel a kind of tingling rush through all my limbs. Honestly, I'm not sure if it's real or if I'm imagining it, but hey, close enough, right?

I open my eyes and nod. "Got it."

My eyes must have adjusted to the dimness, because I can see much more clearly now. It's not just brighter, it's *sharper* somehow. Lily's biting her lip like she's trying not to laugh at me, which is nicer than Elinor and Andrew, who are both snickering openly.

"I guess it's working," Lily says diplomatically. "The energy thing, I mean. Your hair is standing up."

David frowns. "That's… uh. Sure. Okay. So the next step is to transfer that sense of awareness outside your body. You can feel your inner energy—now see if you can feel the energy flowing through the world."

I close my eyes again to keep from being distracted. I'm sure this will be trickier, because the world doesn't have a "heartbeat" for me to start with, but shockingly, it's so much easier. As soon as I focus my awareness on finding "energy" flow—and I assume that's the magic—it's there. It feels so amazingly natural and wonderful. I can't help but smile as it tickles around me.

When I open my eyes this time, it's to find all my teammates, even Gideon, clustered around David, who's frowning. Lily looks worried. Andrew and Gideon are whispering to each other.

"What's wrong?" I ask. Fuck, have I already done something wrong or caused a problem? I haven't even tried doing anything yet!

"Nothing," David says. "This is, uh, just going more smoothly than I expected. I assume you can feel the magic?"

"Yes! Fuck me, it's amazing. Is this what you guys feel all the time? It's almost like being in water, only not."

"That's a weirdly good comparison," Lily says, smiling encouragingly. "It's surrounding us and touching us all the time, adjusting and reacting to movements, like water does, but unlike water, it doesn't hamper movements."

"If you two are done being philosophical," Gideon interrupts, "can we get on with this?" He's staring at his phone now, his thumbs tapping at the screen, and doesn't even bother to look up as he speaks. Seriously? Has there ever been a bigger asshole in the history of assholes?

"Sure." I load as much sarcasm as I can into the word, but he doesn't seem to notice. How dare the top of his head be so attractive? Those horns... ungh. I shiver all over.

"Are you okay?" David asks immediately.

My face gets hot. Thank fuck he can't tell what I'm thinking. "Yeah. Sorry. It's, uh, I'm just not used to feeling magic, I guess." I frown. That felt… wrong. "No, I mean… I'm not used to being aware of feeling magic. Huh. It's always been there, hasn't it? I've always been able to feel it, I just didn't realize."

David smiles and opens his mou—

"Are you still fucking talking?" Gideon demands, putting his phone in his pocket and turning his dark gaze on me.

"Gideon," David and Lily chorus reprovingly. Andrew elbows him.

"Not cool."

"Yeah, yeah. Sorry. Can we move on?"

I hate him. I finally, *finally* understand now what people mean when they talk about hate fucking, because I can't stand the sight of him, want to stab him in the face, but would also fuck him again in a heartbeat.

Although, honestly, right this second, I'd fuck anyone. Being aware of magic has kicked my teenage-again horniness right up, and I'm so glad our office dress code is casual and my jeans and untucked shirt—and the dimness in the room—hide my hard-on.

"Let's move on," I say with gritted teeth. "David, what's next?"

"You need to visualize a ball of light. Phil says I should make sure to tell you *not* a ball of fire or anything else that might be hot or dangerous. A cool, light-only ball."

I snicker, because balls, and nod. "No fire. Got it." I hadn't really considered a fireball anyway, but yeah, I can see how some people might and that would be very bad.

"So visualize the ball, and then you need to use words to direct the energy to form the ball."

Uh… "Like… what words? Do I just say, 'Make a ball'? 'Use words' is not a very clear instruction, David."

He grimaces. "It's different for every person, apparently. Spells aren't universal, which might be why humans are so quick to give up when they try it. Developing your own spells for everything is a lot of work. Phil does say that it helps to use rhythm—so sing the words or rhyme them. The more words you use, the more opportunity to build the magic, so 'make a ball' is probably not enough words, especially since you're not used to doing this. Remember, this isn't like my sorcery, where I take natural-born ability from within and direct it. You're trying to harness and utilize the magic that makes up the universe. It's going to feel different."

I refrain from pointing out that I have no idea how his sorcery "feels" to begin with, so I wouldn't know if it was different or not. Instead, I take a deep breath. I can smell the sharpness of the antiseptic the cleaners used and underneath it, the remnants of someone's lunch… tacos? Never mind. "Here goes."

I close my eyes again and visualize a cool, white ball of light, focusing on it until the image is clear and crisp in my mind, then I imagine the magic I can feel all around me swirling together to create that ball, open my mouth, and sing, "La-la, di-da, ha-ha, ball of light we are; rah-rah, tee-tah, bah-bah, ball of light we are."

I know even before I open my eyes that it didn't work. I can feel the magic against my skin, ebbing and flowing, swirling, whisking about, but none of it reacted at all to my visualization or words.

I sigh and look at David. "What went wrong?"

A shout of laughter bursts out of Andrew, but before he can say anything, I point at him and declare, "No picking on my awesome skill as a singer/songwriter."

"I don't think it was the words, anyway," David says. "I've seen humans perform spells before, and even with the ones that didn't work, there was at least a stirring of the magic around them. This time, it… well…."

"It didn't react at all," I finish. "Yeah, I noticed."

He hesitates.

"What?" I ask. "You can tell me what I did wrong, David. I won't learn otherwise. I can take it." I can't really, but I'll pretend I can and then go home, curl up into a ball, and nurse my shattered ego later. It's already pretty bruised because I can't get the magic to respond.

"You didn't actually do anything wrong," he says. "I'm a bit baffled, honestly. I expected it to take a lot longer for you to be able to sense the magic at all— based on all my reading and what I've been told, we should have spent this whole session working on that and not made a lot of progress. It should have taken a few days of intense concentration before you even began to feel it. So… you're advanced there. You sensed it as easily as any of us. But maybe that means it's going to take a little longer for the rest."

"You should try again," Elinor suggests. "Now that it didn't work once, there's probably less pressure. And practice never hurt anyone, right?"

"Right. Okay." Try again. Just like the first time I tried to ride a bike and fell off. I need to get back on and keep at it until it all comes together.

I ignore the little voice at the back of my head whispering that the bike at least moved a few feet before I fell off.

Closing my eyes again, I envision the ball of light and picture the magic that's kissing my skin streaming toward it, building it up. "Magic ribbons winding up, wind into a ball. Magic ribbons lighting up, light the ball for me." I half chant, half sing this time, but it loses impetus toward the end, because there is absolutely no reaction from the magic.

At all.

I sigh and shrug as I open my eyes. "This is frustrating. I can *feel* it all around me, but it just goes on its merry way and ignores me. It's like those stupid arcade machines—the candy bar is right fucking there, and you've got the tools to grab it, but somehow, you still can't."

"Interesting analogy." Andrew sounds like he's choking, and I know he's trying not to laugh at my choice of spell words.

"Hey, it fits. Also, if you think you can make up a better spell on the spot, I'd like to hear it."

He opens his smirking mouth, stops, then closes it, consternation crossing his face.

"Yeah, that's what I thought," I sneer.

"You might just need to sit with the magic for a while," David says, but he doesn't sound at all sure. "I'll give Phil a call tomorrow and see if he's got some insights."

"If you don't mind," Gideon interrupts, "I have a theory. It's really off the wall and probably wrong, but…" He shrugs.

Ugh, I just want to ruffle his feathers. How dare he be all calm and cool when I'm frustrated and flustered?

"By all means, let's hear it." I sweep an arm in his direction. "The floor is yours."

His smirk is just as irritating as Andrew's. "The day after you got drunk and made an idiot of yourself, when you got up, your hair was sticking up just like it is now, and you said it was always like that in the morning."

I wait, but he seems to be done. "That wasn't a question."

Elinor snorts. Gideon rolls his eyes. "Sorry. Does your hair really always stick up like that in the morning?"

"Is it relevant?" Are we really standing here talking about my hair? Also, I'd really like to fix it now that I'm not playing with magic anymore. I lift my hands to smooth it down, but it seems particularly stubborn right now, and I don't want to fuss with it while everyone's watching, so I drop my hands.

"Yeah, actually. So…?"

He's so fucking sexy. Annoying. I mean he's annoying, not sexy. Though he is sexy too. "Yes." I sound like a petulant child, but there's no way to fix that.

He nods. "And you can feel the energy flowing through your body now that you're thinking about it?"

"Yes." He seems to be waiting for me to say more, so I add, "It's kind of tingly."

David looks up sharply. "Tingly?"

"I don't know how else to describe it," I say helplessly, spreading my hands. "Is that not normal?"

"I don't know," he admits. "It might just be a terminology thing, but nobody else I've spoken to ever described it as 'tingly.' They talk more about a glowing feeling or a warmth."

"You've already said how the magic feels to you," Gideon interrupts, dragging my attention back to him. "And we've seen that you can't influence it at all—"

"Wait, you've *seen*? You can see magic?" I'm instantly jealous. When this life is up and I transition to the spiritual plane, I'm going to make sure everyone knows that my next cycle on the physical plane will *not* be as a human.

"No, I mean that we could sense that the magic didn't react to your attempts. 'See' was the wrong word. Sorry."

Well, that's a bit better. I still don't want to be a human in my next physical life. We kind of suck. "So what does that mean?" Does he have a point? Is he going to reveal this theory before we all grow old and die, which will probably happen sooner for me than the rest of them. Although... they are all considerably older than me. My online research on Andrew puts him at least over eight hundred years old.

And isn't that a disturbing thought?

"That means I've asked someone to come and weigh in on my theory. Here he is now."

And sure enough, when I look to the door, the lucifer is standing there. He reminds me again of a neat, unassuming accountant, only slightly more interesting with his gentle smile and the twinkle in his eyes.

"Percy, hey," Elinor says, sounding surprised. "I didn't know you were still here."

"I was supposed to leave hours ago, but one of the human heads of state called in a panic. Apparently news of pregnant couples disappearing is starting to trickle through to the humans." There isn't so much as a note of censure in his voice, but I still feel the words like a blow.

"We'll get right back to work," I assure him. Fuck, what an idiot I am to make the others waste time trying to teach me to use magic, of all things.

"You can't work all the time; you'll burn out," he says quietly. "I know how many hours you've all put in on this, and how many more are coming." He studies me. "Does your hair do that often?"

Oh, fuck! How embarrassing. I try again to smooth it down, but it's just not happening. "Yeah, uh, sorry. I've been trying to use magic, and I guess connecting to my inner energy has…" I give up on both trying to explain and trying to control my hair. I guess I'm still too in tune to my energy. "I don't normally come to work like this, sir," I promise.

His gentle smile flashes into a grin. "I'm sure you don't, but it doesn't matter if you do. And please call me Percy."

Call the lucifer by his name? "Sure." I smile weakly. "Uh, thanks."

Gideon steps forward. "It was your hair that got me thinking, Sam. David, correct me if I'm wrong, but humans don't usually have that kind of reaction to their own life energy, do they?"

I look at David. They—*we* don't?

He makes a face and shakes his head. "Not that I've ever heard. Your reaction all around to your inner energy and to magic overall was not quite what I expected."

"I asked Percy to come and have a look. Because of his position, he's able to see how magic interacts with beings on a molecular level." Gideon meets my gaze levelly, and for the first time since our hookup all those years ago, he seems... open. Like he's not being an asshole on any level.

I turn in a circle on the spot, looking for something I can hold on to. A chair? I would give everything I own for a chair right now.

In the next instant, someone's shoved a chair at me and Gideon is holding my arm, directing me to sit.

"I don't understand," I mutter. "There's... something wrong with me? On a *molecular level*?" I'm not just human, I'm a defective human?

"That's not what I meant," Gideon rushes to assure me. He's crouched in front of me, holding my hands, and the warmth and rough texture of his skin race through me, giving my stupid hormones the wrong idea. My dick, which had finally subsided in shock a moment ago, begins to stir again. "I don't think there's anything wrong with you. I— Can we just let Percy have a look? It might be easier to explain after. I could be completely wrong. You might just need to practice more to use human magic."

His dark gaze is locked on mine, intense, earnest, and I slowly nod.

After all, what can it hurt?

Gideon lets go of my hands and stands, and a moment later, the luci—Percy is pulling up a chair and sitting in front of me.

He smiles, and it's immensely reassuring. "This won't hurt," he promises. "You probably won't even feel it. If you do, it will be similar to the sensation of magic —which Gideon tells me you're very aware of."

I nod. "I'm ready."

"What I'm going to do is look at you through a filter of magic. It shows me things that my regular eyes can't see—the genetic markers of your species, special talents and abilities, personality traits. It's not something I do often because it *is* an invasion of your privacy. So I need your permission."

"You have it." And I plan to grill him intensely later —politely, of course, since he *is* the lucifer—and find out all about myself. If I have a special talent I don't know about, I'm going to learn.

He smiles again, and a moment later I feel the caress of the magic… intensify. I can't think of another word to describe it.

Percy's smile dims a little, and then puzzlement crosses his face, followed by concentration. Finally, he sits back.

"Well?" Andrew demands impatiently, and I start. I kind of forgot everyone else is still in the room.

Percy shakes his head. "Sam, in the nicest possible way, I have never seen anyone like you before."

"It doesn't matter how nicely you mean it, that still doesn't sound good." Maybe I am defective?

"Is there a reason he's both so aware of and yet unable to manipulate magic?" David asks.

"Yes." Percy blows out a breath. "He's… not really human."

I blink.

Did he…?

What?

The room spins.

"Whoa, Sam!" someone shouts, and then hands grab me and pull me back into the chair I was sliding out of. I shake my head firmly, dispelling the dizzy blackness.

"I'm okay," I manage. "Sorry. Uh. Just a shock. Could I…?" I swallow. "Could I have some water?"

"Of course!" Lily goes to the sink while Andrew takes my pulse.

"I'm glad you're here," Gideon says calmly to him, a steadying hand still on my shoulder. "I wouldn't even know what a human pulse rate should be."

"Should he be checking for human or something else?" Elinor asks worriedly. "Sam, what's your usual pulse rate?"

"I don't know," I mutter. I've done advanced first aid courses. I know what the baseline is for every species, but for some reason, I never really measured my own. I've had checkups before, though, so I assume it was normal for a human.

Which, apparently, I'm not.

"It's a little fast for a human, but he has just had a shock," Andrew says, letting go of my wrist. "I have no idea if it should be different, though."

Lily gives me a glass, and I gulp the water down gratefully. "More?" she asks when I hand the glass back, but I shake my head.

"No, thank you." I look at Percy. "Could you explain, please?"

He spreads his hands. "I will, as much as I can. But I think we need to be more comfortable. Let's go to my office."

I obediently follow along down the hallway toward the elevators, then crowd in. Percy's office is upstairs, on a floor that is, interestingly, less secure than the floor the investigators are located on. I let my mind wander to thoughts of why, mostly so I don't need to think about the fact that I'm "not really" human.

A hand slips into mine and squeezes.

I jerk my head up and look into Gideon's face. He's not smiling, his expression its usual glowering mask, but he meets my gaze, and something there is infinitely reassuring. He squeezes again, and then the elevator dings, the doors open, and he lets go of my hand.

The office assigned to the lucifer is spacious and comfortable, with a living-room-like seating area that can fit us all. I opt for the couch rather than an armchair, so I don't feel alone. It's stupid, but I really don't want to be isolated in any way right now.

Percy settles into an armchair and looks at me. "I'm sorry to have given you such a shock," he reiterates. "It's actually shocking for me, too. I've never seen any situation like this before."

I just nod.

"You said he's not human," Elinor says, "but wouldn't we have noticed that? He smells human. He's been working here for five years. What is he if he's not human, and how did nobody know?"

"It's complicated," Percy reiterates. "Really complicated. He *is* human… but not really."

"You're killing me here, Percy," Andrew says, and Percy shakes his head.

"I know. Let me try to explain. I'm still getting my head around it myself." He pauses, looking into the distance as though thinking. "The best way I can think to describe it is that his shifter side—oh, you're a shifter, by the way—"

"I knew it," Gideon gloats, while I try to wrap my brain around the fact that *I'm a shifter, I'm not human*.

"How did you know?" Elinor demands, standing from beside me and planting her hands on her hips.

"Hellhound or felid?" David asks.

"Wait." Gideon holds up a hand and digs out his phone. A second later, he's showing everyone something on the screen. Eyes widen, and Lily says, "Oooh."

"Do I get to see?" I snap.

"In a second," Andrew promises. "Percy, is Gideon right?"

Are they fucking serious? *In a second?* This is my identity we're talking about. Or my alter-identity. Fuck, how does it work? Especially since I apparently can't shift.

Or maybe I can and I just never have because I thought I was human?

This is too confusing.

"Gideon's right," Percy confirms, and Gideon turns the phone in my direction at last. On the screen is a photo of some adorable baby cheetahs, their fluffy hair standing up.

"Does… uh, this might seem like the wrong thing to focus on, but felid shifters don't have fur that stands on end like that, do they? Is, uh, is mine part of my…." I can't think of the word I want to use.

"They don't," Percy confirms. "At a guess, I'd say your hair is doing that still because of your age. As a shifter, you're still very young. But as I was saying before, the best way I can think to describe it is that your shifter side is dormant."

"Dormant?" Gideon's word is sharp. "Community genes don't go dormant to human genes."

I try to remember everything I've read on this subject. When humans breed with any community species, the community genes dominate. The baby is born without any human DNA at all, which doesn't make sense logically, but I'm told it comes down to magic. On the other hand, when two community species procreate, the child can take genetic material from either or both species—for example, a baby born of a vampire and a shifter may be mostly shifter but have a need to ingest blood.

Percy sighs. "I don't believe it was a natural occurrence," he says heavily. "In fact, I think Sam may be a child of an earlier genetic manipulation experiment."

I can literally feel the blood rushing away from my head, and I sway, extremely thankful to be sitting.

"Say what?" I whisper.

"There's no other way to explain it, Sam, I'm sorry. It looks like the tiny particles of matter that make you up are wearing human disguises. You were, for all intents and purposes, human, but the… let's keep calling them disguises for now, they're starting to degrade. It looks like they've been doing it for a long time, but very slowly. I don't know if it ever would have gotten to the point that your shifter side came out naturally before you died of human old age."

"This is just surreal. You're saying that my cells or genes or whatever are wearing human suits? Like the old parable of the wolf in sheep's clothing?"

He pulls a face. "Somewhat. Honestly, I find it difficult to understand it myself, and even the magic seems… disconcerted. And angry, which tells me this wasn't any kind of human spellcasting."

I rub my forehead, feeling a headache come on. "Remind me why?"

"Because if a human had done this, they would have had to use the magic that makes up the universe," David explains. "And the magic would know it had been done. Whereas a sorcerer utilizes their personal magic from within themselves, which can't be monitored, so to speak."

"It can be traced, though," Andrew says grimly. "Did you get any sort of signature?"

"Yes, but it was… muddled. I think there may have been several sorcerers involved. It will take time to sort that out, and I don't feel that's our priority this very second." Percy leans toward me. "Sam, are you okay?"

"I'm freaked the fuck out," I admit, not even caring that I just said "fuck" to the lucifer. "What does this *mean*? What's… is something going to happen to me?"

"I'm not sure," he says, "but we'll do everything we can to make this easy for you. I have a few questions, if I may?"

I concentrate on breathing evenly and nod. In the next moment, a warm, hard hand is pressed to the back of my neck and Gideon's huge, solid presence comes to stand at my side.

"Has your hair really always stood up like that, or did it begin at a certain time?"

I stop and think about it. "I… I think it began when I was in middle school? I remember complaining about it and my mom saying it was probably because of hormones. I don't think it happened before then." That was back when I still had a mom.

"Anything else that could be considered unusual?"

I wince but decide to come clean. "I don't know if this counts, but you said that I'm still young for a shifter —how young?"

"You're an adult, if that's what concerns you," Elinor assures me. "Our brain development is complete at around twenty-five, same as humans. But our bodies are a little different, probably because of our longevity. Those reproductive hormones you had as a human wouldn't kick in for a shifter until aro— Oh."

Andrew cackles. "Been feeling horny lately?" he teases. "World of Wangs getting a workout?"

"*What?*"

"World of what?"

"Andrew, please don't sexually harass Sam," Percy interjects before that rotten vampire can explain. The others look disappointed. "Sam, you're in your late thirties, right?"

I nod. Gideon's hand shifts against my neck, an extremely comforting presence.

"That's about the age most shifter species become fertile. With you actually being a shifter, it makes sense that you'd be feeling more… sexually aware right now."

I clear my throat. "That's been the case. So… great. But I still don't understand any of this, really."

"It's complicated," Percy says again. "Really complicated. And parts of it are still unclear. What I know for certain is that you are a felid shifter. That's visible to me when I look at you on a cellular level. But there are human cells in your system as well, and they seem to be holding back your shifter side. It's still there, but dormant. You can't access it. Those human cells are degrading, though, which is what tells me more than anything, even if there weren't also sorcery weaves around them, that they're not supposed to be there, and small parts of your shifter self are coming through—like your hair and hormones, I suppose. There seems to have been a bit of an acceleration to the degradation today—

I'd say that might be a result of trying to use magic? David?"

David nods. "Definitely. He was able to feel his own energy so much faster than we expected, and he said it tingled. Shifters often describe their animal as a tingling inside them."

"Did it feel like a rush of goose bumps under your skin that just got more and more intense, until your whole body was alive with energy that wanted to burst out?" Elinor asks.

I think about it. "Sort of. The goose bumps, yes, but it didn't really feel like it wanted to burst out." I bite my lip. "Is that bad?"

"It's probably the influence of the sorcery weaves in the human cells," Percy says reassuringly. "The bursting out part that Elinor refers to is the surge of energy before shifting. Since the human cells prevent that, you wouldn't necessarily feel it—yet." He takes a deep breath and meets my gaze solidly. "You have two options here that I can see, Sam. We can leave things as they are and see what happens. As I said, the human cells may not fully degrade before you die of old age, which means you'd live your life mostly as a human. As you get older, certain felid tendencies might come out. Or the cells could degrade faster than I expect, and you could develop felid tendencies over the years, perhaps even the ability to shift. I don't know, and for your safety and the safety of the community, we'd ask you to have regular checkups to monitor the situation."

"Yeah, of course," I mutter. A future filled with uncertainty—even more so than usual? Sounds about normal for me. "And the other option?"

"We try to unpick the sorcery weaves and remove

the human cells, allowing your shifter biology to come forward."

My head spins a little, and I'm glad I'm sitting down. Gideon's palm burns against my neck, a wonderful anchor to reality.

"This is some weird-ass coincidence," I blurt, not yet ready to address the other part. "Of all the humans in the world, I'm the one who came to work here, despite having absolutely no connection to any member of the community. Harold had to get special permission to interview me. And now we find out that I'm actually a shifter who was tampered with? Right in the middle of a case that's probably about genetic tampering? I mean… what are the odds?"

Andrew gets up and begins pacing. "It is weird. The thing is, we don't know how existential magic really works. We don't know when and why it's going to step in and do things. Maybe… maybe it was trying to bring you back to the community? No," he answers himself. "Percy said the magic was surprised when it realized what had happened to you." He shrugs. "Maybe it is all just a huge coincidence."

"Does it matter right now?" Lily asks gently. She comes to sit on the coffee table in front of me and takes my hands. "It might be something we'll never know. And I'm a little more worried about how it is that you can genetically be a felid and yet our background check for you shows only humans in your family tree."

Ooops.

I wince and withdraw my hands.

The vibe in the room becomes more alert. "Sam?" David asks.

"So, uh, my official background is not technically…

correct. Parts of it aren't entirely true."

Gideon's fingers twitch on my neck.

"But there are still only humans in my family tree," I rush to assure them. "I swear. I knew nothing about the community until the day I came in to interview with Harold."

Lily looks utterly bewildered. "What parts aren't true?"

I look up at the ceiling and purse my lips. "Well, my name is Sam… but my last name's not Tiller. Well, it wasn't. It is now. Legally, I mean."

"You changed your name?" David's frowning. "That should still have been in your file."

Fuck, this is not an easy conversation. "Yeah, except the way I changed it wasn't exactly legal. There's this guy… I paid him a fuck ton of money for a new identity. And for him to hack some systems and have the old me listed as dead."

Gideon's hand tightens. Andrew, who'd stopped pacing to listen, sits. Just… folds right up and sits his ass on the floor. "What?" he asks.

"Okay," David begins, then stops. "Okay," he says again. "This is obviously going to be a long story. Sam, are you up to telling it now?"

It's kind of late… but the more I think about it, the more likely it seems that in my old life, I was the result— victim?—of some kind of genetic manipulation plot. And that might turn out to be important and relevant to our current case.

"Yeah. It's… Thinking back, it seems like my life could be some of the missing puzzle pieces we need, and wow, that sounds so dramatic and egotistical."

Andrew, still sitting on the floor, laughs. It's an

almost hysterical sound. "Sam, you're a felid shifter sorcerously disguised as a human on a genetic level. I think it's okay for you to be a bit egotistical right now, since we've never known anyone like you to exist."

Good point.

"So, my birth name is Samuel Mills. I grew up in a blue-collar neighborhood in a small town. My dad worked—works? I don't know what he's up to now. Anyway, he was a mechanic, and Mom was a waitress at a café. We lived within our means, but my dad complained about it a lot. Said he deserved to live better than that. My mom would always tell him to be patient, that things would change once I was eighteen. I can't even remember the first time I heard that—I always knew that when I was eighteen, I was out. I'd have to look after myself. And then as I got older, I wondered why they thought their lives would change so much, because they weren't spending *that* much money on me. I mean, I had new clothes when I grew out of the old ones and food to eat and all that, but my friends at school had bikes and videogames and got birthday presents."

"You didn't get birthday presents?" Lily sounds shocked.

I shake my head. "I didn't even know when my birthday was until first grade when someone asked me. I had to go home and ask Mom."

"So your parents were pricks," Andrew declares, and I shrug.

"They weren't loving. I was safe and they made sure I had what I needed, but there was never anything more than that. Except they were kind of obsessive about medical care, which even as I say it seems like a huge red flag I should have mentioned before." Fuck, how could I not have realized? Eyes wide, I look at Percy. "Someone came to our house every month to take blood and give me a checkup. Every month as far back as I can remember."

"Samuel Mills, you say?" David says, going to the lucifer's computer. "What were your parents' names and where did you live?"

I tell him, and then as he starts searching, I continue, "When I was about twelve, I found the massive stash of cash hidden in the attic and realized that was how they planned to live large. I was pissed that they were saving all this money to enjoy after I moved out. And then I wondered where it was coming from, since stacks of crisp hundreds don't usually grow on trees. The more I thought about it, the more I became convinced they had to be doing something illegal. Being twelve and an idiot, I started trying to figure out what that could be, but they were totally boring. There were no late-night absences, no unexplained packages… no strangers visiting. You know, just the doctor that came every month." I sigh. "It makes sense now. They weren't really my parents, were they? Or if they were, they just saw me as an investment opportunity. Someone was paying them to raise me." I can't believe this. It's a puzzle I didn't even know existed, and yet the pieces are falling into place. I lean forward to put my head in my hands, control the dizziness, and Gideon's hand falls away from my neck.

I instantly feel a thousand times dizzier. I sit back up and tip my head to look up at him. He seems to know what I need without me having to say a word and sits on the arm of the couch, his side pressing against mine. I sigh in relief as the world stabilizes again.

"If you were actively trying to ferret out secrets and didn't notice that they weren't human, then they were probably human, which means they weren't your parents. Or… at least, one of them wasn't." Lily sounds thoughtful. She gets up and joins David at the desk, filching a notepad and pen, which she begins writing in.

"So… how did you end up faking your death?" Andrew asks.

I smile bitterly. "When I was fourteen, I came out to them. My dad—fuck, I don't know what to call him now. My foster dad? Anyway, I never knew it because he was such a distant parent, but it turns out he was a ginormous homophobe. He went completely off his nut, screaming about how he never signed on to raise… someone like me." I refuse to use *that* word. "My foster mom told me to go to my room, and when she thought I was out of hearing, she started telling him that it was just a few more years and then they'd never have to see me again and their lives would be so much better. Which, in retrospect, reinforces the idea that they were being paid to raise me, but at the time…." I shrug. "I was angry and scared and I just figured… why not leave now? What was the point of staying? So that night I packed a suitcase and left."

They all wait.

"Yeah, so I packed the suitcase with the money in the attic instead of clothes. I figured, in my angry four-teen-year-old way, that I deserved a cut. I took maybe half of it, but I didn't realize until a few days later how much that really was. Hundreds add up fast, you know? So when I realized that people were looking for me, I thought they'd found out the money was missing and were using the police to find me so they could get it back. Which might have been true, because my foster dad really wanted that better life, but knowing what I know now, I'm guessing that monthly visit from the doctor played into why they wanted to find me."

"And rather than give them the money back and then quietly leave after the furor died down, you changed your identity?" Andrew's looking at me like I'm either crazy or a hero.

"In the time before I knew they were looking for me, I discovered just how hard it is to be underage and alone. I had cash, but most hotels wouldn't give me a room without an adult or a credit card. And the ones that would were not exactly safe for a scrawny kid. Even riding the bus a couple towns over got me suspicious looks. I wasn't exactly tall for my age, and people have one of two reactions to a kid alone: they either want to make sure you're okay or take advantage in some way. I needed that cash to bribe my way into an apartment somewhere and support myself until I was older. So I went to the nearest decent-sized city and tried to get lost in the shuffle. They kept finding me somehow, though—and now I know how—and I had to move six times in that first year. Then I met this guy who knew someone who knew someone who helped LGBTQ kids on the run to disappear. I thought it was sus, but he turned out to be a legit do-gooder and was doing it for free for kids who were at risk. I got him to do a really thorough job for me and paid him a boatload of cash as a thank-you. I mean, the guy was doing good work, right? So Sam Mills was in a fire at an abandoned warehouse where over a dozen homeless people died, and Sam Tiller was born—and moved clear across the country. I had ID, enough cash to bribe my way into a safe place to live, got a part-time job while I was 'being homeschooled,' and deposited that money into a real bank account. By the time I turned eighteen and 'graduated,' I had a pretty legit life. Once I had a decent job that would cover living expenses, I used some of the money to buy my apartment, then donated what was left to an LGBTQ charity. And that's it."

"Fuck me," Andrew says. "You make it sound simple."

"How much money did you take?" Elinor asks.

"It turned out to be a little over two and a half million." Looking back as an adult, it gives me the creeps to think of a kid in that situation—more so now that I know what I was actually on the run from.

She whistles. "Well, you can feel good about what they thought you were worth," she says, "but that's probably about it. David, any luck?"

He pushes back from the desk. "Yeah, but I doubt any of it is real. It's bare bones. Definitely nothing medical in there. Your foster parents are listed as your biological parents, which we know isn't true. They reported you missing, and the next update after that is your death certificate. Your guy did good work—it looks completely real. We'll trace anything that looks usable, but I don't think we'll get a lot out of this."

A pang of regret tightens my chest. "So there's no way to know who my parents really were?" I mean… they might be dead. Or, worse, they could have sold me. Or one of my foster parents could be my actual parent, which means they basically did sell me.

Or I could have been stolen from them.

Part of me, the part that always wanted loving parents, really wants it to be that last one.

"Not easily," Percy says, "but since one of your parents is a shifter, we can do some DNA tracing and at least identify which felid clan you're from. From there, we'll be able to narrow it down a little further."

"We're investigators," Gideon says. It's the first time he's spoken for a while, and the sound of his voice is almost startling. "Just give us time."

Percy sighs. "We need to keep this quiet for now. There are some people who'll need to know, but let's not stir things up too much. Maybe this is what we need to get ahead of the cults." He smiles at me. "Do you want to take a while longer to decide what you want to do?"

I take a deep breath and shake my head. "No. It's… kind of a scary decision, but I want you to get rid of the sorcery. No, wait—what will happen when you do?"

"I don't know," Percy says honestly. "People don't usually become shifters as adults. You may have to learn how to shift the way you would have as a teenager, or it might… be a little uncontrolled. You may retain all your human traits, or your shifter instincts might take over. If you want to think about it a little more, that's fine—we'll need some time to arrange things. This is complicated sorcery, and it's someone else's, which makes reversing it even more complex. Plus, I think it would be a good idea to have another felid here— someone alpha, who could help if your shifter side takes over."

I bite my lip. I don't like that so much is unknown here, but on the other hand, do I really want to live the rest of my life as someone's science experiment? There're a lot of unknowns to that, too.

"Make the arrangements," I say firmly. The pressure against my side increases, and I look up at Gideon. He's not smiling, exactly, but something about his expression is softer.

"Okay," Percy says. "David, can—"

"Of course," David interrupts. "I'll make some calls. I don't want to make you feel like a lab rat, Sam, but we'd like to try and get a signature off the weaves before we take them apart. That will help us track down the perpetrators."

"Of course." I want to know who did this. Why. Where I really come from. And if it's connected to the current kidnappings, how we can stop it.

"Let's pack it in for the night," Percy declares. "Gideon, I know you've been frustrated about the lack of traction in the kidnappings, but I don't think you'll achieve anything further tonight, and really, this could be a development that changes your direction."

Gideon nods. "I agree."

"Before we go," Lily interjects, "I just want to run one thing past the group." She holds up the pad she's been drawing on. "David, Percy, this is something I want you to keep in mind when you're examining and reversing the weaves. If you can confirm it, it might get us somewhere."

"Let's hear it," David says, leaning against the front of the desk.

"The thing I was wondering is, why would you go to the bother of disguising a shifter—or any member of the community—as a human on a genetic level. Like you said, it's complicated magic. Assuming this is related to those megalomaniacs intent on the community blotting out humans, we can tentatively say the benefit is human-level fertility. Sam, have you ever had a fertility test?"

"Uh, no. Impregnating women has never been high on my to-do list."

Andrew laughs so hard, he snorts. Ever seen a centuries-old silver-hottie vampire snort with laughter? It looks wrong. He's supposed to be dignified.

"Would you mind giving a specimen before we reverse the weaves?" Percy asks quietly. "I'm sorry, I know this is invasive, but…."

"It's fine," I assure him. "Set it up for tomorrow?" He nods, and I turn back to Lily. "Wait, so if I'm following your train of thought, you're saying that I would be as fertile as a human, but the genetic makeup I pass on to any offspring would be shifter?"

"I *think* so," she says, making a face. "It's only a theory. But what would be the point otherwise? You've gone your whole life with no magic and no shifter abilities—how would that further the cultists' goals?"

"That's something we can try to verify in the weaves," David assures us. "What else have you got there?" He points to Lily's pad, which does seem to have a lot of writing and hand-drawn flowcharts on it for just that one theory.

"No, the rest waits. I need to do some more thinking, and I want to see if I'm right about this first bit."

David looks like he's going to argue, but Percy steps in, saying smoothly, "Then let's call it a night. We'll meet back here at eight tomorrow—that should give you all time to rest and check on your caseloads before we start. I'll arrange for a doctor to give you a full checkup, Sam, if that's okay, and then we'll look at reversing this sorcery."

I blow out a breath. Wow. "Sounds good." And it *does*.

CHAPTER EIGHT

IT'S NEARLY MIDNIGHT, and I've been sitting cross-legged on my couch, just staring at my phone, for half an hour. I got home, changed into pj's and brushed my teeth, decided I was too wound up to sleep just yet, and… that's it.

I really want to call Alistair. He's my best friend, and this is a huge development in my life. But… it's late. And this is supposed to be kept quiet.

And what if it changes how he sees me?

I hate myself for even thinking it, for doubting Alistair's friendship and integrity like that, but… the little voice at the back of my head is persistent. Plus, I've heard Alistair gripe about cats a million times. There's somewhat of a rivalry amongst shifters.

Ugh. This is ridiculous. Alistair has high-level security clearance and he's *my best friend*. If he finds out about this later from someone else, he's going to be hurt.

I hit the call button and lift my phone to my ear. It only rings twice before a sleepy voice growls, "What's wrong?"

I open my mouth to say, "Nothing," but the word gets stuck in my throat.

"Sam?" He sounds more alert now. "Where are you? Are you okay?"

"Yes," I manage, because I am. Mostly. "Uh, you're not going to believe this." Should I tell him to come over? It's really an in-person kind of conversation, but it's late. We both have work tomorrow.

"Not going to believe what? Are you still at the office?"

"No, no. I'm home. So, tonight David tried to teach me how—hey, how come you never told me humans could do magic?"

Silence. I can almost see him blinking as he tries to process that.

"I never thought about it," he says finally. "Most humans don't bother to learn, so I only sometimes remember that you can."

"I can't," I inform him. "David tried to teach me how tonight, and it didn't work. To cut a long story short, Percy used the magic to check why, and it turns out I'm not human."

The silence this time is longer. I wait him out.

"Have you been drinking?" he asks finally. "Did someone slip you some brew?"

"No." I bite back a laugh. This is fun.

"The lucifer used magic to check why you couldn't do human magic and it's because you're not human?" he summarizes.

"That's right."

"Okay. Sure. I'll bite. What are you then?" There's heavy sarcasm in his voice.

"Felid shifter."

There's no silence this time; instead, he yowls, a sound of pain.

"Alistair? You okay?"

"Yeah," he grumbles. "I thought you said you were a felid, and I stubbed my toe on the doorframe."

I snicker. "Seriously? You can't walk and talk at the same time?"

"Not when it's dark and you're saying stupid shit."

I wince. "It's not stupid shit, Al. And aren't you supposed to be able to see well in the dark?"

"My eyes are mostly closed because it's late and I was asleep. Wait… what are you talking about? Are you *serious*?"

"Alistair, I swear, everything I've said is completely true. I didn't wake you up just to play a joke."

There's a crash in my ear, and then distant swearing. I wait, and a second later Alistair's saying, "Sam? Sorry, dropped the phone. You're… you're a *cat*? I thought you were human! You smell like a human. How are you not human? Fuck, I need to sit down."

"It's the weirdest story, Al. And it's classified, so keep it to yourself." I give him a quick rundown of everything that's happened tonight. Surprisingly, he only interrupts to ask questions four times. When I'm done, he sighs.

"Wow. I can't believe you're a fucking cat."

I knew he'd get stuck on that. "Seriously? That's what you're focusing on?"

"It's important," he whines. "When they turn off the human part, you're going to smell like a cat."

"Turn off the human part?" I ask incredulously.

"You know what I mean." He sighs again. "Well, fuck. I guess I'll just have to get used to it." He pauses. "How are you? Freaked out?"

"Yeah, a little. I mean… I'm a shifter. This is so weird."

"Want me to come over?" I hear movement. "I'm coming over."

"No, it's fine. I'm fine. We both have work tomorrow." That's weak, and I know it. Truth is, I don't really want to be alone with my thoughts right now. I haven't talked about my parents—foster parents—to anyone, ever, before tonight. I don't even think about them if I don't have to. But I feel bad dragging Alistair out in the middle of the night to, what? Hold my hand?

Someone knocks on my front door.

I glance at the clock. It's after midnight. I'm definitely not expecting anyone. Fuck me, what if it's the cultists? What if they've finally tracked me down after all these years and come to take me back?

"Al, there's someone at the door," I whisper.

"Now? Don't open it," he demands. "I'm on my way. Go lock yourself in the bathroom."

A laugh bursts from me. I can't help it—the thought of cowering in the bathroom, waiting for Alistair to come and rescue me from what's most likely a neighbor with a problem, is just that ridiculous. "Let me check the peephole before we both overreact," I suggest dryly.

Gotta admit, though, I tiptoe over to the door and hold my breath as I peer through the peephole, as though whoever is on the other side will hear me breathing and… I don't even know what they'd do if they heard me breathing. Knock again?

"Oh." The surprise is clear in my voice.

"Who is it?" Alistair asks. The aggressive note is gone; he must realize it's not anybody to worry about.

"Gideon," I say, sliding back the chain and undoing the bolt.

"Gideon? Who's— Gideon *Bailey*?"

"Yes." I turn the key in the lock and open the door.

"What the fuck is Gideon Bailey doing at your place at this time of night?" my best friend demands loudly.

Very loudly.

From the twitch of Gideon's lips, loudly enough for him to have heard.

"Hi, Gideon. Everything okay?" I lean against the doorjamb, trying to be casual.

He eyes me. I instantly feel like an idiot. It doesn't help that this is the moment when I remember that my pajama pants have a rip in the thigh, right near my groin, and the T-shirt I'm wearing with them is bleach stained. My professional image suffers a huge blow, and I sigh, straighten, and step back. "Come on in."

In my ear, Alistair says, "Sam, what's going on?"

As Gideon steps past me into my living room, I tell Alistair, "It's all good here. I'll talk to you tomorrow." Tomorrow, the day of reckoning. "Um…" I bite my lip and look at Gideon's back. "Hang on." Pulling the phone away from my face and covering the microphone, I say, "Gideon, do you think it would be okay if Alistair is there tomorrow? When Percy and David are trying to reverse the sorcery weaves, I mean?"

Don't get me wrong, I like my new team. They've been great. But for a life-changing—literally—experience, I want Alistair there.

Gideon seems to consider it. "Yeah. They might have to ask him to leave if your cat reacts badly, but they'll probably kick most of us out if that happens, so…" He shrugs.

"Thanks." My smile feels shaky. Fuck. What if my cat reacts badly?

Nope. Not thinking about that now. I lift the phone back to my ear. "Hey, Al, can you make some time to be there tomorrow when they turn off the human part?"

Gideon makes a sound that might be a laugh, but I steadfastly don't look at him.

"Of course," Alistair says immediately. "I'll pick you up tomorrow morning."

Something in me settles. "Nah, you don't need to do that," I assure him. "I've got other stuff to do first anyway. I'll let you know when we're… ready."

"Sure?" He sounds dubious.

"Positive. Go back to bed, and I'll see you tomorrow. Thanks, Alistair."

"And you're sure you're okay with the demon there? You never said, what's Gideon Bailey doing there?"

"I'll find out in a second, won't I? Good night."

"Good night, cat. I can't believe you're a cat," he mutters, and then the line goes dead on my chuckle.

I toss the phone onto the couch and turn to see where Gideon's got to. I'm not really surprised to see him in my tiny kitchen, moving some things around in my pantry. I've seen him reorganizing everyone's desk at the office about a million times over the past couple months.

I wince.

"Yeah, sorry, I might not have put everything back exactly where you arranged it after I used it." I'm not exactly a keep-the-pantry-organized kind of person.

"Better that way," he says without turning around. "Gives me something to do."

I hover near the peninsula counter that separates the

kitchen from the living room, then finally just sit on one of the barstools. He's obviously not going to tell me why he's here until he's sorted through whatever problem is clogging his brain. Fuck knows, he's probably got a shit-ton to think about.

There's something oddly soothing about watching Gideon rearrange my pantry. I find myself being lulled by his movements, and soon I rest my head on my arms on the counter. My eyelids feel so heavy. I'll just let myself drowse for a few minutes until Gideon's finished.

Next thing I know, the world is flipping upside down. I open my eyes and find myself staring at a very nice ass.

What an amazing way to wake up.

Wait… I know that ass. I've been admiring it for weeks.

Covertly, of course.

"Gideon?" I mumble sleepily, wondering if I'm actually awake or just having a fabulous dream. "What are you doing?"

In other words, why am I draped over his shoulder?

"I didn't want to wake you, so I'm carrying you to bed." I feel his voice rumble through every inch of me that's touching him.

"Oh. Okay." I like this. This is good. If it is a dream, I'm just going to enjoy it.

I'm flipping again, and then the soft but firm feel of my mattress is under me. Do I care that he now knows I don't make my bed? Not really.

I snuggle under the covers and let my eyes close. "Thanks," I mumble.

"You're welcome," he replies, and the warm, amused tone almost makes me want to open my eyes again and see if he's actually smiling, but I'm too sleepy.

I'm just on the edge of sleep when the covers lift and the mattress dips behind me. My eyes snap open. Is Gideon... getting into bed with me?

The general shifting of the mattress and the "getting settled" rustling noises would indicate yes.

I turn over and sit up. "Dude, what are you... do... ing?" He's lying on his back, one arm behind his head, his naked chest on display. Frankly, I'm going to congratulate myself for not drooling.

I'm not, right?

No. It's cool.

"Going to sleep," he says, like I'm an idiot to even ask. "I didn't think you'd want to be alone tonight."

Aww. My whole body just melts into a puddle of goo.

No. Wait. There's something about this that's not right.

Boundaries! That's it.

"That's sweet, but you can't just climb into bed with me, Gideon. That crosses a great big fat line."

"If I was sleeping in the guest room, you'd still be alone," he points out in a reasonable tone. "And this bed is huge. You haven't even noticed the pillow between us."

I look down, and nope, I hadn't noticed, but he's put one of my extra pillows in the center of the king-size bed. My resolve wavers.

"It's still creepy," I declare, "even if you're trying to be thoughtful."

He sighs. "Would it still be creepy if I'd done it to make sure you didn't throw up in your sleep and choke on your own vomit?"

"Why would I throw up in my sleep? I'm not dru —" My eyes go wide. "No way! You slept in my bed when I was drunk and unconscious? Gideon, that's creepy!"

"Choking on vomit was a concern, remember? And anyway, your guest room bed is tiny. How were Andrew and I supposed to share that?"

I scrub my hands over my face. I can't believe I slept a whole night with Gideon in my bed. I can't believe he doesn't see why this is a problem.

"You're missing the point," I snap. "It's *not okay* for you to decide we're sharing a bed without asking me first. It's definitely not okay for you to sleep in my bed while I'm unconscious and unable to defend myself!"

He sits up. "Defend yourself? From me? I'd never hurt you." There's a surprised tremor in his voice.

"Gideon, that doesn't matter. What matters is that you're invading my personal space while I'm vulnerable. You can't do that without permission."

He closes his eyes and takes a deep breath. "You're right. I'm sorry." His eyes open again, and his remorse is clear. "I hadn't thought of it from that perspective, and that was wrong."

"Thank you." I'm actually pleasantly surprised that he's apologized. His hotness factor just multiplied about a thousand times, something that my dick definitely notices. "For what it's worth, I get that your intentions were good, and I appreciate you thinking about my well-being."

He flips back the covers. "I'll go sleep in the guest room."

"No." I sigh and lie down. "I know you're here now. And you're right, this bed is big enough that we'll never even come into contact. Plus I stripped the bed in the guest room after that night and haven't made it up again." Or washed those sheets, but he doesn't need to know that.

"Are you sure?" He hesitates. It makes me like him more.

"Yeah, I'm sure."

I feel him moving around as he settles in again, but I resolutely don't look over. His presence, even with nearly two feet of space and a pillow between us, fills the bed—and my senses. I can't believe I never knew he was there that time, even if I was blind drunk and unconscious.

This is going to be a long night.

I WAS WRONG.

As I open my eyes almost six hours later, I marvel over what a great sleep I had. Something about the sound of Gideon breathing and his overwhelming, protective presence was incredibly soothing.

I roll onto my side and study him. He's on his back, which gives me a fantastic view of his profile. It's like he was chiseled from stone, his face is so perfect. Sleep has relaxed his features, and he's even more attractive—still severe-looking, but softer. More vulnerable. True to his word, he's still on his side of the bed and the pillow is in place between us. A tiny part of me—the part that wants to lick him all over—is disappointed about that.

I'm glad he's still asleep, though, because this gives me the opportunity to look at him. I rise up onto my elbow and take in the glory that is his naked chest. Demons are naturally more muscular than other species

—well, more bulkily muscled. Most shifters have a lot of muscle, but it's leaner. Demons tend to be built broader, and Gideon seems to take very good care of himself. He's ripped, even for a demon.

My mind wanders a little as I admire the dips and planes and ridges of his gorgeous, furry chest. Gideon's an enigma. My online searches on him got a lot of hits, even if there was little actual information. He keeps his private life pretty quiet, and the combination of that secrecy plus his looks and professional reputation drive the team's fanboys wild. The girls too, I imagine, but the one thing he never even tried to keep secret is his prefer-ence for men. There's a lot of gushing over him in the forums and some pretty racy fan fic. What I actually know about him is limited.

He's somewhere between a hundred and fifty and two hundred years old. His exact age is unclear.

He was born and grew up in Europe, then came to the US when he was appointed to this team—about forty or fifty years ago.

Prior to that, he worked in investigative offices in five different countries.

His family is important. I don't know the exact details—I never really looked into it. But they're prom-inent amongst demons.

He's seriously good at his job, although his interper-sonal skills can be lacking sometimes.

He's empathetic enough to have realized that I didn't want to be alone last night and caring enough to have come over to stay with me.

He's an insanely good fuck.

"Are you done ogling me?"

And he's awake and aware that I'm staring at him like a creeper.

"I'm not actually looking at you," I say loftily, my cheeks burning. "I was staring into space and thinking. You just happen to be in my line of vision."

His dirty chuckle tells me he's not buying it. Unintentionally, I look at his face.

He's smiling. The soft, amused expression transforms him, and my lips part in shocked wonder.

Would he murder me if I kissed him?

Probably.

And it would be a baaaaaaad idea. We're leaving the past behind us. I have to work with him. He doesn't want a relationship—not with me, anyway.

Bad idea.

Stop thinking about it, Sam.

"What are you thinking about now?" he asks in that rumbly morning voice that makes my morning wood just a little bit woodier. Can he read my mind? Fuck, I hope not.

"Uh, just that it's time to get up. Big day today!" Crap. It *is* a big day. They're going to try to reverse the sorcery that makes me seem human, and nobody knows what will happen or even if it will work.

That kills my erection.

I start to throw back the covers, but Gideon's hand shoots out and captures my wrist.

"Sam… it's going to be okay. You're going to be fine." The firm, definite statement is reassuring. I turn back to him as he sits up.

"Do you really think so?"

He nods. "Yes. Even if something doesn't go as

planned, we will fix it. You're going to be *fine*." He leans in, and before I realize what he's doing, he's planted a kiss on my mouth. There's no tongue, but he lingers a little, and when he pulls back, I suck in a shaky breath. "I promise," he whispers, his face still only inches from mine.

I nod. "Okay."

And I feel better.

CHAPTER NINE

IT'S ALMOST MIDMORNING by the time we all gather again in the lucifer's office. We were supposed to be there earlier, but there was another kidnapping overnight—a couple we knew nothing about, which is better than it being one of the ones we were trying to protect, but still. While everyone else chased down those details and checked on their other cases, I had the pleasure of a medical exam. The doctor Percy called in is nice, but a full checkup, including blood and semen samples, is not my favorite way to spend a morning.

"You've been a good sport," Dr. Sims says to me at last, packing away the equipment she brought with her. We're in Percy's office, where we can be guaranteed privacy. "And without lab results, I can tell you that you appear to be human in every way. We'll see what the lab says about that. I'm keen to get a look at those results."

"You're not the only one," I mutter, pulling my pants back on.

"Are you concerned, Sam?" she asks gently. "I want to remind you that you don't *have* to do anything."

"I know." I sigh. "Thank you. I'm a bit… nervous, but I do want to move forward. I don't think it will help anything to leave things as they are. It's just going to weigh on my mind."

She nods. "All right, then. I'll let everyone know we're ready." She slips out, closing the door behind her as I finish buttoning my shirt.

Barely a moment later, there's a knock on the door. "Come in," I call, bending over to lace up my shoes. I hear the door open and close, but nobody speaks, and I straighten to see a man I've never met before studying me. He's a shifter, I can tell that, but I'm not sure about species. Based on his height—only a few inches taller than me—his slim build, and the fact that he's come in here, I'm going to guess felid. I'm further going to guess that this is the alpha Percy asked to sit in.

I can't wait until I have shifter senses and will be able to know all these things with a sniff instead of having to guess.

"Hi? I'm Sam."

He tips his head to the side, still examining me. "I know. You really do smell human. If it was anyone but Percy, I'd think they were fucking with me." He extends a hand. "I'm Aidan." Only the faintest hint of an Irish accent is apparent, but it still gives his words an almost musical cadence. That, combined with the name, tells me exactly who he is. He's not just an alpha felid, he's the shifter species leader. Like the role of lucifer—and god—the roles of species leaders are assigned by the magic. Aidan has been shifter leader for only fifteen years, and *all* shifters—felid and hellhound—answer to him.

I shake his hand, a little nervous now. This man has

flown a long way to be here, and he's going to have a lot of influence on my life soon. If he decides I'm not really shifter material... I don't actually know what will happen, because there has never, ever been a situation like this.

Huh. I'm a freaking history maker.

"It's good to meet you," I manage, and he grins suddenly.

"Relax, man. Well, if you can. This is a helluva situation." He wanders over to sit in one of the armchairs, and after a second's hesitation, I follow and take up last night's post on the couch. Was that only twelve hours ago? "I thought you might have some questions for me."

I shrug. "About a million," I admit. "But I can't remember most of them right now, and the ones I can, I don't think you can answer. Mostly, I'm worried about what will happen right after they... do it."

He leans back. "You're right, I can't answer that. Not definitely. We've no idea what will happen. I've had a think and decided the best option is to prepare for you to react like a hormonal teenager. Percy tells me you're at about the age to be entering your fertile cycle?"

"Yeah. To be honest, though, I don't really know what that means." Am I still a child in shifter terms? That's kind of creepy, since I've experienced some very adult activities as a human.

"It's a bit different for us than for humans, from what I understand. We basically undergo two periods of, let's call it puberty—one is related to brain chemistry and physical growth and takes place during the teen years. Our young develop the ability to shift when they're toddlers but are mostly unable to control it. Their parents and other, stronger adult shifters restrain that ability on their behalf. This is partly to prevent them from exposing us to humans, but mostly it's to protect them. Spontaneous, emotion-driven shifting takes a lot of energy and can be very wearing on the body, leaving it susceptible to ailments and diseases. Our childhood mortality rates dropped an incredible amount once we instituted this practice."

"How long ago was that?" I ask, fascinated.

"Six or so thousand years ago," he answers so matter-of-factly that it takes me a moment to realize he didn't say sixty, or even six hundred. "Once they become physically stronger and their psychological development allows it, usually at around age fourteen, we remove that restraint and let them learn to control their own shift. It's a highly volatile time as brain chemistry adjusts to switching back and forth between humanoid and animal forms. Dominance begins to emerge, and a lot of social connections form and disappear. It's a difficult time in any shifter's life."

"Exactly like a human's teenage years."

Aidan nods. "Pretty much. Some biologists theorize that's why we don't have sexual puberty until later, after we're fully adults. Dealing with being a shifter is difficult enough. It would be even harder if we were still doing it 'the natural way' and not restraining children's shifts. The first fifteen or so years of their lives would be a fight for survival between the two sides of their selves." There's a note of disgust in his voice.

"That sounds like there are people who want to go back to the old way," I venture.

His sigh is frustrated. "Of course there are. People who think they know better than thousands of years of research and insist on risking their children."

"Like human anti-vaxxers," I mutter. I guess some things, like stupidity, cross the species barrier.

"Anyway, whatever the reason is, we don't experience sexual puberty until we're in our late thirties, early forties. Since our brains are fully adult by then, we're mostly better equipped to deal with the hormonal surges."

I think about that and compare what I've been feeling lately to what I felt as a teenager. He's not wrong. The arousal and urges are the same, but the constant insecurity isn't there.

"I, uh, I don't know what Percy told you," I start hesitantly, "but I seem to be going through sexual puberty now. The thing is, I already had it when I was a teenager." I spread my hands. "I don't know what any of this means."

"I wish I could give you an answer," he says. "The best I can come up with is that the human cells hiding your shifter side gave you the same growth experiences that any human would have had, but now that they're starting to break down, you're getting the shifter ones."

I bite my lip. "So... since I won't have learned to control my shift or gone through all the dominance development and stuff... I'm basically going to have two puberties at once?"

He winces. "I don't know. I hope not, for your sake, but on the flip side, I don't want you to be denied your shift."

I rub my hands over my face. "I guess we won't know if we don't try."

Leaning forward, Aidan reaches out and takes my hand. "I'm prepared for you to be the most volatile, aggressive shifter possible when they lift the magic. I *can* help you control yourself. That's why Percy called me instead of someone closer. No matter what happens, I will help you."

I nod, swallowing down my trepidation. "Okay. Okay. Thank you."

He studies me for a moment longer, then says, "I've also started the investigation into who your parents might be. There's not a lot we can do until the DNA results come back, but we're tracking down all reports of lost or stolen cat children from around the time you were born until you were about three or four." He shrugs. "It may be that your parents are involved in the cults and willingly took part in this... whatever it is they're doing, but we shifters tend to be very possessive and protective of our children, and I think it's far more likely they 'volunteered' other people's rather than use their own."

Something inside me perks up. "So you think it's possible I might have a real family?" Who would actually give a shit about me? Because that might be nice.

"I can't promise," he warns. "But even if it turns out your parents are cultists, we'll be able to trace your family line. You might gain some grandparents or aunts or cousins."

I lean back against the couch and tip my head back to study the ceiling. "At the very least, I'll be able to fill in the part of the form at the doctor's office that says 'family history.'"

He snorts. "Sam, I hate to break it to you, but your doctor is probably going to be government assigned for a few hundred years. They'll have your history, believe me."

I shiver a little, but in a good way. "A few hundred

years," I marvel. The reality hits. "Except we don't know if I'll actually live that long or just end up with a human lifespan." Man, this whole being the subject of genetic manipulation thing sucks. "I guess we should get on with it." There's only one way to find out what will happen, and that's to live through it.

"Before we do," Aidan says, "I want to make sure you know that we're glad you're here."

It's like being slapped—only good. Just this sudden, shocking *wall* of feeling. I don't know what to say.

Luckily, he's not done.

"Regardless of what happens once the magic is reversed, you are a shifter, and you're welcome among us. I imagine there will be a lot for you to learn and take in. I'm going to stick around until we can see how things go for you, and hopefully by then we'll have an idea of which clan you belong to and can get you settled with them. But whatever happens, you'll have a place with us. We'll help you acclimate to being a cat." He smiles at me, and I get just a hint of his alphaness. It's a comforting warmth in the air.

I smile back. "Thank you. That means a lot." I take a deep breath, then stand. "I'm ready."

THE ROOM IS CROWDED. My team is here, plus Alistair and Percy, of course. Dr. Sims and a nurse. Aidan. And two powerful sorcerers here to help David and Percy with the reversal.

"How would you feel most comfortable?" David asks me. "Sitting? Lying on the couch?"

I consider it. I don't think I could handle lying down

while everyone towers over me. I'm usually one of the shorter people in the room anyway; there's no need to make it worse. I'm not sure standing would be good, though—for one, I don't know how long this is going to take or if it's going to have a physical impact. I mean, it will, but…

"Sitting," I decide. It seems the better option all round. I pick an armchair and settle myself. "Is this okay?"

Percy smiles reassuringly. "It's fine."

There's some more preparation, during which most of the observers are banished to the far side of the room. Dr. Sims, the nurse, and Aidan are the only nonparticipants allowed to stay close, just in case I need them. I try not to think about what it would mean for me to need the doctor. We had a quick conversation earlier about the possibility that I might feel pain or have an adverse physical reaction—like cardiac arrest—during the reversal. I've been assured that they can definitely keep me alive in that case, which is a silver lining, I guess? We also talked about ranking pain levels. They're hesitant to introduce any kind of pain relief into my system until the procedure is done, in case it influences anything, but of course if I'm in agony, they won't make me stay that way.

So… yeah, feeling a bit nervous right now.

"Okay," Percy says. "Are we all ready?"

"Yes," David says, and his friends… fuck. I forgot their names. You'd think, considering what I'm about to let them do to me, that I would remember who they are.

Deep breath, Sam. This is fine. This is okay. I can just ask their names again. They look like they're concentrating, though. Maybe it'd be better not to interrupt right now. I'll just call them Tall and Eyebrows until we're done. Really, that guy's got the best damn eyebrows I've ever seen.

Am I rambling? I might be a bit nervous. I turn my head and glance across the room to where the others are. Gideon meets my gaze, and the solid strength there settles me.

"Sam." I look up at Percy. He smiles reassuringly. "What I'm going to do is filter the magic so they"—he nods to the three sorcerers—"can see what's been done. Then we'll work on reversing it."

I nod. "Okay. I'm ready." I feel like I've been saying that a lot.

In the next moment, I feel the warm wash of magic, the same as last night when Percy did his examination.

"Oh!" Tall exclaims, surprise written all over her face.

"Fuck," David says, and I try to remember if I've ever heard him swear before.

"You told us what to expect, but…" Eyebrows shakes his head. "This is extraordinary. Obscene, but extraordinary."

"You can see the threads of sorcery now?" Percy checks, and Tall nods.

"Yes," David replies. All four of them are looking at me, but… not. Looking beyond me?

Looking *into* me. That's so fucking creepy.

"You're right, Percy, there's several distinct signatures here, but the way they're woven together makes it difficult to pinpoint them."

Eyebrows pushes his sleeves up, as though preparing for physical work. "Hopefully we'll be able to get a good sense of them as we unravel this shit. Where do you want to start?"

I tune them out as they begin talking about crap I don't understand. I should probably pay attention, since they're going to be doing stuff to me, but I can't get my brain to focus properly.

"Sam?" That's David. I flick my gaze toward him. "Could you focus on your inner energy, the way you did last night?"

"Sure." That might actually help my brain work better. It felt almost meditative when I did it yesterday. Closing my eyes, I let the thrum of my heartbeat take over. Blood rushes to all my extremities and back again, a cycle of life and energy. A low-level tingle itches under my skin, not as strong as last night, but there.

"That's interesting," Eyebrows says. "You can actually see the sorcery degrading when he channels his inner energy."

"Most humans are unaware they can even do this," Tall responds. "It was probably something they felt safe not to guard against when they were designing the weave."

"It works in our favor, anyway. Let's grab some pieces before they disintegrate and see if we can identify the perpetrators. Sam, are you able to maintain this focus for a while?" Eyebrows speaks directly to me for the first time since we were introduced.

"I think so," I say, slitting my eyes open. It has no effect on the thrum of energy through me, so I open them properly. "It feels easier today, good, like stretching."

He nods. "Excellent. That makes sense—it's your shifter side waking up. Those of us in the community are used to being aware of our inner power. Let us know if you start to feel any strain, but I think that, given enough time, most of this sorcery will just break down under the pressure of your true self. That should make it easier for us to reverse."

"That's good." I let my eyes drift closed again and concentrate on the energy. It's kind of mesmerizing. Soothing. I can hear the murmur of voices as the others discuss what they're doing, but I don't bother trying to make sense of it. There's a faint rushing noise beneath it all.

"Sam?"

I lift my heavy eyelids and look up into David's smiling face. His features seem sharper… clearer, somehow. "Yeah?"

"We've gotten enough to identify the sorcerers involved and also to see exactly what they've done here. Now we're going to try unraveling the rest. I need you to pay attention and let us know what you're feeling."

Ah, the scary bit. Great. "Okay."

"Are you still okay to keep up the energy flow? Because we think that will make it easier."

"Sure. It's not any effort at all anymore."

David exchanges glances with the others.

"Could you ramp it up a bit?" Tall suggests tentatively.

I shrug. "I could try." I direct my focus back to the energy. It's been flowing without any direction from me for a while, so now I actually concentrate on the thrum of it, encouraging more intensity. The tingle picks up, racing a little faster, and the tiny hairs all over my body stand on end.

"That's sped it up," Tall says with a lot of satis-faction.

"If I may," a new voice says, and I open my eyes again. It's Aidan. "I could compel his shift."

"No!" Alistair snaps from across the room, and I turn my head to look at him. Elinor has a firm grip on his arm, but his face is livid. She doesn't look happy either. Gideon steps up beside her and bends his head to ask her something.

From the way the others stop to consider, I know this is a big deal.

"What does that mean?" I ask.

Aidan meets my gaze. "It's a serious thing," he says solemnly. "I would force your animal side to come forward. Shifting is difficult and takes a lot of energy at the best of times. To have it forced is very uncomfort-able, both physically and mentally. I definitely don't like the idea of having your first shift be that way."

So why did he suggest it? "Oh. You think calling my cat forward will make what's left of the sorcery fall apart." That kind of makes sense.

He shrugs. "It's a theory. Your scent has changed over the past hour or so—the human is fading, and the cat is coming out. I think there's enough of your shifter self discernible for me to call the rest out. I'll leave it up to the experts to say whether it would be a safer option than trying to unpick the sorcery."

"Percy?" David asks. He's worrying his lip with his teeth. "The weaves are degrading naturally under the pressure of Sam's shifter energy without impacting him at all. I'm confident we can handle unraveling them, but we don't know what those booby traps will do if we inadvertently trigger one."

Booby traps? Maybe I should have paid attention. "Wait," I say. "Can I just…? So, if Aidan forces me to shift, it'll be… what? A bit painful? Make me feel… sad? Anxious? Help me out here."

"Painful," Aidan agrees. "It's something your body can do naturally, but instead of you doing it, I'd be forcing it on you—like how most people can reach up behind themselves and scratch the middle of their back, but when someone yanks their arm back, it hurts."

"So painful but not cripplingly so?"

"Right. But there's a degree of mental discomfort too. You'll feel anxiety, and it will probably linger for a few days. You may also get emotional."

"Sounds fun," I mutter. "Okay. But it's likely that in return, this will dissolve all the sorcery with no consequences?"

"We *think*," David is quick to stress.

"The other option is for you all to pick apart the sorcery and potentially set off some kind of booby trap?"

"Yes."

"And we don't know what those booby traps would do?"

He exchanges glances with Eyebrows and Tall. "No. We could examine them a little more closely to get an idea, but that will take time, since we want to be careful not to set any of them off."

Well, fuck.

Either way, this is not going to be fun for me, but the decision seems kind of obvious.

"You're all the experts," I say, "but right now, my vote is for Aidan to compel the shift."

"Sam," Alistair starts, but Percy's already talking.

"I think that's the best option also. The magic seems to concur."

"Wait," Gideon says, frowning.

"That's what we'll do, then," David declares.

"It's best if we clear the room," Aidan advises. "We don't know how Sam will react to his first shift."

"I'm not going anywhere until I've talked to Sam!" Alistair shouts. I turn to look at him. He's got his hands balled into fists, and it seems like he's right on the edge of his own shift. Elinor is hissing something at him, but I can't make out the words.

"Okay," I say. "What?"

He stomps over. "You need to think about this seriously, Sam. I trust the species leader to take care of you, but a compelled shift is *awful*. Your first shift will be hard enough anyway without having to deal with the aftermath of it being forced. I'd be a shitty friend if I didn't warn you against this."

Nervous butterflies erupt in my gut. Could it really be that bad? I look at Elinor, who followed Alistair. She makes a face, but nods.

"It's really bad, Sam. We pretty much spend our lives trying to avoid it."

Fuck. I look over at David. "If you had to guess, what do you think those booby traps do?"

He shakes his head. "I don't know. But… for a booby trap like this to be triggered, a sorcerer would need to be probing your genetic makeup. I'd say the purpose of the trap is to protect the sorcerers involved and maybe hide the exact extent of the work. I doubt we would have been able to get as much information as we have without Percy's help—and without the weaves having degraded as much as they have. If they'd been in perfect condition, we wouldn't have even been able to *see* them without Percy."

"You're talking in circles, David," Tall says impatiently. She meets my gaze squarely. "If I was guessing, I'd say setting off one of the traps would cause a self-destruct in the remaining weaves."

"Which are tied to me on a molecular level?" I'm not sure if that's the right turn of phrase. Honestly, I don't even know what a molecule really is. But the very thought of something inside me self-destructing makes me feel sick.

"Yes."

"Then fuck no," Gideon declares. "You can't put him at risk that way. And I don't like the idea of forcing him to shift, either. There has to be a way to do this that won't *hurt*."

I push aside the warm, fuzzy feeling his concern brings and turn back to Alistair. "Which would be worse, a forced shift or the possibility of me melting into a puddle of goo from the inside out?"

He looks at the sorcerers. "What are the chances that you'd actually trigger the booby traps?"

"Fuck off!" Gideon roars.

I can't believe Alistair's even asking. I just want this fucking sorcery *out of me*.

Eyebrows spreads his hands. "We'd try really hard not to, but there may be more than we can even see. Let's say a maybe… ten, fifteen percent chance?"

"I don't think it would be quite that high," David says bluntly, "but if it were me, I'd go for the forced shift. I've heard they're horrible, but nobody's ever died from one, have they?"

Alistair shakes his head reluctantly. "Not that I'm

aware." He glances at Aidan, who also shakes his head. "Fuck, okay. I wish it didn't have to be this way." He steps back. "I have to wait outside, Sam. Your cat might not like having a hellhound in the room."

"Why are we not trying to think of a better solution?" Gideon demands.

I ignore him. Am I going to lose all sense of self? "But it's you," I tell Alistair. "Won't I know you?" I turn to Aidan, slightly panicked. "Won't I know my friends?"

"Probably," he assures me. "But you've never shifted before, and the circumstances aren't ideal. We don't know how your cat is going to react at first, so we're going to minimize the potential for problems. Remember?"

Yeah. All right. He did say something about that before. I nod, huffing out a breath. "Wow, I thought I was ready, but I guess this is… Can we just do it and get it over with?"

"All right, everyone, clear the room," Percy announces, and there's a ring of authority in his voice that startles me. I knew he was the lucifer, and everyone defers to him, but I never really thought about the fact that he's *in charge*.

He smiles at me. "For what it's worth, the magic is strongly indicating that this is the right decision, Sam." He defers to Aidan. "Dr. Sims, Karly, and I are going to stay. Does that work for you?"

Aidan nods. "Nobody else, though." He raises an eyebrow at Alistair, who huffs.

"I said I was going." He grabs me in a hard hug. "Ugh, you smell like cat."

"You'd better get used to it," I manage. Unless I die, of course. They said that had never happened, but hey,

I've been setting a record for firsts in the past twenty-four hours. Why not add another to the list.

He puts his hand on my nape and squeezes. "I'll see you in a few minutes."

Is that all this will take? I hope so. I nod, and Alistair lets go and makes a beeline for the door. "Hurry up, all of you," he yells. "Don't drag this out longer than it has to be."

Elinor grabs my hand and gives it a squeeze. "You'll be fine, Sam. See you soon." She goes after Alistair. Lily comes to give me a kiss and a hug, then she and Andrew leave as well.

"I'm sorry this wasn't easier," David tells me. "We're going to find the people who did this to you." And then the sorcerers are gone too.

We all look at Gideon. He's standing a few feet away, legs planted, arms crossed over his chest. He doesn't look like he's on his way out the door.

"Gideon?" Percy prompts.

Gideon shakes his head. "I'm not leaving him."

Aidan frowns and opens his mouth, but Gideon cuts him off. "Not. Leaving."

His intimidating, massive presence makes this all seem a little bit less scary.

"Let him stay," I say, almost without thinking about it. "If that's okay?"

Everyone looks to Percy, who's studying Gideon with a considering expression. He glances at me, back to Gideon, and then finally says, "Fine. But don't interfere."

Gideon nods sharply and seems to settle more comfortably into his I-can-kick-your-ass stance.

Percy smiles at me. "Sam, are you rea—"

"Sam, shift!" Aidan commands, and there's something in his tone that makes my bones ache.

But nothing happens.

Disappointment settles in my stomach. "Maybe there's not enough of my shif—" I cut myself off with a shriek as my whole body comes apart, the energy inside me *pushing*, bursting out—

CHAPTER TEN

Hurt.

All over.

Strange smell.

Not clan.

Danger?

Smell.

Clan. Alpha. Safe.

Strange smell. Danger?

Protect alpha!

Open eyes. No alpha? Up. Sore. Alpha danger? Snarl.

"Sam?"

Big danger. Protect alpha smell.

"Sam, it's me."

Snarl.

"Stay in that chair, Gideon. He's all cat right now."

Snarl. Protect.

"Sam."

Hurt. Whine.

"Sam!"

My awareness snaps back. What the fuck? What…

Whoa.

Like… whoa.

I think… I think I shifted.

I'm achy all over. I feel… different. My vision is… weird. And either I'm sitting on the floor, or I'm a cat.

I look down.

Paws.

Yep. Safe to assume I shifted.

I look back up and allow my weird vision to focus on the others in the room. Aidan is just a foot away, watching me intently. Percy is standing near Dr. Sims and the nurse. Gideon is leaning forward in his chair, his gaze fixed on me.

"Sam?" Aidan asks, and I open my mouth to answer, but only a rumbling sound comes out. Relief crosses his face. "He's back," he says, then sits on the floor right beside me and opens his arms. "How're you feeling?"

I practically crawl into his lap. There's something in me that just wants to snuggle up to him and be safe.

"You're okay," he assures me. "I've got you. Do me a favor—blink twice if you can understand me clearly."

I blink twice, and his smile breaks out as he scratches the back of my neck.

"Great. You've shifted into an adult cat, which is great, and there doesn't seem to be anything wrong. The human smell is completely gone—you're absolutely, one hundred percent shifter."

I rub my head against his chest. I don't know why. This is just… surreal.

"I want to see how your coordination is. Could you walk across to Gideon, please?"

Part of me hates the idea of leaving the safety of Aidan's touch, and I whine… then movement catches my attention, and I look over at Gideon again.

Without consciously deciding, I wiggle out of Aidan's lap and take a step toward Gideon—

—and stumble sideways.

Frowning, I stabilize, shake myself out, and try again.

This time, I trip and actually fall.

Aidan laughs. "Looks like you're a full-grown adult with the coordination of a first-time shift."

"Is that bad?" Gideon asks.

"Only in the sense that he'll need to get used to his cat. All shifters go through this—but usually we're teenagers."

I put my head down on my paws. I have to learn how to walk? How fucking annoying.

"Come on, Sam—it's not that bad. Let your cat do the work. You're trying to walk like a human, and that won't work with four legs."

Sighing, I push myself back up to my feet, which feels different from usual, and try to take a step without thinking about taking a step.

It doesn't work, and this time I collide with the coffee table. My snarl of pain is actually pretty cool to hear, and I try to do it again.

"If I may?" Percy asks Aidan, who nods. "Sam, focus on your inner energy."

I give it a try—it feels exactly the same as when I was human, only… tinglier.

I take a step.

And then another.

Hey, this isn't so hard after all!

On the next step, I stumble. Okay. Maybe don't get cocky just yet. Still, I manage to make it across to Gideon and rub my cheek against his thigh, mostly because I want to know if it's as muscled as I think it is.

It is.

He puts a hand on me and bends forward. "You're beautiful, Sam."

There's a sharp knock at the door, and I whip around, fall on my ass, scramble back to my feet, and snarl.

"Relax, Sam," Aidan says, letting a bit of the alpha seep into his voice, and the panicky feeling—*danger! Danger!*—recedes a little. "Those are your friends, remember?"

Oh. Right. Wow, those cat instincts sure are sharp.

"Percy, could you ask them to come in one at a time? Hellhounds last. He's still very reactive, and I don't want there to be any incidents."

Percy goes over to the door and lets himself out of the room. I back up until I'm touching Gideon's legs, then sit.

"Uh, Sam," he murmurs, and there's a thread of laughter in his voice. "Could you move over just a few inches? You're a beautiful cat, but just a bit too big to sit on my feet."

I chuff and glare at him over my shoulder. In response, he wriggles his feet out from underneath me.

The door opens, and I whip my head back around. Percy comes in and moves to stand beside the doorway. Lily follows him, and then he closes the door.

Her eyes land on me, and a huge smile lights up her

face. I suddenly realize that I can smell her—not just *her*, but her species. I can clearly tell that she's a succubus. I don't know how or why, but I just can.

I inhale deeply, and it sinks in that I can smell everyone in the room. Gideon, behind me—demon.

Percy—felid shifter. Lucifer. That has a smell of its own.

Dr. Sims—sorcerer. The nurse—demon.

Aidan—felid shifter. Alpha. Leader.

Briefly, I ponder the difference in scent between Percy and Aidan. It's subtle, but there. I wonder if me learning to be a cat will include explanations on reading scents and what they mean.

"Sam? Look at you!" Lily steps closer, then looks to Aidan. "Can I go to him?"

He's studying me. "Yeah, but keep it slow. No sudden movements. His protective instincts are very close to the surface."

Lily comes slowly across the room—so slowly that I get bored waiting for her and get up to go meet her. She gets down on her knees and opens her arms. "Can I have a hug?"

I'm still snuggled up to her when Percy opens the door and David slips in.

And then Andrew.

And then Tall and Eyebrows. They all exclaim in excitement when they see me, and my cat stays calm, mostly just intrigued by all the new scents.

But now I want Alistair. I go over to the door and nudge Percy. He glances at Aidan.

"Okay, Sam, but come over here first."

Chuffing my impatience, I obey. If he wants close in case I go gonzo, I really can't argue with that.

Percy sticks his head out into the anteroom, and a moment later, the door swings wide and Alistair and Elinor cautiously enter. My best friend's gaze flits around the room before it locks on me.

"Wow. You really are a cat," he murmurs, and then a huge grin breaks over his face. "Your fur is standing up on your head like a cub's," he teases.

Really? Oh, fuck me! Why didn't anyone say? I try to use my paw to smooth it down, but I'm pretty sure it doesn't work.

Alistair comes toward me, moving carefully but not that slowly, and sinks down to sit beside me. "All good, Sammy?" He offers a hand for me to sniff, but I've already clocked his and Elinor's scents. They're shifter, but different from Percy and Aidan and me. Part of me wants to wrinkle my nose and swipe at him because of it, but mostly it's just different and he's my best friend.

I knock his hand aside and swipe my rough tongue over his cheek.

"Hey! Eeew!"

Once the laughter tapers off into chuckles, Aidan says, "I think it's time for you to shift back, Sam. You need to practice shifting back and forth, and I imagine you all have a lot to do today."

Oh.

He's right, of course, but I kind of like being a cat. Plus, if I can't talk, I can kind of hide from everything that's still unanswered. And I've gotten tons of hugs. The hugs are nice.

And Gideon called me beautiful and I got to feel him up. Sort of.

I growl.

Aidan raises a brow, but Alistair slaps me lightly across the muzzle.

"Show some respect," he chides. "You don't talk back to the leader like that."

I stare at him incredulously, and he shrugs.

"Shifter etiquette is consistent across all subspecies. You might still be young in shifter years, but that's no excuse for bad behavior."

Okay, now I have to shift back just so I can laugh in his face. Is this the same Alistair who thinks "behaving" is for other people?

My look must communicate what I'm thinking, because he sighs. "It's different with the leader. Trust me. Now come on, it's time to shift back."

Huffing, I turn my back on him and look up at Aidan.

"He's right," my alpha tells me. "But you get a pass this time because you've never been taught the rules. What you need to do now is focus on your inner energy. Let it build in you until it feels as though it's going to explode out. Then visualize your human self and let the energy go."

He makes it sound so easy, but what if I fuck it up? Am I going to be some kind of weird half cat, half human? Or… how detailed does the visualization of my human self need to be? If I don't imagine my toenails, am I going to lose them? And then will I get them back next time I shift, or will I be forever doomed to walk the world as a toenail-less freak?

"Relax," Aidan chides, as though he can tell what I'm thinking. "This is natural for you. You can't fuck it up."

I'm not sure I entirely believe him, but it's worth a

shot. I focus on my inner energy, and it swirls forth faster than ever before. The tingling feeling is stronger, vibrating under my skin, making my fur stand on end. I close my eyes and picture my human self—with my hair neatly styled, thank you very much—wait until the tingling is so strong I feel like my skin is going to split, and then just… let it split? It's a weird sensation that I can't fully describe, but my energy bursts out of me, and I can actually feel myself changing. It's not the most pleasant experience. Not as painful as before, but still uncomfortable.

And then it's over.

Panting a little, I blink and look down at myself. Back to human.

"Wow." I sway a little bit. Every muscle in my body aches.

"Time to sit down," Alistair declares, taking my arm and pushing me down onto the couch. I cling to his hand.

"How do you feel?" Aidan asks, coming to sit on my other side.

"Fine. Tired. That was… surreal."

"Since you never expected to be able to shift, I'm sure it was. You did very well."

"Really?" My insecurities swarm to the surface.

Aidan's smile is warm. "Really. You have a lot more control than most cats shifting for the first time—aside from those initial few minutes when your cat was in complete control. Don't try shifting again unless I'm with you, just in case that wasn't a one-off."

My eyes widen as the implications of that hit me, and he rushes to assure me, "It's not likely. But there's no harm in making sure, yeah?"

"Yeah." I nod. Honestly, I'm not even sure what he's talking about. "My cat was in control? What does that mean?"

Alistair squeezes my hand. "Exactly what it sounds like. Sometimes, when the human side of us can't handle what's going on, the animal side takes over. It's a defense mechanism and usually only happens after a trauma. We're not actually animals in the purest sense when we shift—we retain our human faculties and just merge them with our animal senses and instincts."

I try to understand. "So… after I shifted, there was some time that I don't remember?"

Alistair looks across me to Aidan.

"Yes," the pack leader confirms. "Just a few minutes. You were disoriented, seemed a bit frightened. I called you back—it's similar to compelling a shift, but more psychological."

It's creepy to think that I wasn't in control of my body, and worse, I have no memory of it.

"If you don't mind," Dr. Sims says quietly, "we should get another lot of samples now that Sam is no longer human in any way."

"Samples?" Does she mean more blood and semen? Panic closes my throat. I can't let her near me with a needle, I can't. A little voice in the back of my head chides that she already took samples once today and there's nothing to worry about, but it's drowned out by a wave of fear. "No. Nonono."

"Sam?" Gideon gets up from his armchair and comes toward me. I launch up from the couch and into his arms, the sudden impact sending him back a step as I cling to him and bury my face in his neck.

"Don't let her near me. Don't. Please don't let her near me."

"Whoa. What's going on?" someone asks.

"Anxiety. Maybe paranoia," Aidan says, sighing. "It's a side effect of the forced shift. I'm sorry, Doctor, but it's probably best if you don't try to take those samples today."

"Of course," *she* says. I open one eye and turn my head slightly so I can see her as she makes her way toward the door. I can't trust her, not for one second. She might try to double back. "Call me when he's ready. We'll process the other samples in the meantime."

"Thank you," Percy says, and I turn my attention to him. He invited her here. Maybe he's in on it with her? Maybe he's just been pretending to want to help me.

I try to climb Gideon.

"Okay, Sam, I've got you," he murmurs. "Nobody's going to hurt you. You're safe."

"You don't know that," I hiss. "We don't know who we can trust!"

"I'd be offended, but he's really not himself right now," Andrew mutters. *The vampire.* In my head, all the stuff I've learned about vampires in the past five years tangles with the fiction from my pre-community life. I can't remember what's true and what's not. I can't remember if vampires are to be trusted.

"Sam, I need my hands free to protect you best," Gideon says softly in my ear. "So I'm going to put you down. You can stay right next to me, all right?"

I don't want to let him go, but he's right. I unwind my legs from around his waist and reluctantly drop to my feet, turning around so he can protect my back and I can watch everyone else.

"Sam, do you know who I am?" Aidan asks, and something in me relaxes. The species leader is here. He can keep us safe.

"Yes, of course. Aidan."

"Good. There's a lot going on here, so I think you'll be safest if you go home while I deal with it. Who would you like with you?"

My gaze flits around the room. If he can't come with me... who can I trust?

"Gideon," I say, even though I'm not really sure why. I just know he'll help me.

Alistair moves restlessly, and I bite my lip. Something in me wants to say his name too, but he's a hellhound. Am I sure I can trust him?

Gideon's a demon, and you're trusting him, inner me points out. "And Alistair," I add, and curiously, nearly everyone looks relieved.

Maybe he is in on their plot. Maybe I've just invited the enemy into my home, where Gideon and I will be vulnerable.

"That's great," Aidan says. Does that mean he doesn't know Alistair might be a risk? Or is he certain it's safe?

Alistair would never turn on you, inner me says, and I decide to trust him. It. Myself.

"Let's go, then," Gideon says, taking my hand and tugging me toward the door. "I'll walk with you, Sam, and Alistair will have our backs. We'll take his SUV. Is that okay?"

"Yes." I'm not sure if it is.

We get to the door and Gideon reaches for the knob, and I grab his wrist. "No. Stop. Can you hear them? They're out there." They're waiting for us. "We can't go out there without a plan. We have to take them down to get through." Behind us, I can hear the others murmuring. Plotting against us? Preparing to join forces with those outside?

"Don't worry, Sam, I have a plan," Alistair says confidently. I look up at him, but his gaze is fixed across the room. He knows. He's realized that everyone else has been compromised.

I lean forward and whisper to him, "We have to rescue Aidan."

His attention comes to me, and he nods. "Absolutely. My plan takes that into account." His gaze drifts back, and he nods again.

"Sam, could I have a moment of your time?" a voice says, and it's such a beautiful voice. I just want to listen to it all day. I turn around. Andrew is walking toward me, smiling, and he's sooooo pretty. I smile back. "I just need you to come and lie down on the couch for a few minutes. Come on, this way."

I follow Andrew over to the couch. I would do anything for him, because he's so nice and friendly and beautiful. I want to curl up in his lap and let him feed me grapes. He could ask for so much more than just me to lie down, but if that's what he wants…

I stretch out on the couch. Andrew kneels on the floor beside me, still smiling. "Thank you, Sam. That's exactly what I needed. You've done a great job." I can vaguely hear other people talking, but they're not important. The only thing that's important is Andrew and making sure he's happy with me. "Just lie there for a few minutes and rest. You can close your eyes if you like. I'm going to tell you about what I did last weekend."

I let my eyes drift closed as Andrew begins talking

about brunch and laundry and tennis. His voice is so nice. I'm going to lie here and bask— Ouch!

My eyes snap open in time to see Dr. Sims step back, a syringe in hand. I flail on the couch as panic swirls up, but then Andrew says, "It's all okay, Sam. Everything is just fine," and it recedes. For a moment longer, I lie there, absorbing the calm of Andrew's voice, and then my head gets fuzzy and my vision doubles. I close my eyes again.

CHAPTER ELEVEN

I OPEN my eyes and stare at the ceiling. I'm in my bedroom—I can see my dresser from the corner of my eye. But I'm not exactly sure how I got here. Fuck, please don't tell me I got drunk again.

My head still feels a bit fuzzy from sleep, so I take my time and run through what I can remember. I shifted —I'm a cat! Then I shifted back. We were talking about monitoring my next shift... Dr. Sims wanted to take more samples... and I freaked out.

Wow. What was wrong with me? I went totally conspiracy theorist. I can clearly remember everything I was thinking, and none of it makes any sense. It's like I really believed everyone was out to get me.

The last bit's a little unclear, kind of soft focus. Andrew must have been using his charisma on me— there's no other reason I would have gone from completely paranoid to wanting to curl up in Andrew's lap like a puppy. I'm not thrilled about it, but I can see why he had to do it—I was fully prepared to assault someone to "escape."

"You're awake."

I prop myself up slowly, letting my head adjust to the movement, and look at Gideon leaning against the door-frame. "Hey. Uh, how long have I been out?"

He straightens and comes into the room. "Just a couple of hours. Dr. Sims gave you a mild sedative, just enough for us to get you home and settled." He takes my wrist and puts his fingers to my pulse.

"I feel fine," I say, trying not to wince as I remember how I clung to him like a monkey does a tree. I'm not exactly sure what's going on with us—barely civil colleagues, friends, something more?—but I *am* sure that was embarrassing. "Uh, listen, I'm sorry—"

"Don't be," he says. "Nobody blames you. A compelled shift brings out some weird behavior. Alistair and Aidan warned you beforehand, remember?"

I huff a laugh. "Yeah, but I didn't realize it would be like *that.*"

"So you remember?" He sits on the edge of the bed. "How are you feeling now?"

"Embarrassed," I admit. "I remember thinking all those things, and none of them make sense."

"That's good," he says. "It means the paranoia has passed. Apparently there's a chance it might recur for the next few days, so we need to keep an eye out. Some-one's going to stay with you until we're sure we're clear."

"Okay." I'm not really upset by this. I don't want to be alone right now.

"Are you hungry? Alistair made this stew thing that's pretty good, and you haven't had lunch."

I sit all the way up. "He made his grandmother's stew? Awesome." No way am I missing that.

Gideon's mouth quirks in an almost smile. "I'll tell

him to dish some up for you. Take your time." He leans over and drops a quick kiss on my mouth that leaves me stunned. By the time I've got my wits back, he's left.

I follow his advice and take my time making a trip to the bathroom and stretching my achy muscles. I'm not sure if that's a side effect of shifting, the drugs, or both, but it's only minorly uncomfortable. Like the day after a workout when you haven't done one for a while. I have a lot of experience with that feeling, since working out regularly is not something I believe in.

I finally amble down the hall into my living room. Alistair is in the kitchen, ladling stew into a huge bowl, but Gideon is nowhere to be seen.

"Hey," my best friend says, grinning. "You look less crazy."

"Thanks," I reply dryly. "You always know just what to say." I slide onto one of the stools at the counter and take the bowl and a spoon from him. "Where's Gideon?"

"He had to go, now that you're awake. There are some things he needs to follow up on for the case you guys are working. He said he'd be back later… which gives me time to ask you what the fuck is going on with you and him."

I shovel in a spoonful of food. It's about twice as big as it needs to be, because I have no idea what to say and I need a couple minutes to think about it. Also, how dare that bastard run away after kissing me!

He just watches me, smirking. I glare at him while chewing, then finally swallow.

"Well?" he demands.

"Nothing. I don't know," I admit.

"Really? Because he's stayed over here twice now.

The whole office is talking about how protective he is of you. Today, he refused to leave you. You trusted him over everyone else in that room, including me. And he insisted on bringing you back here and staying until you woke up, even though there are a million things he should be doing. So… what's it all about?"

I put my spoon down and hesitate.

"I knew it! There is something."

"Not really. I honestly don't know. We… so the thing is, before I started working for CSG, he and I hooked up one night. I didn't know he was a demon, of course. And then I got the job, and it just seemed really awkward. He didn't know how to deal. I didn't really, either. We decided to pretend it never happened. But… sometimes I think there's something there. I mean, he's insanely hot, and his natural state might be asshole, but he can be really sweet sometimes."

"Sweet? Gideon Bailey? *Sweet?*" Alistair's jaw is practically on the floor.

"Yeah. Don't get me wrong, he's still a dick a lot of the time, but sometimes…" I shrug.

"That's just too weird." He shakes his head. "And I can't believe you hooked up with him and never mentioned it to me!"

"It was before I even knew you," I remind him. "Besides, if I'd told you, you would have just made the awkwardness worse. Which is why you are going to swear not to ever say anything about this conversation. Or write anything down. Or give anyone a knowing look. Or communicate in any way that this ever happened."

He squints at me. "Are we sure the paranoia has passed?"

"Yes. I just know you really well. Swear, Al."

Sighing, rolling his eyes, he says, "Fine. I so swear. Spoilsport. Hey, I asked the doctor and Aidan if I could give you some brew, see if you still react to it like a human, but they said to wait a couple days. So I put some in your fridge. Do *not* drink any until you get the all-clear, but I'm having one now." He turns and opens the fridge. "Because I need a drink to be able to deal with the concept of Gideon Bailey being sweet."

"Don't be an ass," I mutter and take another big spoonful of stew.

Although... does he have a point?

Either way, I don't know what the fuck is going on with me and Gideon.

"So if you don't know what's going on with you and Gideon," Alistair says, almost as though he can read my mind, "what do you *want* to happen?" He leans against the other side of the counter, an open bottle of brew dangling from his fingers.

"Why do you ask the hard questions?" I complain, scowling at my stew. He's ruining it for me.

"Is it really a hard question, or are you just too chicken to answer it?"

"I'm not chicken!" I shovel in more food.

He smirks. "Typical cat, just a big chicken at heart. I should have guessed years ago that you weren't human."

I almost choke on the stew, the urge to laugh is so overpowering. By the time I've safely swallowed my food, I'm still snorting out chuckles.

"Seriously, dude? How old are you, six?"

"You're still dodging the question."

Fuck. He's right. I hate when that happens.

"Fine." I put down my spoon again. "What do I

DEMONS DO IT BETTER

want to happen? I want us to hook up again. I want to spend three days in bed with him *not sleeping*, only leaving the room to refuel for the next round. And I want to be the person being whispered about at the office because someone saw us sneaking out of a meeting room together. Is that what you wanted to hear?"

My annoying best friend laughs. "Is that the truth?"

I glare at him. He grins back. It's so fucking annoying, but I can actually smell his smug satisfaction. Shifter senses are awesome, but not when they magnify my best friend's irritating glee.

Finally, I give in with a sharp nod. Alistair puts down his bottle and *claps his hands* like a douchebag.

"I hate you."

"You love me," he counters. "Now, do you *just* want to fuck Gideon until you're both wrung dry, or do you have *feelings*? Like, do you want a wham-bam-thank-you-Sam experience, or are you dreamily planning your happily ever after?"

I grab an apple from the fruit basket beside me and throw it at him. The bastard nabs it—fucking shifter reflexes—and tosses it in the air, catching it casually. "I'm going to take that as a 'yes, Alistair, I have so many feelings and I want to settle down into domestic bliss.'"

"You know, sometimes I really wonder why we're friends." I sigh. "I don't know. I mean, sometimes, yes, I think about how sweet Gideon can be and wonder whether he actually likes me and whether he'd be a good boyfriend. But I barely know him, and anyway, we work together. Crazy hot sex is maybe doable, but anything more would just be asking for trouble."

He doesn't reply, which leads me to think that I must

be right and he just doesn't want to admit it, but when I look at him, he's staring over my shoulder toward my front door, an expression of mixed horror and amusement on his face.

Suddenly, I'm afraid to turn around.

I know what I'm going to see.

But surely I couldn't be that unlucky?

Surely fate wouldn't humiliate me like that? After all, I just found out that I'm a living genetic experiment. My family and my culture were torn from me before I even knew they existed. Haven't I been through enough without having to deal with the mortifying burden of having my colleague, who I have to work with every day, know that I want him to screw me through a wall and cuddle me afterward?

Slowly, cringing, I peer over my shoulder.

Sure enough, Gideon is standing in the open doorway, arms crossed, face blank in his usual scowly way.

I groan and drop my head to the counter, thankfully having the presence of mind to push my bowl out of the way first. Because that's really the only way this could get any worse, right? If I landed face-first in a bowl of stew?

"Uh," Alistair says, and part of me notes with vicious satisfaction that he sounds completely flustered. "I thought you were going to the office?"

Really, Al? You can't come up with anything better than that? For a desperate moment, I hope really hard that he didn't hear anything incriminating. How long was he standing there? Maybe he just came in at the end and thinks we were talking about someone else.

"Percy called. Since Sam's awake, he wanted to know if we could set up operations here. He didn't say much, but I think there might have been a security breach."

I sit up so fast, my head spins. "A security breach?" I whirl around to face him. "At the office? By who? What did they get?"

"I don't know yet," he replies patiently. "Percy was brief, which could mean he was in a hurry, or it could mean that our cell phone encryption has been compromised. I won't know more until I can talk to him in person."

The rest of his words sink in. "He wants to set up operations here?" I look around. "It's not exactly spacious. I mean, it is for me to live in, but if the whole team plus equipment is here…" It'll be really crowded.

"Sam," he says, "I've told you exactly what I know. Percy wants everyone to meet here in two hours, and he specifically said I shouldn't come back to the office before then, which is a pretty big indicator of a security breach of some kind. So all we can do is wait to see what he tells us in two hours."

I'm still processing that when Alistair's phone chimes. He pulls it out of his pocket, and his face goes grim when he sees the screen. "Jim," he says, then looks at me. "He wants to know if I'll go fishing with him after work."

I gasp.

"What?" Gideon asks, crossing the room toward us.

"It's code," Alistair explains. "One time, we all got insanely drunk and decided we should have a team code in case we were infiltrated by body snatching aliens."

"What?" Gideon asks again, and this time he sounds a little incredulous.

"It's better not to know," I tell him. "But I think this

is a pretty clear sign that things aren't right at the office."
I shake my head. "What the fuck could have happened
between this morning and now?"

"I'll meet up with Jim and find out," Alistair offers.
He holds his phone out to me. "Unlock it, please."

I take it and punch in the code.

Try again.

Crap. "What was the passcode again?" I must have
gotten it wrong.

"498… ohhhh."

I look up. "What?"

"Uh… 498652." There's a half-amused, half-pitying
expression on his face that concerns me, because who
knows what's going on in his head?

Shaking my head, I punch the digits in. I could have
sworn those were the ones I put in before, but—

Try again.

I stare at the screen. What the—

Oh.

Oh, *fuck*.

Tossing Alistair his phone, I look around frantically
for mine and spot it on the coffee table. I practically
shove Gideon out of the way to get to it.

And yep, sure enough, my code doesn't work. Nor
does my fingerprint. And since I don't have the latest
phone, facial recognition is not an option. "Fuck!"

"Yeah. Sucks, right?" Alistair commiserates, holding
his own phone up to his face. I glare at him. Before
facial recognition, shifters were forced to rely on old-
school cell phones rather than smartphones. A lot of
shifters still have to, since the latest generation smartphones aren't exactly cheap. I'm lucky, because I need a
smartphone for work purposes, so I can claim the cost

back, but that still leaves me unable to access my phone without help until I can get my hands on the latest model.

"What's wrong?" Gideon asks, coming to stand by me. I shove my phone in his direction and recite the code.

"Could you unlock that for me, please?" I'll disable the passcode until I can upgrade.

Comprehension crosses his face, and he bites back a smile as he unlocks the device and hands it back. "Ask Andrew to grab you a new one," he suggests. "He's out at the latest site and probably needs to pass a mall on his way here."

"I couldn't ask him to do that," I protest, quickly turning off the phone's security. "These things are expensive."

Gideon shrugs. "I'll ask him then. Don't worry, Andrew can afford it, and it's not like he's not going to get the money back."

Alistair interrupts before I can reply, holding up his phone so I can see a text string. "I'm going to meet Jim," he says. "I'll keep you in the loop."

"Be careful," I warn, following him to the door.

"I will," he promises. "You too. Don't open the door to strangers."

I roll my eyes, because come on. I'm not an idiot. "Gideon's here," I remind him, and he nods.

"That's the only reason I'm willing to leave." He walks out and shuts the door before I can retort, and I glare at it.

"I'm not incompetent," I declare... to the door. "I'm nearly forty years old. I've been looking after myself since I was fourteen."

"Nobody doubts your competence," Gideon says from behind me, and I jump and whirl around, despite knowing that he was there. "But until we know more, we have to assume that our enemies would do anything to get you back. You're valuable, and that means you get protected." He lifts a hand and clasps the back of my neck. "You also underwent a traumatic experience this morning. The people who care about you are allowed to be worried."

And just like that, I'm hard.

Seriously.

He said people care about me and put his hand on my neck, and my dick took that to mean "let's party!"

This whole second puberty thing is getting old fast.

Worse… my face is getting hot. I'm *blushing*. And there's no way Gideon can miss that. Which reminds me that he walked in while I was telling Alistair how much I wanted to do him.

He must be able to read my mind, because he smiles at me, and it's a wicked, knowing kind of smile, the kind of smile that promises sex and sin and makes my dick so hard, it could pound nails into concrete.

I swallow hard. "Uh, listen—"

"What you were saying before," he interrupts, "about hot sex being doable?"

So he definitely heard, then. Great. Does that mean he also heard the part about me wanting us to be boyfriends, and if so, can I just die of embarrassment now?

Or, judging by the way my heartbeat is speeding up as he leans in, I might pass out due to arrythmia.

His mouth is on mine in the next breath, before I fully realize what he intends, and then I don't care. This isn't our first kiss, but it's a fuck of a lot hotter than the last one. Before I know it, I've got my legs wrapped around his waist and I'm being pressed against the door while we devour each other's mouths.

An odd sense of déjà vu comes over me. We did this last time too—me against the door with my hands all over him and his mouth on mine. I go harder than concrete just remembering, and he makes a sound in his throat and undulates his hips slowly.

I go off like a firecracker.

As reality seeps back in, I hide my face against his neck. Holy shit. I'm thirty-nine years old, not thirteen. I haven't come that quickly since… puberty.

You know. The human one.

I'm stewing in my embarrassment and wondering how I'm going to disentangle myself and then avoid ever having to look Gideon in the eye again when I feel his breath against my ear and he murmurs, "It's so fucking hot watching you come."

And just like that, I'm hard again.

"Mmm." He moves his hips again, the friction of his dick alongside mine amazing even through our clothes. "Shifter stamina is *much* better than human. Although…" He slides a hand up to the back of my neck and pulls my head up so I have to look at him. "… even shifter stamina isn't quite as good as demon."

I swear, it's only immense self-control and the knowledge that I've embarrassed myself enough for one day that keeps me from coming right this second—*again*. Instead, I close the scant inches between us and bite his lower lip.

"I need to get out of these pants. Wanna help?"

That wicked smile is back. He eases away from me,

and I let my feet drop to the floor. Within seconds, we're both naked, and although it's a relief to get my sticky pants off, it's even better to be skin-to-skin with all of him. We're kissing again, not quite as urgently as before, but it's still arousing. I love touching him—all that glorious smooth skin—and I slide my hands up his body and into his hair.

At the first brush of my fingers over his horns, he jerks and breaks the kiss, gasping.

"What?" I ask. Did I hurt him somehow?

"Sensitive." He sucks in a deep breath and stares up at the ceiling for a second.

Sensitive? What—

I grin. "Wait… are you telling me that your horns are an erogenous zone?"

He clears his throat. "Not exactly. They're a point of sensory input—their purpose is to allow us to teleport safely. Sometimes that makes them sensitive to touch."

"Sensitive good? Or does it hurt?" I don't want to hurt him. Well, not right now, anyway.

Color flares along his cheekbones. "It… doesn't hurt."

"So, if I was to do this…" I reach up and lightly stroke a single fingertip along one horn from base to tip. "…that doesn't hurt?"

He shudders hard. "No." The word seems to get stuck in his throat.

"What about this?" I do the same thing to the other horn. He's panting now and visibly breaks out in a sweat.

"It… doesn't hurt."

"And this?" I close a hand tightly around each horn, covering as much surface area as I can. Gideon makes a sound halfway between a groan and a yell, and the next thing I know, I'm on my back on the floor with his mouth devouring mine.

"Wait!" I pull back from the kiss, although it's seriously one of the hardest things I've ever done. "Let me turn over." I want to have traction to thrust back this time.

Gideon lets me go for the three seconds it takes to flip over and get on my hands and knees, and then he's making that growling sound that gets me so hot and—

"Did you just bite my ass?" I look over my shoulder at him.

"Yes. And if I wasn't so desperate to get inside you, I'd do it again." His big, blunt fingers test my opening. "Fuck. Where's the lube?"

For a split second, I consider telling him to do me without it. After all, shifters heal fast, right? But he's already up and in the kitchen, yanking open the pantry. Moments later he's back with a bottle of olive oil. The sharp scent fills my nostrils, and I just know I'm never going to be able to cook with it again without remembering this moment.

And then Gideon is sliding into me, filling me up, and all thoughts of cooking vanish. He's not as careful with me this time, probably because I'm not human anymore, and I love that he doesn't need to hold back.

"Good?" he grunts, and I don't answer, just shove back on him. We both moan at the sensation, and then he's taking back control, his fingers hard on my hips as he draws back and pistons into me over and over.

The upside of this second puberty thing? My dick has no need of manual stimulation. I'm coming before I know it, so hard that I can't breathe, that I clamp down on Gideon and he yells as he spurts inside me.

Finally my muscles relax and I can take in air. A moment later, Gideon carefully pulls out, and I collapse to the floor, rolling onto my back, panting.

For the second time today, I stare up at a ceiling.

I just had sex with Gideon Bailey again.

Heart-stopping, breath-stealing, sweaty sex.

That was fucking amazing.

"That was incredible," Gideon says, sounding a little short of breath himself. I feel a ridiculous surge of pride that I did that to him.

"Yeah." I can't argue. "Uh, could we not let it make things weird?" Because we still have to work together.

"No weirdness," he agrees. "Especially if we can do it again."

"Abso-fucking-lutely." I don't even need to think about it. "But, ah, could we be… discreet?"

I feel him go still beside me. In the next second, he's propping himself up on an elbow and looking down at me. "Discreet?" His expression has gone back to resting bitch face.

"Well, yeah," I reply, a little uncertain. "I mean, it would be awkward at work…" His face doesn't change. "Andrew, for one, would never let us hear the end of it."

In one swift move that I envy greatly, he goes from lying to standing, towering over me. I stare up at him wistfully. I'm going to look like a clumsy idiot clambering to my feet. I really didn't want to remind him of my lack of grace quite so soon after we blew each other's minds, but I sense some sort of confrontation looming, and lying naked on the floor puts me at a distinct disadvantage.

Sighing, I plant my hands by my hips and heave to sitting in preparation for the awkward scrabble upright. To my surprise, I flow smoothly into a crouch and then stand without needing to grab anything for balance or leverage.

Wow. I guess my shifter abilities have kicked in. This is way cool!

Grinning, I look up at Gideon to share my excitement—I'm no longer a klutzy human!—but his glower quickly kills my smile. Right. He's pissed about something. About me wanting to be discreet.

"Gideon, you've got to tell me what you're thinking," I declare bluntly. "I don't want the whole office gossiping about us fucking, and honestly, I thought you'd feel the same. From everything I've seen, you've always been private about your sex life."

If anything, his face just becomes more grim. I'm suddenly incredibly aware that we're standing naked in my living room, our clothes scattered around us, and our colleagues due to arrive at some random time over the next hour. We really should get dressed and cleaned up.

As if he reads my mind, he bends over and picks up his boxer briefs and puts them on with sharp, jerky motions, very unlike him. I keep my mouth shut and follow suit, even though mine are still wet and sticky—I have a feeling this will go better if my bits aren't exposed. Or at least, I'll feel less vulnerable.

But once we're dressed, Gideon heads for the door.

"Hey!" Suddenly I'm pissed off. Fine, he's angry about something I've said or done. But I've said I want to work it out, and he's not even going to try. Instead, he's going to leave me here not knowing what the fuck is going on while he goes and sulks somewhere, and

I'm not okay with that. "Don't you fucking dare leave!"

He freezes just steps away from the door, his back to me. I hold my breath. Is he going to leave, or will he stay and talk so I'm not confused out of my mind when the rest of the team turns up?

He turns. His regular blank glower is firmly in place. "You're right. Until we know what's going on and if anyone is looking for you, you shouldn't be alone."

I stamp my foot, because yes, I'm at three-year-old-having-a-tantrum level of mad. "That is *not* why I want you to stay, you dickweed! Tell me what crawled up your ass in the last five minutes."

"There's nothing up my ass, as you so charmingly put it."

I narrow my eyes. That smug, supercilious tone of voice is not helping. "Want me to shove my foot up there?"

The glower cracks, replaced by a smirk. "I'd like to see you try."

For a second, I actually consider it. But, sadly, even though I'm now a super cool cat shifter, I don't have a grip on my new abilities, and he's still way bigger than me anyway.

"This is stupid," I say instead, swallowing my anger. "I don't even understand why you're mad."

"Really? You really don't understand?" He scoffs disbelievingly, but I shrug.

"No. I don't. One second everything is fine, and the next, you've got some bug up your ass because... what? You want to brag to the office that we're fucking? I just don't get it."

His jaw literally drops. Like, his mouth is wide open

enough that I could shove a hot dog in there, bun and all.

Or something else…

Pushing aside the naughty little voice, I start to ask what the matter is *now*, but I'm interrupted by a heavy knock at the door. "Sam! Gideon? It's me."

Impossible to mistake Andrew for anyone else, and his timing is typical. Crap. Aside from being in the middle of a very important conversation, I really need to use the bathroom—pulling on underwear right after sex without a condom is not ideal. Plus, the place stinks of sex, something that's much more apparent to me now that I have a shifter sense of smell.

Before I can yell for Andrew to come back in half an hour, Gideon has closed his mouth, pivoted, and is opening the door.

"Fuck," I mutter, turning and beelining to the hall-way. "I'll be back," I call over my shoulder. I can't deal with Andrew without cleaning up first. As I escape to the bathroom, I can hear him asking Gideon what we've been up to with a gloating, amused undertone. Damn my improved hearing. I'd prefer not to have heard that.

When I rejoin them (after procrastinating for as long as I could, but unfortunately, there wasn't much to do in the bathroom, especially since Gideon seems to have rearranged it again while I was unconscious), Andrew smirks at me from where he's planted himself on the couch and says, "Glad to see you're back in top form."

Ugh. "Thanks." This is exactly why I didn't want people to know. The not-so-subtle jokes will be next. For some reason, people feel it's okay to joke about your sex life as long as you're not in a relationship with the person you're having sex with.

I'm about to change the subject and ask him what the fuck is going on at the office when he holds up a box. "I got your new phone."

"Oh." Gideon must have texted him while I was talking to Alistair earlier. "Uh, thanks. How much do I owe—"

"Don't worry about it." He hands me the box with one hand and waves the other dismissively. "I'll put in an expense claim for it. We can't have you unable to use your phone."

I sink down onto the ottoman and pick at the shrink wrapping on the box for a second before giving up. I'm not going to fumble with this now. Setting the box on the coffee table, I smile at Andrew. "Thank you, I appreciate it."

"Anytime." He grins and glances between me and Gideon. "So—"

"Do you want something to drink?" I offer desperately. "I'm sorry, I don't have any blood on hand, but I could get you a soda or something? Coffee? Or Alistair put some brew in the fridge."

His grin widens, and he cocks a silver eyebrow. "Brew? Really?"

I can't help the chuckle that escapes me. "Yeah. I'm hoping it won't ever affect me that way again, but I won't know until I try it, and apparently, I'm not supposed to do that just yet."

He nods. "Until we can be sure there's no remaining issues from your time as a human and the forced shift, it's better to be safe, I guess. But now I'm wildly curious to see how you'd react." He tips his head and studies me. "How are you feeling?"

Awkward, this is very awkward. Especially with

Gideon glowering at us from the kitchen. "Uh, fine. Listen, I'm really sorry about how I was acting in the office. I know you and the others wouldn't hurt me."

He pats my knee. "Yeah, we know. Don't worry about it. And I'm sorry I had to put the whammy on you. I'd normally never—"

"I know," I interrupt, because Andrew might be a big kid sometimes and might like to push boundaries, but deliberately using his charisma to take away someone's will is not his style. He was protecting me and the others—they could have taken me down physically to give me the shot, but that would likely have ended up with someone—me—getting hurt. "You left all my memories intact, Andrew. I know exactly what happened, and it was the best option." Vampires have the ability to wipe memories, but they can't replace them. So if you haven't been drinking or drugging and suddenly find yourself missing time, there's a good chance a vampire's been messing with you.

"Okay, good. I'm glad you're back to yourself."

I lean forward and prop my elbows on my knees. "What's happening at the office?"

His expression turns hard. It's an unusual look for him, and it makes me want to shiver. Suddenly I'm reminded that he's an old vampire and very powerful.

"It's bad shit," he says grimly. "I was just telling Gideon. Someone hacked our case files for the kidnappings, and the only reason we knew was because they dumped the whole lot into the printer queue—probably accidentally."

"Are you sure it wasn't one of us that did it?" I know they would have checked that, but still… "I've acciden-

tally hit the print button a few times. It might even have
been me, this morning."

He shakes his head. "No. The time on the printer
puts it at eleven forty-three this morning."

Which was when everyone who had access to those
files was in Percy's office, *not* accessing them.

"Fuck." I wrack my brain, trying to remember the
protocols for this situation. It's literally never happened
in the five years I've worked there—not for case files,
anyway. There's some inter-team rivalry, so occasionally
people will hack another team's vacation roster or something, and everyone tries to hack the fantasy sports
league, but case files are sacrosanct. Hacking a case file
is cause for prosecution, and prosecution in the community is a little different from in the human world—for
one thing, most judges are vampires, and they're legally
permitted to use charisma to ascertain the truth.

"Candice on reception found the files. She told us
she was pissed at first that someone was tying up the
printer for so long, and then she got curious because
nobody had come to check on how it was going, so she
looked at some of the documents. As soon as she realized what they were, she pulled them all together and
made sure nobody else saw them."

I frown. "She thought it was an accident?"

He nods. "Yeah. Or that one of us had sent them to
print before going into the meeting."

"No way. This case is top-level confidential. If we
wanted to print anything for it, we'd use the secure
printer in Percy's office. Or at least the printer on our
floor." Not the massive printer that services reception
and everyone else.

"She thought we'd picked the wrong printer—that's

why she waited to say anything. She wanted to slip the files to us quietly so nobody would get into trouble." He grimaces, and I can't help but agree. That's really sweet of her, but the fact is, she should have flagged it immediately. The longer the delay after a hack, the less chance there is of catching the culprit. "As soon as she came in with the trolley-load of paper, we saw the time stamp and locked down the building and the system."

I rub my hands over my face. "I'm trying to remember what the procedure is for this, but I'm coming up blank," I admit.

Gideon comes over to sit in an armchair. "First, lockdown. Then identify the point of entry and the hacker, if possible."

I look at Andrew. He shakes his head. "We managed to find out that the hacker gained entry to the system using a clone of Lily's account. There's a definite digital fingerprint on the clone, but it wasn't one that's been identified before. When we ran a check through the system, we found that same fingerprint on about a dozen other cloned accounts dating back for the past six or so months."

"How did they even manage to clone the accounts? Aren't they supposed to be protected against that?" I shake my head and hold up a hand before he can reply. "Never mind." My tech knowledge is limited to what I actually use to get through the day, plus I know that the community tends to interweave sorcery among regular practices—like genetic modification and network security. It makes things work differently than what I was used to and also opens up options that wouldn't be available "the human way." "So somebody with advanced sorcery and hacking abilities has been basically walking through what is supposed to be the most secure system on the planet and looking at whatever data they like for half a year?" This is not good. "And we have no idea who they are?"

Andrew shakes his head.

I search for a silver lining. "What are the chances that it's some bored college student who's doing it just because they can and who we can recruit?"

"This isn't a movie, Sam," Gideon snaps, and it's like a slap. Even Andrew looks surprised.

Awkward silence blankets us until Andrew clears his throat and says, "That's something we might have considered, but the files that have been accessed were all highly classified and quite specific. There wasn't any of the aimlessness we would have expected if this wasn't deliberate targeting."

I look between them. "I feel like I'm missing something. Can we guess who it might be by the files they accessed?"

"Yes." Gideon's the one to answer. "The others should be here soon. They'll hopefully have some more information." The firm way he says it tells me I'm not going to learn anything else right now.

"Okay. What does this mean for the office? Are we offline until we can work out exactly what we're dealing with?"

Andrew shrugs. "Basically. Everything's been shunted to backup servers, and now that we know what we're looking for, we've been able to ensure they're clean and secure. We'll keep checking them, too. But there's a strong possibility that the access is coming from within the office—either a member of staff or some kind of remote device that's been planted."

"Like a camera or a keystroke reader so they were able to get a password into the network and then jump around from there?" I'm trying to understand how it would work but basically just guessing.

"Yes, but with sorcery in the mix, it doesn't have to be electronic and they don't need to be able to read or see the password. The 'device' could be literally anything that can hold a sorcery weave." Which means almost anything. "A team will go in and sweep for both electronics and sorcery weaves. Every member of staff will undergo the same sweep before they're allowed into the building for the next few months at least, and there are going to be some more background investigations. This is going to cause chaos."

"And cost a lot of money," I add. A thought strikes me. "How sure are we that sending the files to the printer was an accident?"

They both stare at me.

"Think about it," I say defensively. "They've been in the system without anyone noticing for six months, and then suddenly, when they're in what's currently the most sensitive file we have, they get clumsy?"

Gideon expels a sharp breath and stands, pacing back and forth. "You're right. We're in the middle of an urgent and time sensitive case, and now we can't access the office, our network access is limited, and we're distracted by the intruder." He looks around, then heads back to the kitchen and opens the pantry.

"This is a distraction?" Andrew asks incredulously. "Fuck, whatever they're up to must be big if they're willing to sacrifice a hidden mole. They're losing their access to our systems."

"Unless they have another access point? But there

would be too good a chance of us finding it now that we're looking. You're right, it's safe to assume they're going to do something big." I scrub my face with my hands. I can't believe how long this day has been, and it's not even close to over.

My front door opens right then, and we all whirl toward it. A snarl I didn't know I was capable of tears from my throat, and my hands tingle painfully.

"Whoa!" Elinor holds up her hands. "It's just us. Sorry, I didn't think how on edge you'd be."

I exhale in relief as Andrew comes out of his half crouch and retracts his fangs from bite-ready. Damn shifters and their ability to ignore locks.

Oh, hey, that's me now! I'll never have to worry about forgetting my keys again. At least something good came out of today.

My hands are still aching, and I glance down at them—and shriek.

"What?" Andrew barks, head whipping toward me. The others swarm in through the doorway, searching for the threat.

"My hands!" I hold them up so everyone can see.

I have claws.

Like… actual claws. They're two inches long, look razor sharp, and protrude from the ends of my fingers. The skin is a little bit torn and bloody, but not as badly as I would have thought—I seem to be healing around the claws.

"Wow!" Elinor bounds forward and takes my hand to examine it more closely. "A partial shift. That's way cool, Sam. Not many shifters can do this."

"Great. Um, I'll get a bit more excited about that after

you tell me how to undo it." The achy feeling is starting to fade, and yeah, this is way cool and feeds my inner super-hero geek, but hiding claw-tipped fingers from the human world is not something I want to dedicate my life to.

She shrugs. *Shrugs*, like this is no big deal!

"No idea—like I said, this is something not many of us can do. Aidan was right behind us, though. Even if he can't talk you through it, he can probably force them to change back."

"No!" Gideon's exclamation is sharp as he comes back into the living room. "No more forced shifts. We're not even sure he's over the last one."

"Gideon's right," Percy says calmly. "But I'm sure it won't be necessary anyway. This is something Sam does naturally. He just needs to be shown how." He comes over to stand beside Elinor and takes my hand, turning it over to see the claws from all angles. "Not every shifter can partially shift, Sam, but those who can say it feels just the same as a regular shift, just on a localized scale. So connect with your energy and visualize your hands the way they should be."

I bite my lip. What if it all goes horribly wrong and I end up with paws, or no hands at all?

Percy smiles that gentle, knowing smile of his and looks me right in the eye, and I sigh.

"Okay." Closing my eyes, I breathe deeply and concentrate on my energy. It's even easier this time than last time, faster and stronger, and in just a few seconds, it's ready. I visualize myself with human hands and let it burst free.

My hands ache with that same strange discomfort as before, but when I open my eyes, I once again have ordinary fingers with ordinary fingernails. There aren't any signs that they were ever anything else.

I turn them over, checking closely. "There's not even any cuts or dried blood," I marvel.

"That's how it should be," Aidan says beside me, and I jump.

"Fuck me! When did you get here? And can you not ever sneak up on me again, please?" I slap a hand to my chest, where my heart feels like it's beating out of control. "In fact, new rule! Nobody is allowed to enter my apartment unless I let them in. There will be no more unexpected claw events."

There's a round of coughing and clearing throats—Andrew is the only one with the balls (or temerity) to laugh outright. Aidan smiles and takes my hands, checking them carefully.

"A partial shift, huh? The first time is usually an emotional reaction—fear, shock, something like that."

"The locked door opening while we were talking about invaders?"

"Invaders?" David asks. "I guess it fits, but it seems a bit dramatic."

I glare at him. "Really? You want to get picky about terminology *now*? Go ahead." I fling my arms wide. "Let's have a debate about the nuances of language."

"Whoa." He holds up his hands and takes a step back, eyes wide. "Nope. Sorry. I'll just go see what kind of organizational system Gideon's using for your pantry."

"Anyway," Aidan says, sounding like he's trying not to laugh and pulling my attention back to him, "your instincts reacted to protect you by giving you claws.

Because it was a completely uncontrolled shift, I'm guessing you ended up with some tearing and bleeding?"

I nod, suddenly a little overwhelmed. There's so much I have to learn about being a shifter. And with all the other crap going on at the moment, I don't know where the time is going to come from... or if I'll be able to learn what I need before I need it.

"In future, you should be able to shift certain parts of yourself at will, the same as you'll be able to shift entirely into a cat. We'll practice," he assures me, no doubt seeing my doubtful expression. "How are you feeling?"

I heave a huge, dramatic sigh. "I'm fine. Physically, I feel great, and there's been no paranoia or anxiety since I woke up. I'm embarrassed as fuck, though."

"Don't be," he tells me. "It was brought on entirely by the chemicals that flooded your brain as a result of the compelled shift and has absolutely nothing to do with you or your ordinary behavior."

Lily pushes forward, and I realize how crowded it is. My living room is a great size for one or two people, and can handle four or five relatively comfortably, but eight, even with David and Gideon in the kitchen, is beyond cozy. Maybe we should rearrange the furniture to make it more comfortable?

"Sam," Lily says firmly, "you're awesome. We love you. And we're so touched that you've let us be part of such a momentous time of your life." She puts her arms around me and hugs me tight. Since she's inches taller than me—like most people—my face is smashed into her neck. I can smell her perfume, a blend designed not to irritate sensitive shifter noses, her underlying succubus species scent, and something else that's uniquely her. It's warm and comforting but strong as steel. Just like her.

I hug her back. "Thanks, Lily." Even if I'm not sure I had a choice about including them in everything that's happened in the last twenty-four hours—fuck me, is that all? It feels like eternity—I'm glad they're here. I may not have known them all that long, but they've made me feel welcome and accepted, something I was missing for a long time. Alistair and my old team began the process, but part of me always remembered that I was forced on them. I was Harold's last resort for the team that had scared off all their admins. And while I have no doubt that they grew to love me, there's always a little voice in my head telling me that if they'd had a choice back then, it would never have been me.

This team, though… they came to me. They chose me. They wanted me, despite me being human, *because of* me being human. That meant more to me than even I realized.

So I squeeze Lily tight, because she's the heart of the team and one of the closest friends I've ever had, and I breathe her in and file that scent in my olfactory memory under "comfort." Then I let her go and smile.

"We should rearrange the furniture so we can be comfortable. And then we have work to do."

CHAPTER TWELVE

BY THE TIME we reorganize the room and set up laptops and a printer and hook in to the secure backup server, we're all starving, so I order takeout for us and we eat while discussing theories.

"Let's assume this is all connected," David says thoughtfully. "Anything else would just be too coincidental. We've made greater headway in this case than our opponents expected us to in this short time. In order to distract us, they've sacrificed their source on the inside. We're now scrambling to defend our systems and are unable to use the office until we're certain it's secure."

"We're definitely on the back foot," Lily agrees. "But do they know about Sam? Because if he's one of their early experiments—sorry, Sam—we're still ahead of their game."

I wave to indicate that I'm not offended. "Did any of you log anything we've done since last night in the system?"

Heads are shaken all around. "The request for a medic to do a DNA profile went through the usual process, but your name wasn't attached to it," Percy says. "They might think we're doing some kind of genetic investigation that connects to the case, but that would be all."

"But Dr. Sims would have had to log the samples," Andrew points out. "Fuck. We need to—"

"No." Percy shakes his head. "I asked Dr. Sims to log them under an anonymous numeric code. Sam is, as far as we know, the only one of his kind not in enemy custody. We need to protect his identity until we can be certain he's safe, and that means only the people who were in my office this morning can know."

"That's good," Gideon calls from where he's arranging mugs in the kitchen, because he's done the pantry twice already today and he needs to stay within earshot. "That means the only way they can know about Sam is if there was a device in one of the rooms we were in."

We all exchange glances, because that's highly possible. "What rooms?" Elinor asks. "Percy's office, of course. Uh, the antechamber? We talked a bit about what was happening while we were waiting there. Not in detail, but enough for someone who knew about the genetic experiments to put it together."

"The break room," David adds. "Our office?"

I shake my head. "Not unless one of you said something today. Last night, we were only talking about me learning to use magic while we were in the office. It wasn't until we were in the break room that we realized that wasn't going to happen."

David sighs. "We're overlooking something important. The device might be something one of us is carrying around."

There's a crash as Gideon drops a mug. My stomach churns as I look around and see the same dawning horror on everyone's faces. Phones. Watches. Jewelry. Fabric can't hold a sorcery weave for more than a few hours, but leather can, so shoes and belts are a possibility. Pens—Andrew has a beautiful platinum pen that lives in his pocket and goes with him everywhere. Tablets. Laptops? Fuck, did we leave the office because it wasn't secure, only to bring the leak with us?

"Calm down," Percy says. "Our equipment was screened before we left the office, remember?"

"What about personal belongings?" Gideon growls, coming to hover protectively near my chair. I immediately feel safer.

"I'll check them now," he replies, because that's right, Percy can use the magic to see hidden sorcery. Thank holy fuck that he's on our team. "Empty your pockets and bags, please."

There's a scramble to obey. It's creepy as fuck to think that someone might be watching or listening to us. Worse still is the thought that they might be planning to kidnap me and perform experiments.

"I'm completely a shifter now," I declare loudly. "No human DNA left."

Everyone looks at me weirdly.

"What? I just want it clearly understood that since the results of the experiment are gone, there would be no benefit to any kind of invasive testing or vivisection or anal probing."

Andrew coughs. "Really? No benefit to anal probing?"

My face goes hot, which means it's probably traffic-light-red, but I pretend I have no idea what he's talking about and very carefully don't look at Gideon, who just snorted a laugh, the bastard.

"Well, anyway," Lily says, trying to keep the peace, "it's perfectly clear that there would be no benefit to vivisection or… anything else."

"There's always a benefit to 'anything else,'" Aidan murmurs wickedly, and part of my brain wants to smack him, but the rest cringes away from the idea of smacking my species leader.

Some things were easier when I was human.

Percy, who's been methodically examining the items presented to him, says, "It looks like we're clear. Sam, did you bring anything home with you today?"

"Uh…" I look around. "My phone." I point to it. "And I'll get my shoes for you to check. I didn't have anything in my pockets." I look at Gideon. "Did you and Alistair grab anything else of mine?"

He shakes his head. "No, we basically just brought you. We didn't even bother with your keys—they should still be on your desk."

"I packed them in with Sam's stuff," Elinor volunteers, "but that was all scanned when we left the building."

"The phone is clear," Percy tells us.

I race off to find my shoes, and a few minutes later we're all sinking into our seats with relief.

"So we're secure right now," Lily says. "But we have to assume that we weren't while we were at the office."

Everyone looks at me. I think I might throw up.

"Sam is never alone," Percy orders, and there's a thread of steel to his voice that I'm not used to hearing. "Doors and windows are always locked."

"That's not going to protect him against shifters,"

David points out, rubbing his forehead. "I can set up a security barrier of some kind—something that will react to anyone entering who has bad intentions. It's a complicated weave, though, and will take time."

"How much time?"

He makes a face. "A couple of days. Less if I could get someone to help, but…" He shrugs helplessly.

"But we don't know exactly who we can trust right now," Elinor finishes.

Panic rises. "What do you mean? Like, we can't trust *anyone*?" That can't be right. The people we work with have all been through stringent background checks. They're dedicated to protecting and serving the community.

"Sam." Gideon's hand squeezes my shoulder and he crouches beside me. "All we know right now is that there's a leak somewhere in the office. Someone hacked the system, and someone presumably planted a device or devices. Percy can use the magic to check each and every person's loyalty and intentions, but it's time-consuming and exhausting for him. Right now, we know we can trust the people in this room and the head of security and his team, who are right now sweeping the office for devices."

"And Alistair?" I clutch desperately at that emotional straw.

Gideon hesitates, but Percy says, "Alistair is fine. I don't even need to use the magic to check him—his concern and protectiveness for you are so strong that I can sense them."

I sag with relief.

"Uh, Sam," Gideon says, "have you heard from Alistair since he left?"

"No, I—" The panic is back as I scramble forward to grab my phone. "There's no message from him."

"Wait, what?" Elinor asks. "What's going on with Alistair?"

"Send one," Gideon orders me. "Use whatever that code was, just in case." While I'm carefully composing a text about fishing and groceries, trying to stay calm long enough to remember the code, Gideon runs down what happened for the others.

I send the message and then stare at the screen, praying for him to text me back. "Should I call?" I ask.

"No," half a dozen voices chorus.

"It's easier to trip up during a conversation," Andrew adds. "Plus, tone of voice can be a big give-away. Let's see how he responds first, and then we can decide if you need to call." He gets up and goes to get the box holding my new phone, which I moved to the kitchen counter when we were rearranging the furniture.

"Let's get this set up while we're waiting," he says. "David, can we rig a panic button feature?"

"Yes." David goes to join him. I keep staring at my phone. Gideon perches on the arm of my chair, watching over my shoulder, and I lean against him, taking comfort from his solid warmth.

On the screen, three dots begin to dance.

"He's typing!"

Elinor crowds in on my other side, and the three of us watch my phone as the room falls silent.

Can't bring your groceries tonight. Fishing a bust. Jim used wrong bait.

"Fuck!"

"What does that mean?" Elinor asks, mystified.

"Even if you hadn't told me, I'd know he's not talking about actual fishing. Alistair hates to fish."

"It means he and Jim are in trouble. The grocery part means they're being followed. I think."

"You think?" Aidan asks incredulously. "What good's using a code if you don't remember it?"

"It's not an official code," I defend, "and none of us was sober when we came up with it. We've mostly used it as a joke since."

"Wait." David comes back from the kitchen. "Alistair thinks he's being followed? Why would they do that if it's our case that they're interested in?"

"Maybe it's not," Gideon says, but he sounds unsure.

"It can't be Sam, can it?" Lily asks. "Following Alistair to get to Sam, I mean. Even if they know they're friends, these people had access to our system. Sam's address is in there."

I wince.

"Your address isn't in there?" she guesses. "How did you manage that?"

"It's an old habit," I mumble, "from when I was running and hiding. The address I used is for the local post office."

"A post office box?"

"No, just the street address of the post office."

Percy shakes his head. "That's probably got tax implications," he mutters, then adds, "never mind. So it's possible they're following Alistair to track you down, then, which means they know something about you. We just don't know what."

"What do I tell Alistair? Can we help him?"

"If your code can find out where he is, Gideon and I

will go back him and this Jim guy up," Andrew says. I look up at Gideon, who nods.

"We'll dump Jim somewhere safe and get Alistair back here without anyone following," he assures me. "We're going to need all hands on deck to figure this shit out."

"Okay, gimme a sec." I turn my attention to texting. The location part of the code is the trickiest, and I want to make sure I don't fuck it up.

"While you two are doing that, I'm going to get back to tracing the signatures from the weaves today," David says. "We need to confirm who's behind all this if we're going to figure out exactly what they're doing."

Alistair texts me back almost right away. "He's going to meet you at the cinema complex at the mall in Eastside. Cinema six."

"Good choice," Andrew approves. "That place is huge, and it's got three or four entrances. Ready, Gideon?"

"Sure." Gideon kisses the top of my head and then stands up and heads for the door as if he didn't just metaphorically throw a live grenade into the room.

Andrew just smirks and follows him out, but Elinor shrieks, "What the fuck was that?"

The door closes.

Those remaining turn to me.

I shrug, my face on fire. "It's nothing." So much for discretion. I mean, I know he was pissed about that, though I'm still not sure why, but I didn't think he'd just throw me under the bus and leave.

"I'm sorry," Lily says slowly, "did you just say that Gideon Bailey showing you affection was *nothing*? Perhaps you're unaware that Gideon doesn't show affection, ever." She's grinning widely. "I'm pretty sure this is not nothing. In fact… I'd go as far as to say it's something."

"I love you, but I will hurt you if you don't shut up," I tell her. "I can do that now. I have super cool shifter skills."

She just laughs.

"Stop trying to change the subject," David says, coming to sit on the coffee table right in front of me. "Is something happening with you and Gideon?"

I cast a desperate look at Percy. "We really all should get to work."

"Of course," he agrees, "as soon as you tell us what's going on." He smiles that gentle smile of his, but mischief lurks in his eyes.

I sigh. "Fine. Gideon and I hooked up. I asked him to be discreet, which pissed him off for some reason, and he's clearly exercised his revenge by siccing you lot on me."

"You asked him to be discreet?"

"And you don't know why he's pissed off?"

"Oh, my sweet summer child." That's Elinor. She reaches out to pat my arm. "You've hurt his feelings. I know that's hard to believe, because there are many people who don't think Gideon *has* feelings, but it's true."

I… what?

I look between them, at the varying expressions of indulgence and sympathy.

"But… we agreed to do it again." My face is on fire. "I just said I didn't want to be the subject of office gossip. Why would his feelings be hurt?"

Aidan laughs. "I don't know Gideon all that well, but

my guess is that he doesn't care if people gossip about the two of you because he *likes* you."

Likes me? Like… *likes* me, likes me?

Whoa.

Lily's still grinning at me. "I love this for you! Gideon can be rough around the edges, but he's such a good man. And really, I don't know why any of us are surprised. He's been nicer to you over the past few weeks than he is to anyone."

David makes a surprised agreeing noise. "You're right. It's hard to tell, because Gideon's idea of nice isn't like most people's, but I bet if this hadn't all happened, we would have ended up seeing an office romance slowly bloom."

I shake my head. "I… need to think about this. And talk to Gideon, I think." Because if he's interested in more than just a fuck…

I push down the excited hope. I hadn't realized until now that I wanted more than sex and friendship from him.

"Okay," Percy says firmly. "Now it's time to work. We can gossip about Sam and Gideon when all the kidnapped couples are safely home."

WE'VE ONLY BEEN SLOGGING through the data, looking for patterns or things we've missed or *anything* that could give us a hint who we're looking for, where they are, and exactly what they're doing, for about twenty-five minutes when David says, "Fuck yeah!"

Elinor chokes on her coffee, coughing and hacking and gasping for breath. Not to be mean, but I'm so, so glad it's not me doing it for once. I pound her on the back until she can breathe almost normally. I can't blame her for reacting that way, though—David hardly ever swears. It really has an impact when he does.

"You found something?" Percy asks, getting up and going to hover behind David.

"Yeah, I've got the names of the three sorcerers who created those weaves in Sam—"

Lily cheers, scrambling out of her seat to go see, and Aidan starts to ask something, but David waves for them both to be quiet.

"—*and* they're all known associates of the Coalition for Community Advancement."

"Who are our main suspects in this case." Suddenly dizzy at the thought that we might be getting some-where, I lean back in my chair.

"Yep. I've also managed to wrangle some more information about the purpose of the weaves. It's fasci-nating, really—completely obscene and chilling, but amazing work."

"Before you give us a quick rundown," Percy inter-rupts, "is what you've found sufficient for us to raid all known CCA compounds?"

David nods. "Yes."

The community doesn't require warrants in the same way the human world does—the lucifer's authority is generally enough—but some of these cults have very wealthy and influential members who are good at kicking up a fuss if they get raided too often, so usually it has to wait until there's a really good reason and a decent amount of evidence. Percy doesn't have to worry about reelection, but he does depend on wealthy members of the community to support charities and welfare projects for those less fortunate.

"Okay." Percy pulls out his phone and taps at the screen for a few moments, uses his thumb to authenticate something, then turns back to us. "I've given the order. The teams are preparing, and we'll need to join them, but give me an overview first."

Oh fuck, oh wow, oh shit, there's going to be *raids* tonight. We might actually find the missing couples!

"It was done in vitro," David begins, looking me right in the eyes. "Sorry, Sam. From what I can see, the weaves started out a lot more basic but developed as you did. That's how they were able to bond so completely with you. Our own research on fertility tells us that when a member of the community and a human become pregnant, the fetus does initially retain some human DNA. That changes slowly over the second trimester, and by the third, there's none left."

"That's the magic stepping in to ensure continuation of community species?" I say. I know this part, but it still comes out sounding like a question.

David nods. "Exactly. These weaves are incredibly complex, and they seem to have… for want of a better word, 'captured' the human DNA before the magic could remove it. This part is a little unclear to me, since we don't know exactly how the magic does this, or even exactly what it does—whether it switches human DNA out with community, or changes it, or what. It seems to me that the CCA might know more about this than we do, which means…" He trails off and looks at Percy.

"They've been doing more experimentation on fetuses," the lucifer says grimly.

David spreads his hands. "It's just a guess, but I can't

see how else they'd know. Our information comes from noninvasive research. To find out more, they'd need to be taking samples from and performing experiments on fetuses in weeks thirteen to twenty-eight, which is something we've never really done because of the risk to the pregnancy."

Lily sighs and shakes her head. "Okay. So the CCA potentially understands what the magic does to ensure that babies aren't born human, and they've used that knowledge to warp the process?"

"As far as I can see, yes. Rather than the human DNA being discarded or switched out, it's captured by the weave and used as a disguise of sorts—but not really. Maybe more like a suppressant? Sam's shifter DNA was forced into dormancy and he appeared fully human."

"To what end?" Aidan asks intently. "I know the CCA advocates for community dominance over humans. What's the benefit of turning our babies into humans?"

"I can't be certain until the samples Dr. Sims took are tested, but my guess is that Sam's fertility while he appeared human was at human level. Despite his underlying shifter DNA, that humanity would breed through to the next generation. Or at least that was the aim."

I blink. "Wait. You're saying that if I'd somehow impregnated someone while I thought I was human, the baby would have been born human, even if the mother was part of the community?"

"I think that's what they were hoping to achieve. I don't know if they were successful."

Aidan shakes his head. "Maybe I'm being stupid, but that doesn't make sense to me. Why are they breeding humans if they want to eradicate them?"

"They're playing a long game." David sighs. "Again, I'm only guessing, but my take would be that what they did to Sam was only phase one. Phase two would be taking samples from Sam and others who were part of their program last time around and refining the weaves so they don't affect all parts of DNA—just fertility. They would have done that while they were waiting for their subjects—sorry, Sam—to grow up enough to start reproducing. Samples from the next generation would show whether the weaves succeeded in producing human children. I'm going to say they did, which means—"

"Fuck," Aidan interrupts, his eyes wide.

David nods. "Exactly. This latest mass kidnapping is to see if the newer versions of the weave will work to change only fertility instead of everything. They'll be able to test for that within twelve months, although if it was me running the experiment, I wouldn't consider it a success until the children went through puberty."

My head is spinning as I try to grasp this. I don't know a lot about biology, but I didn't think DNA and genes worked that way… I guess magic and sorcery have a huge part to play in this?

"So," Lily begins, "theoretically, within twelve months the CCA will have developed community DNA that has human-level fertility?"

"Theoretically, yes," David agrees. "Unless my extrapolations are completely off track."

"Would it be possible for them to then… I don't know what term to use. Apply? Could they apply or transfer that to adults to improve fertility?"

"Again, theoretically… yes. Once they know what more fertile DNA looks like in each species, they could potentially develop a weave that would make that change in an adult. The same way we've developed weaves that change cells containing chronic or genetic diseases."

Lily rubs the bridge of her nose. "So they could conceivably rally people to support them by dangling improved fertility as a carrot."

"I'm so confused," I admit. "I know what they're doing is wrong, but increasing fertility isn't a bad thing overall, is it?"

Percy smiles sadly. "Remember that our lives are longer than humans', and we're harder to kill—we heal faster and are susceptible to fewer life-threatening illnesses. When you factor in our lifespan to a comparison between fertility rates, we're actually just as fertile as humans. Well, we are when we mate within our own species. Cross-species mating can be a little more difficult. But even knowing how long their lives are, people get impatient and want things *now*, especially things like babies. Or they want their babies closer together. So the concept of improved fertility will appeal to a lot of people."

"But it will increase community population levels." Which doesn't sound bad in and of itself, but there would definitely be a change in world dynamics if humans were suddenly outnumbered. The CCA could potentially achieve their goal without ever even stating it or using the word "human," simply by appealing to the community's desire for babies.

"And we don't know how the magic will react to that," Percy reminds me. "There's a reason for the current population balance. The magic protected us when it looked like humans would wipe us out. If things go the other way, it may very well step in again, and we might not like the result."

"This is so complicated," I mutter. "I feel like I'm doing a jigsaw puzzle without a picture of what the end result should be."

"Well," Percy stands, and we all follow suit, "hopefully these raids will give us a clearer picture. Sam, I'm sorry, you need to stay here, and someone's going to stay with you."

I sigh. I'm not really surprised by that. I never expected to be included in the actual raiding—I'm not trained for that—but if things were running as usual, I would have been in the control center. Potentially having a target on my back, though... "Fine," I concede. "But nobody else needs to stay."

"I disagree," Percy declares with a steely look. He's so mild-mannered, it's easy to forget that he's literally the ruler of the world and is able to wield existential magic. And then he'll whip out his authority like now, and I'm sharply reminded.

"I'm with Percy," Aidan says. "Sam, even putting aside the fact that you're likely one of the CCA's earlier test subjects and they'd probably want to retrieve you, a lot of shit has happened to you in the past twenty-four hours. You may still not be past the reactions to the compelled shift this morning. Leaving you alone would be stupid."

A glance around the room shows a lot of sympathetically agreeing faces. I shrug. "It's your call."

"I'll stay," Lily volunteers. She smiles at me. "Sam and I will hold down the fort. Just don't forget to update us."

"Regularly," I add. "Don't leave us sitting here wondering all night."

"Will do," David promises. He holds out my new phone. "Here—switch your SIM over and start using this. I've set up a panic button feature. Hit this button"—he indicates the power button—"three times fast. It'll send a panic alert to all of us on the team and automatically activate the GPS so we can find you."

"If someone's kidnapping him, they're unlikely to let him bring his phone," Elinor says, frowning. "But I guess it's a start."

"We're investigators, Elinor," David says dryly, already halfway to the door as I sink back into my seat, clutching my new phone. "Once the panic button alerts us and gives us his initial location, we'll be able to find him. I'll call Gideon and tell him and Andrew to bring Alistair and meet us."

"Be discreet," Percy warns, following him. "We still don't know whether our phone encryption has been compromised. Take care, Lily, Sam. We'll check in."

And with a jumble of goodbyes, they're gone, leaving me and Lily alone in the suddenly empty-feeling apartment.

CHAPTER THIRTEEN

IT'S NEARLY three hours before Lily's phone rings.

Three. Hours.

To say that I'm wound up would be like calling the Pacific Ocean a bit of water. I mean, I get it, first they were prepping, then they were actually raiding, and they didn't really have time to be giving us a play-by-play. But seriously, would a text while they were en route have hurt?

Ugh.

Anyway, Lily answers practically as soon as the ringing starts, before I've managed to scrape myself off the ceiling. My shifter instincts may need some honing, because her reaction time was way better than mine.

She's uh-huh-ing and yes-ing, but she makes eye contact with me and smiles and nods. Part of me relaxes, and I wait impatiently for her to end the call.

"It's all good," she says finally. "Raids in three compounds were successful. They found the kidnapped couples—the final count hasn't come in yet, but Andrew says it looks like all of them. They also made a ton of arrests and confiscated heaps of research and records."

I sag in my seat, the last modicum of stress deserting me. "Good. Okay. That's great. Uh, did he say whether the couples had been… uh, experimented on?"

She grimaces. "Unfortunately, they're not sure. The couples were all forced to give blood and tissue samples, and they were all examined more than once, but nobody told them what was going on, so they don't know anything. We'll have to hope the interrogations and records can tell us more."

Nodding, I process that. The thing about sorcery is that it doesn't necessarily require surgery. I didn't think to ask David earlier if the genetic adjustments could have been made nonsurgically.

"I need the bathroom," I realize suddenly. The adrenaline is seeping away, and my body is reasserting normal functionality. "I'll be back. Uh, did they say if they were coming back here?" I edge toward the door, trying not to squirm. That would be totally uncool, and as close as Lily and I are, she'd never let me forget it if I danced from foot to foot like a kid.

Of course, she'd also never let me forget it if I wet my pants.

"They're not sure yet. Andrew said they were still processing the compound and overseeing the removal of evidence."

"Sure." I give up on maintaining dignity and make a mad dash for the bathroom. Lily's laughter follows me down the hall.

I've done my business and am washing my hands when my skin begins to tingle. My inner energy is rising, crawling beneath the surface, my cat pushing, pushing.

A side effect of the compelled shift? Fuck, am I going to spontaneously shift? I have to get out of here—the door is closed, and Lily will come looking for me eventually, but I really don't want people saying "Remember the time Sam spontaneously shifted and got trapped in the bathroom?"

I shut off the water, swipe my hands with a towel, and open the door. It's not until I'm halfway down the hallway that I realize I can smell more than just Lily in the living room.

Strangers.

In my apartment.

Fuck.

What do I do? Is Lily okay? I have to make sure she's okay, but… I'm pretty sure I'm smelling three different strangers. Maybe more. There are a lot of scents in the apartment right now, since there were so many people here earlier, and I'm still not used to filtering them.

I would be useless against three assailants. Let's face it, I wouldn't be much good against one. But I have to help Lily.

And I definitely can't stand frozen here in the hallway. If I can smell them, they can smell me. The only advantage I have is that my scent is all over the apartment, so they may not yet have realized that I'm in the hallway now and not the bathroom.

Or that I'm here at all? Could the residual layers of scent have thrown them off? Maybe Lily told them I went with the others? Maybe they're not shifters and can't smell me at all? How do the other species differentiate between each other? Why did I never ask?

Fuck. I don't know what to do. I wish Gideon was

here. I wish they'd all come back right now and save the day. My stomach is all twisty and heaving.

Oh my fuck, I can't believe I'm this fucking stupid! The panic button. Where's my phone? Is it… did I leave it on the coffee table or on the kitchen counter? I took it with me when I went to get water, because I didn't want it out of reach in case it rang.

From the living room, I hear movement.

Fuck.

Fuck.

Think, Sammy. Sweat trickles down my spine.

I had it in my hand when I went back to work. I was checking the screen every two minutes.

The vague sounds of movement turn to footfalls, incredibly light, but still audible to my shifter senses.

Fuck. My brain won't *work*.

It was beside my laptop. I kept looking at it. So it's probably still—

No. I put it in my pocket so I'd feel it vibrate but not be tempted to look at it all the time.

I fumble in my pocket, and yes, it's still there. Panic is clouding my brain. I'm starting to feel lightheaded as adrenaline pumps through my system, but the footsteps are coming closer.

I don't bother pulling the phone out, just feel for the button. Three times, David said. Three times fast.

There's a short, sharp vibration in my hand, and I pray that's a sign of success and not the phone asking me to input a passcode.

The light at the end of the hall is blocked out.

It's too late to worry about the panic button.

Seizing every last iota of courage inside me, I charge toward the figure.

I need to see if Lily is okay. Maybe my charge will distract them and the two of us can make a run for it.

The figure makes a startled noise, and then I'm ramming into it with all my weight and the power of my running start behind me. It's not much, and he's huge—demon, maybe, or hellhound. I don't have time to analyze his scent—but he wasn't ready for me and stumbles back a few steps, enough for me to get past him and into the living room.

And skid to a stop.

There aren't three of them.

There are five.

And there's no way Lily can make a run for it, seeing as she's lying bound and gagged on the floor, eyes closed, bleeding from her head.

Fuck. *Fuck!*

What do I do?

Make a decision.

They've already started moving toward me when I spin and dart toward the slider out to the tiny balcony. I'm four floors up, but cats always land on their feet, right?

I hope so, because there's no way I can take on five of them, but I can hide, get the others here, and rescue Lily. Maybe if they're all searching for me, I can double back and help Lily before the others even get here.

Resolutely ignoring the fact that I have no idea where I'm going to hide—I'll worry about that once I'm out of arm's reach—I get the slider open and make it out onto the balcony.

Two more steps, then jump up on the rail. Hope that shifter instincts will help me do that, because there's no way human me could ever have done it. Should I shift? Do I have time for that?

One more ste—

A hand catches the back of my shirt.

No.

I tear free and stumble forward, but then there's a tight grip on my arm and a blow to the side of my head that makes my ears ring.

I blink and yank forward. I'm so close. I just need to get free.

Forcing back tears of frustration, I struggle hard against my captor's grip as I watch the balcony railing move farther away. The asshole drags me back inside and another guy—also huge, but an incubus—closes the slider and flips the lock, adding a few seconds to any further escape plan I might have.

I'm dragged over to the sofa and shoved down. My new shifter reflexes kick in and I manage to land reasonably gracefully, then bound back up to my feet.

The asshole shoves me down again. "Stay there." He sounds pissed, but so am I, and I'm back on my feet instantly, glaring at him, daring him to shove me again.

The backhand I don't see coming knocks me to the floor. I lie there, my cheek on fire and my eye feeling like it's going to explode out of the socket. My ears are ringing again, and I can't quite get my brain to focus.

Hard hands grab my arm and haul me to my feet. I sway slightly, my head spinning violently, but manage not to throw up or fall over. I'm shoved back onto the sofa.

"Do as you're told, and it will hurt less."

I swallow down bile but don't bother to respond. My gaze lands on Lily, still unconscious—I hope. I've never stared at a woman's chest so hard—or at all—in my life, but finally I make out a tiny movement. She's breathing. That's enough for now.

One of the other invading bastards moves toward me, and I look up, blinking away the dizziness.

It's like someone just knocked me over again.

I lean forward and vomit, and I'm so off-kilter, I don't even care about the rug or the fact that some of it's on my feet.

Because I know this man.

Only he's not who I thought he was.

The distinct scent of a sorcerer cuts through the tang of vomit, and in the next second, a hand grips my hair and yanks my head back.

"Hello, Sam."

I stare up at my childhood doctor.

Fuck.

CHAPTER FOURTEEN

I'VE HAD SHIFTER senses for less than a day, but already, losing them is agony. Before we left the apartment, my captors blindfolded me and inserted shifter-strength nose and earplugs. Then, for good measure, they put a bag over my head. I can't see, hear, or smell, and I'm freaking out. Everything feels surreal—every movement exaggerated—and if it wasn't for the solidity of whatever I'm lying on, I think I'd go insane.

Every time the lack of sensory input from my eyes, ears, and nose starts to overwhelm me, I beat back the panic by focusing on the hard, slightly vibrating surface under me. I think I'm in the back of a van or truck. Maybe an SUV? And we're in motion. But I can't tell how long it's been or where we're going or anything like that. Time seems to stretch out. How long is this taking?

I make myself take a deep breath of the musty air inside the bag and begin slowly counting in my head.

One…

Two…

Three…

Four…

Five…

By the time I reach ten, I'm calmer. Don't get me wrong, I'm still freaked the fuck out, but I can think. The panic isn't whipping away my sanity.

I just have to focus on the solidness under me and the beat of my pulse in my aching face.

Okay. Think.

My hands and feet are bound, but unlike Lily, I'm not gagged. Probably because gagging someone who's wearing nose plugs is a good way to suffocate them. But before we left the apartment, they told me that if I made a sound, they'd kill Lily. Given that all my neighbors are human and wouldn't be able to help, I wasn't prepared to risk Lily's life or theirs. Instead, I focused on dragging my vomit-splashed feet as much as possible, leaving a scent trail for the others to follow. My feet are all scraped up now, but my street has CCTV cameras, and I know Percy can access them. With a strong scent trail to show the team where we were loaded into the vehicle, they'll be able to identify it and track it faster.

I hope.

Because unfortunately, they did pat me down and take away my phone. The last I saw it, it was on the coffee table beside Lily's, which was lit up with a call from Gideon. Our captors briefly considered having me answer it and say Lily was in the bathroom, but then decided I couldn't be trusted and that silence would be more benign.

Of course, they don't know that I'd managed to get an alert out. Lily not answering in these circumstances isn't benign at all.

So… team alerted. Scent trail left. Lily alive. Panic

held at bay. There's nothing else I can do until we get to wherever we're going.

I've been trying really hard not to think about the fact that Dr. Tish is a sorcerer. It's just a guess on my part, but I'd say he's one of the sorcerers who created the DNA-altering weaves. I wish I'd asked David their names when he said he'd worked it out.

Not that it really matters.

What's important is what they know. They obviously know that I'm no longer human... but do they know what we know? Or did we manage to keep it secret?

And what does Dr. Tish plan to do with me? If they were beginning phase two of their plan, then they wouldn't need a phase one subject—would they?

I'm still turning it all over in my head and trying to work out what the best stalling tactic would be while I wait for the others to find us, when I feel a change in acceleration. We're slowing down. That makes me realize that we've been moving at a steady pace for a while now, no stopping and starting. We must have left the city a while back. I wish I hadn't let panic overtake rational thinking earlier—if I'd been more aware of time, I could make a guess now as to what direction we went in.

Too late for that.

The vehicle slows even more, and then finally comes to a stop. Sharp, edgy butterflies take flight in my stomach, and I take a deep breath of musty bag air. I need to be ready for anything.

The vehicle rocks slightly, and I find myself straining in a desperate attempt to sense *anything*. My only warning is a slight displacement of air over my bare feet, and then I'm being hauled up and dragged out.

There's dirt under my feet, not pavement or gravel. Dirt and stones and sticks. That's another signpost seemingly pointing toward a rural location. Then my feet hit wood as I'm hauled upward again—steps?—and now there's… concrete. Or maybe stone.

And it stretches endlessly.

The panic starts to rise, but I force it back down.

No. Count.

I need to try and judge the distance from the entrance to wherever I end up, so I begin counting, matching the pace to the jostling rhythm of my captors' steps as they drag me along. I'm glad I'm not being carried, as this at least gives me contact with something fixed, but my feet are getting really banged up by all this dragging.

Finally, *finally*, I'm dumped on the floor. The side of my face hits it, and the pain flares again. I lie there, the gritty, cold surface beneath me a lodestone, it and my aching cheek my only contact with reality. In the next moment, someone hauls me to a sitting position and yanks the hood off. Cool air filters over my face, and I gasp it in, shivering. I hadn't even realized how stuffy and musty the air in the bag really was until this second.

Next, the earplugs are yanked out, then the nose plugs. My senses come screaming back online, the rush of input almost painful after being without, yet so, so welcome. It's a pain I will gladly embrace. I struggle to sort through what I'm smelling and hearing—a voice giving orders, others responding… the soft hum of some kind of machinery. An air conditioner? I can smell Lily close by and at least three others. Dr. Tish, and one other who was in my apartment. Underlying everything is the sharp bite of disinfectant.

The blindfold is whipped off, and I squeeze my eyes shut against the bright light.

"I've dimmed the lights," Dr. Tish says. "Open your eyes."

I consider disobeying, but ultimately it serves my purpose to see where I am—and make sure Lily's okay. So I squint one eye open, checking the light level, and when my retina isn't seared, I open the other as well and take a quick look around. I appear to be in an office-slash-lab. There's an exam table, a wall of racks containing test tubes and petri dishes, some medical-science-looking machines, a long stretch of stainless steel counter, a desk with a computer, a small seating area, and two big demons—including the asshole who hit me —standing guard at the door.

And Lily. Lying on the floor on her side a few feet from me, eyes open and alert, still bound and gagged but looking utterly focused.

Relief floods me. She's alive. Lily will know what to do.

"I was very surprised when the news went out about the new member of the lucifer's senior team," Dr. Tish says, drawing my attention to him. He doesn't look any different from my memory of him nearly twenty-five years ago, which makes sense, since he's apparently a sorcerer. "How did my dear patient who died so tragically as a teenager end up working for the government? It was especially curious since he was supposed to be human." He eyes me, a certain glint in his gaze scaring the shit out of me. "But you're not human anymore, are you, Sam?"

Okay, that's an obvious one and not something I can get around. I may not know for sure how sorcerers differentiate between species, but I know they can. I shake my head, wincing at the surge of pain the movement causes—my neck, my shoulders, down my arms to my bound hands. "No," I rasp through my dry throat. I stop, cough, and try to clear it.

"So tell me what happened, Sam." Dr. Tish leans against his desk, his expression avid. "Did you change all of a sudden? Or was it more gradual? How old were you when it happened?"

He doesn't know. Whatever information they have, they don't know what we've been doing over the past… fuck, how long has it been now? Still only one day? Or two?

Never mind. What's important is how I can make this work for us.

"I-it happened gradually," I stammer, mind racing. Fuck, fuck, fuck. I wish I knew what had happened with his other subjects. What if he's testing me? What if I say something that trips me up? I need to stick as close to the truth as possible.

And test some boundaries.

I sit as straight as I can, ignoring my screaming muscles. "I'm not telling you anything else until you tell me some things," I declare. My defiance is weakened somewhat by the hoarseness of my voice and the fact that I'm tied hand and foot and sitting on the floor, but hey. You've gotta start somewhere.

Once more, I push aside my fear.

"Do you know what happened to me? Why I'm like this?" There. Let him think I know nothing about the weaves, that we're all completely in the dark about his activities forty years ago.

His eyes narrow. "I'm asking the questions. You're answering them."

I shut my mouth and set my jaw stubbornly.

For a long moment, he stares at me. Then he turns his head to look at the guards. "Kill her."

My eyes go wide, and panic explodes in me as the asshole steps forward, drawing a wicked-looking knife from a sheath at his hip. "No!" *No.* Lily can't die. "No, leave her alone!"

The asshole doesn't even hesitate, walking over to Lily and yanking her upward by the hair, bringing the knife toward her throat. She struggles against his grip and the knife nicks her, the welling blood sending me toward a meltdown.

"No! I'll tell you, leave her alone!" I shout, thrashing around in a desperate attempt to get to her.

"Wait," Dr. Tish says. I can't be sure, but given the fixed way he's staring at me, I don't think he's taken his gaze off me at all.

The asshole pauses.

"Sam, are you ready to tell me what I want to know?"

"Yes," I say immediately. He might be bluffing, but I can't risk Lily. Especially since I'm not planning to tell him the truth.

Fuck, where are the others? Are they tracking us? Was the scent trail I left enough to get them started? Please, please let them be close.

He nods, then gestures to the asshole, who drops Lily and goes back to his post by the door. I wriggle toward her as fast as I can, but she shakes her head, and the cut on her throat doesn't seem to be bleeding too badly.

"I'm sorry," I whisper to her. I'm not that close, so I don't know if she hears me, but her gaze warms slightly and she shakes her head again, so I'm guessing she gets the idea.

"Sam," Dr. Tish snaps, and I turn my attention to him. "You said it happened gradually."

I swallow. "Yes. Uh… first my senses started to get sharper." That makes sense, right? And fits with what happened to me when we started breaking down the weaves. "It-it happened so slowly that I didn't realize, but then one day I-I was at work and I heard—" Fuck, what could I have heard? "—uh, I heard someone who was late for a meeting coming down the hall, and it was then I realized I shouldn't have been able to hear them. Nobody else could."

"And then what?" he prompts. "Wait—I want to record this." He goes around the desk and opens a drawer, pulling out a tiny digital recorder and tapping on the screen. Quickly, he says his name, the date, my name, rattles off a file number—the bastard. I *am not* a file number—then summarizes what I just told him. "Is that correct, Sam?"

I try to remember if I'd said anything different. "Uh, yeah."

He sits in his desk chair and puts the recorder on the surface of the desk. "Continue."

I take a deep breath. "Um, well, after I realized that my hearing was better than everyone else's, I started thinking about it and figured out I was more sensitive to smells and that my eyesight was better. Eyesight was the hardest one to tell, because it was mostly night vision and I didn't go out to completely dark places."

"How old were you when this all started happening?"

Fuck. Fuck. This is the tricky part. Either I'm the exception, and none of his other subjects' weaves broke down, or I'm about to get busted.

Sink or swim.

"I-I'm not sure exactly when it started," I hedge. "I was, uh, thirty-three when I realized." That was well before my first interview with Harold and fits with the next part of the story I'm weaving.

If I get that far.

He nods. "Thirty-three? I wonder if the change was connected to the approach of your second puberty?" He pulls over a pad and pen and jots down a note. "That could have some impact on the efficiency of the current project—a time crunch, perhaps." He seems to be musing to himself, but the words suggest that none of the other subjects changed like I did.

"What happened next?"

I drag my attention back. I'm on slightly firmer ground here, thanks to my work for the last five years. "Other things started to happen. I, uh, lost time occasionally. At first it was always when I was in my apartment, but then one time it happened when I was watering the plants on the balcony." I'm borrowing from a case my old team handled, where a teenage hellhound who had no idea she was a shifter was spontaneously shifting without knowing it. Her single mom worked second shift, so they rarely saw each other in the afternoon or evening, and neither of them knew that the one-night stand that produced her hadn't been with a human. We were called when the succubus who lived across the street saw the kid change and realized that they weren't just standoffish people but had no idea they were part of the community. "The next day, I got a visit from the CSG and they explained that I'd shifted and what I was."

"And welcomed you into the fold, of course." His sarcasm is heavy, and I wonder what his problem is—aside from being a total psychopathic douche, of course.

I try to shrug, but my muscles protest, so I nod instead.

"Hmm. Once you started to shift, did you experience any regression? Periods when you couldn't shift or when you felt human again?"

"No," I say honestly. He doesn't have to know it hasn't been that long. "Do you know what happened to me? Because nobody at CSG has been able to figure it out. Is it an illness I had as a kid? Is that why you visited so often and took all those blood samples?" I want Lily to be fully aware of who he is. She's smart enough to put the pieces together, but confirmation is a good thing.

Dr. Tish looks at me for a long time, tapping his fingers on the surface of the desk—he's going to regret that when he listens to the recording later—and seeming to consider my questions. Finally, he smiles and leans forward, steepling his fingers. He looks like the cliché of every supervillain in every third-rate movie ever made.

"There was no illness," he says. "Not unless you consider having a human mother an illness. Which, I suppose, it is. But in the end, it was what allowed our breakthrough."

I pretend to have no idea what he's talking about, even as the mention of my mother—whoever she is—makes my stomach clench. "W-What do you mean? I-I guessed that my parents weren't really my parents, because neither of them could shift, but… my mother was human? I thought I might have been stolen...." I trail off before I can give myself away.

He waves a hand dismissively, leaning back again. "Not stolen. Too much fuss is made over stolen children. You were purchased."

I gasp. It's like I've been punched. I don't know what's worse, the people I grew up thinking were my parents or the knowledge that my actual parents *sold* me.

Lily makes a low noise, and when I look at her, her gaze is sympathetic. In contrast, Dr. Tish doesn't seem to notice my distress. He's still talking.

"...so we hired a number of human women and gave them a list of approved community men to choose from. Those men were selected by us as having excellent bloodlines and genetic traits that we wanted... which reminds me. Can you partially shift?"

I blink. "I, uh, I've never tried." It's technically true. I'm a little freaked to know that whoever my father was, he was selected for genetic traits. Also, does this mean he doesn't know about me?

Is that surge of hope ridiculous?

Dr. Tish nods and makes another note. "We'll have to try. Anyway, over the following three years, the women had an 82 percent success rate in becoming pregnant. As soon as they conceived, we removed them to a secure facility so the real work could begin." He sounds almost excited now, and I get the feeling I'm in for a long, boastful monologue extolling his brilliance. Not something I'd normally enjoy, but if it gives us the information we need and stalls him while the others find us, I can live with it.

"I don't understand," I say, trying to sound as

confused as possible. "If my father was a shifter, shouldn't I have been born a shifter?"

"That's the genius of our program," he crows. "You *should have* been born a shifter, but our weaves forced your shifter side into dormancy in the womb and allowed the human half to be dominant."

Something about that doesn't seem right to me, but I don't have time to think about it. He starts to ramble about the unprecedented brilliance of his weaves and how the future of the community has been changed forever and humans will soon learn to bow down to their betters. That seems to confirm our theory that this has all been about world domination. I need to get him back on track.

"Wait… so there are others like me?" Could they still be captives after so many years?

"None quite like you, Sam," he says with a look that's completely nonsexual and yet makes me feel dirty and violated. "There were seventy-three modified subjects who lived through the first year. They were all placed with carefully vetted human couples to be raised to legal adulthood. One died in a random car accident, one proved too susceptible to human illnesses and had to be terminated early, and we nearly lost one when the human couple became overly fond of it and tried to run." His cold smile tells me more clearly than words could what happened to that couple. "And then there was you, Sam. Ran away. The couple we placed you with tried to insist that you'd been kidnapped, but with the right incentive, they finally admitted the truth. And then we found your death certificate." He shook his head. "That was a blow. You were just a handful of years from the next stage."

I swallow hard. I never thought I'd be glad that the man who raised me was a raging homophobe. "What was the next stage?"

He shrugs. "Another breeding cycle. We needed to see if the weaves would breed through to the next generation." A wide grin crosses his face. "They did. The last of the subjects from that phase reached legal adulthood last year and were still human." The sudden change from happy grin to scowl is disconcerting. "If I'd known there was a chance the weaves would fail later on, I would have insisted we keep the subjects alive for further testing." My blood runs cold, but he's back to tapping his fingers on the desk. "I wonder if the second generation would also have failed, or if the natural reproduction of the gene pattern will protect it?" He looks back at me. "Do you have children from when you were human?"

Choking down the desire to vomit at the thought of him experimenting on children I don't have, I shake my head. "No. I'm, uh, gay, so it's not as easy for me."

"Really?" He sounds surprised. "I suppose that's why you ran away? We never did find out why."

"Yeah. Uh, so... I'm the only one left from the original, uh, group?"

"You're the only one left from any earlier phase of the experiment," he says bluntly, that cold smile back. "We couldn't risk exposure, so all participants and subjects were terminated once their contribution was complete."

He's so casual while talking about the mass murders of what must have been hundreds of people—the biological mothers, the foster parents, and of course the test subjects from two rounds of experimentation—that the panic I've been keeping at bay begins to creep back in. There's no reason for him to keep us alive… except perhaps to experiment further on me. The weaves were clearly not meant to ever break down, so my existence as a shifter might be something I can use as a negotiating chip.

Somehow. If I can just *think* and work out how.

Where the fuck is my team?

"Your current lack of humanity is slightly concerning. We'll need to run some tests to determine if any of your human DNA remains and try to determine exactly what happened to the weaves. The last time I saw you, they had so successfully bonded with you that you were completely human in every way."

Tests. Okay. Tests take time. Time is what I need right now. "What kind of tests? Blood tests?" I stall, trying to wring out as much information as I can.

"Blood, skin, and semen to begin with. Depending on what we find, we may decide on others."

"That, uh… If I donate samples willingly, is there any chance you could untie me and Lily? My arms and legs are pretty numb."

He stands and walks over to one of the medical units, and I know instantly that I've made a mistake. "Don't worry, Sam. You've told me what I want to know, so there's no need for you to be aware of your misery any longer." He pulls out a small vial and a syringe. "We've found that subjects tend to be more cooperative when unconscious." The ridiculous statement is followed by a little laugh, but I'm too panicked to feel disgust. If he knocks me out, I'll be completely vulnerable. I can't help myself or Lily if I'm unconscious.

I start to struggle, wriggling in a desperate attempt

to… do *something*. Dr. Tish strolls toward me. "Hold him down," he orders, and the asshole leaves his post at the door once more to come and pin me to the concrete floor. With my limbs bound and mostly numb, there's nothing I can do but beg them not to drug me.

It doesn't work.

Dr. Tish injects the contents of the syringe into my neck and straightens. "There you are, Sam. That will just take a moment to kick in." Turning and heading back toward his desk, he adds, "Kill her."

I scream, so loud and so hard that my voice cracks, but already I'm feeling fuzzy and my vision is fading.

The last thing I see before everything goes dark is Lily's blood spraying.

CHAPTER FIFTEEN

My SENSE of smell is the first thing I become aware of as I slowly drift back to consciousness. Undertones of antiseptic, sorcerer, and hellhound are layered around whatever space I'm in.

And there's a human here.

My hearing comes back online next. The faint murmur of electronics. Far-off shouts. And unsteady breathing… not mine.

I open my eyes and stare at the blank, perfectly nondescript ceiling.

And memory crashes back.

Lily.

My chest seizes, squeezing so tight, I can't breathe. Oh fuck, Lily. Tears well up and stream from my eyes, streaking down the sides of my face and into my hair. A sob bursts from me, and I suck in a shaky breath, scrunch my eyes closed, and seize control of myself.

There will be time to mourn later. Now, I need to get out of here.

And make sure Tish and the asshole guard face justice.

Forcing myself to breathe evenly, I open my eyes again and turn my head. There's definitely someone else in here, but either they're too involved in their own trauma to notice I'm awake, or they're giving me time to process. Considering that my nose is telling me it's a human, I vote for option number one.

I'm wrong.

My gaze lands on a young man sitting in a swivel chair about ten feet away. The chair is literally in the middle of the room—there's no desk or table anywhere near it. He's just sitting there, watching me. He looks nervous, though I could have guessed that by the way his breathing hitches and the change in his scent.

"Hello," I croak. I cough to clear my throat, auto- matically lifting my hand to cover my mouth, and realize I'm not tied up anymore. I'm lying on an exam table, but my hands and feet are unbound. I sit up slowly, head spinning, and carefully move my legs to dangle over the side, and then my attention is recaptured by the human —hah, when did I start thinking of them that way?— carefully edging his chair back.

"Uh... hi," I try again. I don't know who he is or why he's here, but I doubt the CCA would have any human members, so chances are, he's a captive or a victim of some kind. And he definitely looks wary of me.

"Hi," he finally says. "Do you... want some water?"

I really do, but I'm hesitant to ingest anything a stranger gives me. Especially here and now.

"I can get it. I need to stretch my legs. Uh, where...?" He points toward a sink on the far side of the room. "Thanks."

Slowly, I ease from the table to the floor, holding on until I'm sure my legs will hold me. My feet are sore. In fact, all of me is sore. Including my balls. Fuck, what did they do while I was unconscious?

Pushing the thought aside, I make my way carefully across the room to the sink. There's a cup dispenser on the wall, and I pull a plastic cup from it—these people clearly don't care a lot about the environment, which is dumb considering how long-lived they are—and fill it with water. Sipping slowly, I turn around and lean against the sink, watching the human. He's standing next to the chair now, fidgeting nervously.

I finish the water and put the cup down. "I'm Sam," I begin, and he jumps.

"Noah," he offers.

Nodding, I wonder what to say next. I can still hear shouting, and I strongly suspect that's a good sign for me, but I won't know for sure unless I check it out. Is Noah going to try to stop me? Is he supposed to be a guard of some sort? Shouldn't a guard have a weapon?

"What are you doing here, Noah?"

He fidgets a bit more, looking away and then back. "I-I can't get out."

I blink. What does he— Is there some kind of biose-curity lock on the door? He's a prisoner too? I look toward the door, but it doesn't appear to have any kind of lock at all.

He follows my gaze, then shakes his head. "No, I mean the main entrance. There are always guards there, and I can't work out how to get past them."

Well, that makes sense. Except… "Who are you, and why are you here *at all*?"

He flushes. "I-I… They were doing tests on me and

some others. I don't understand it. I got home from school one day and my parents were packing and these guys were there. They took me, and I woke up here."

"And they did tests on you."

He nods. "My doctor is here. They did a lot of tests, then they'd make us run on treadmills and smell stuff and all sorts of weird shit. Then one day, the lab assistant came to the dorm room and started giving us these injections. Normally they were really picky about stuff like that—only in the lab, and only when we were strapped to tables—but he just came in and told us to roll up our sleeves and started injecting. He did my three roommates and was about to do me when someone screamed in the hallway, and he and the guard went to look just as one of my roommates collapsed. The other two went down like a second later, and I freaked, because that wasn't normally the way shit happened, so I just collapsed too."

Wait. "You faked... unconsciousness?" I'm pretty sure I know where this story is going, but I don't want to guess wrong and potentially freak him out.

He nods. "That's what I thought I was doing, but it turns out I was pretending to be dead, because they were dead." His voice trembles slightly on the last word.

"And the lab assistant didn't suspect anything? He only injected three, but the fourth magically died as well?"

Noah shrugs. "He was always kind of sloppy. The doctors used to tell him off in the lab all the time."

I shake my head, because I always thought I was fucking lucky after I ran away from home, but this guy is seriously fucking lucky. "And then what?"

He shudders. "They took us to the incinerator. It

was pretty close, but they decided to bring everyone down before they started loading us in, so…" He shudders again, and his expression changes. "I snuck away before they got back."

"And you've just been hiding since?" I can hear how incredulous I sound.

"I can't get *out*," he says, stamping his foot. "This place is huge and it's only half-full, so as long as I keep alert and move around every few days, they don't notice me."

"They don't smell you?" Belatedly, I realize he might not understand and have a frantic moment of panic, because I don't want to be the one to explain it, but he's shaking his head.

"I've heard them say the place still stinks of human, but then they just put it down to the air filtration system." He looks at me warily. "Are you one of them? Because I don't know any other human who knew about the smelling thing."

Fuck. "Uh, I'm not one of them, but I'm not human, either. Although I was. Well, no, I *thought* I was. Although I really was, but… it's complicated. What you need to know is that this isn't a humans vs bad guys situation. It's a good guys who aren't all human vs bad guys thing." The shouting is getting louder, loud enough that he can probably hear it. "Do you know what that's all about?" I wave toward the sound.

"That's why I'm here. The lab assistant was supposed to keep you under, but when the security alert went out, the guards evacuated her to the panic room before she could give you the next dose. They were going to bring you too, but she said she'd gotten the samples and if your friends really wanted you and they managed to get this far, they could have you." He meets my gaze, the hazel of his darkening. "She might change her mind later. The doctors don't like it when their orders aren't followed exactly. But I figured this was the best place for me to be."

My heart leapt when he mentioned my "friends." Finally. "If I get out of here, you're coming with me," I promise. Aside from it being the right thing to do, he probably has a lot of information we can use, considering he's been wandering around a secret research facility for, what... a year? "We need to go find them." I start toward the door.

Noah snorts. "Are you stupid? The guards are still trying to hold them back. If you get anywhere near there, they'll just use you as a hostage."

Uh. Yeah. "Good point."

"We need to wait until the commotion settles, and then I'll sneak out and find out which side won. If it's yours, I'll come get you so your friends don't kill me on sight. If it's not, I'll come get you and we can hide."

I grin. It feels weird on my face, given the circumstances. "My side will win." Percy and the existential magic will make sure of that.

Unless... this is the route the magic wants the world to take?

No. In the past, the magic has always sought to keep humans and the community in balance. This would destroy that balance, so I have to believe that the magic will be on our side. After all, our side only exists in this struggle because we're trying to uphold the mandate set by the magic. If what we're doing is counter to what it wants, Percy would no longer be the lucifer.

Noah looks doubtful, but right at that moment, the lights go out.

"Fuck," I hiss. My eyes adjust quickly, thanks to my shifter senses, and I move toward Noah and grab his arm. He jumps. "It's just me," I say softly. "We need to hide, just in case." I pull him over to the freestanding workstation. It's a shitty place to hide, but it's also the only thing in the room that might work. He stumbles along behind me and crouches when I tell him to, huddling up against the side of the cabinets. I concentrate on breathing, taking in scents and filtering them. When—if—the door opens, I need to know if it's friend or foe—and hopefully, if it's foe, they'll just peer in, assume the room is empty, and move on.

If it was just me, I wouldn't bet on it, but Noah seems to have some damn good luck on his side.

In the distance, the noise has died down. Is that related to the darkness? Or does it mean someone's won?

The lights come back on. Noah starts to stand, but I grab him and pull him back down. The yelling hasn't started again, so I'm guessing that means the fight's over, and we don't know who won. I'm confident, but not stupid.

Well, not always.

We crouch there for what feels like forever, until muscles cramp and the anticipation threatens to kill me. So… maybe ten minutes? And then I hear a sound that makes my heart sing.

"Sam!"

It's faint, shouted from some distance away and muffled by at least one door, but my name is distinct—as is the voice that yells it.

DEMONS DO IT BETTER

There's rhythmic crashing sounds followed by yells of "Clear!" and I realize they're checking rooms, looking for me… and probably any leftover bad guys.

"Sam!"

I stand, pulling Noah up with me. "Come on," I announce. "It's safe now. Just don't move too suddenly until they know it's us." Accidents happen, after all.

"Are you sure?" he asks doubtfully, then jerks to stare at the door.

"Sam!"

They're close enough now for Noah to hear. "I'm sure." We cross the room to the door, but I hesitate. I really don't want to get accidentally hit by a weave or bullet because I startled someone.

"Gideon?" I yell.

All movement outside stops.

"Sam?" Gideon's tone changes. "Sam!"

"I'm coming out. Don't shoot me or anything!" I grasp the doorknob as rhythmic footsteps pound down the corridor, and when we step outside the lab, I see Gideon running toward me, followed by armed enforcers. I take off in his direction, although as sore as I am, it's more like a limping stagger than a run.

That doesn't make it any less sweet when we collide and he snatches me into a hug so hard, I actually squeak.

"Are you okay?" My face is buried in his neck and he's murmuring directly into my ear. I nod, then make myself pull back just enough to answer.

"Yeah. They, uh, took some samples and knocked me out, but…" I trail off, and tears fill my eyes. "Lily."

He squeezes his eyes shut and clenches his jaw. "We know. We… We know." He opens his eyes and lets me go but keeps me close with one arm, raising the other to rub his face. "Percy… He and Lily have known each other for a long time. And the magic gives him some abilities nobody else has."

Fuck. Poor Percy. "Is he okay?"

Gideon shakes his head and smiles sadly. "Not really. I think he'll feel a bit better when he sees you, though."

"Sir?"

Gideon looks over my shoulder, and I turn around in the circle of his arm. One of the enforcers is standing there, Noah firmly in his grip.

"Oh, hey, let him go," I say immediately. "He's human." I feel like an idiot as soon as the words are out of my mouth, and the look the enforcer gives me tells me he thinks I'm one. He's an incubus, and I'm not entirely clear on how they can tell the difference between species, but I know they can. "I mean, he's on our side." I hope. Unless this is a really intricate plan to get a spy into… what? He's a human kid. We're not going to give him high-level access to all our secrets.

Gideon's arm tightens around me. I'm so fucking glad he's here. "Who is he?"

"He's—"

"Able to speak for himself, thank you," Noah snaps, yanking at the enforcer's grip. He'll never get free, but I'm sure it makes him feel better to try. "I'm Noah Cage."

"This is Gideon Bailey," I say, trying to smooth things along. "Uh, Gideon, Noah was brought here and tested upon a while back. He's been trying to get out ever since. It's actually quite a story, but I think maybe he's only going to want to tell it once."

"Yeah, but before that," Noah cuts in, "did you

know about the panic room? Because there should be a lot of people in there right now."

I twist around to look up at Gideon. His face is grim, and my stomach sinks.

"We found the panic room and cleared it," he says. "But several of the higher-level researchers escaped down an exit tunnel."

I don't even bother to ask, because I *know* Tish was one of them. "Why didn't they all escape?"

"There was only one vehicle hidden at the end. Some of the others took their chances in the woods, but we'll find them. The rest figured they had a better chance if they stayed put."

"So it's not over." I just want to crawl into bed and hide.

"It is for now. Come on. The others will want to see you, and there's a lot to talk about."

CHAPTER SIXTEEN

THREE MONTHS LATER

EVERY TIME I walk into our office and see Lily's empty desk, it's like a punch to the gut. For weeks, we left it exactly as it was before she died, but then her family wanted to retrieve her personal belongings, and security started nagging us about it, because apparently they needed to sign off on her file and archive it—which is the most disgusting thing I've ever heard. Lily is *not* a file to be archived—and so we spent an afternoon going through her desk and packing it up. At the time I thought it might be easier once we were done, but I was wrong.

Today, though… today's going to be harder still. Today, Percy wants us to choose a new team member. I can't use the word replacement, because nobody will ever be able to replace Lily, and I feel sick just thinking about it. But we do need another set of hands. We're still dealing with the aftermath of the CCA debacle—

going through all the information we took from their servers and labs, using it to track other compounds and members who escaped the first sweep. Making sure their hack into our system has been shut down. Plus there's the usual caseload—sadly, even with such a huge example of how attempting to take down the lucifer is futile, there are still people trying. So we have a meeting in a few minutes to review the short list of qualified candidates. We each had to nominate three people we've worked with who might be suitable—it was hardest for me, because my experience at CSG has been pretty much only here at head office and only for the past five years as opposed to everyone else's fifty or more... much more.

Gideon comes up behind me and kisses my neck before going to his desk. Discretion is not something he gives a shit about when it comes to me. In fact, he puts his hands—and mouth—on me every chance he gets, no matter where we are. Part of it is because he finds me irresistible, but it's also because he's possessive and jealous and likes the idea of showing people "I'm his." We had a huge fight when he said that, and I ended up kicking him out of my place and not talking to him for a day—okay, maybe it was closer to ten hours—before following it up with a lecture that even I admit was long-winded. He hasn't said it again since then, but I see the smug smirk he gets when he's snuggling me in public. I like being felt up by him, so I let it slide.

At first, I thought there might be trouble with us being openly together at work, but nobody's said anything, and people are really casual about acknowl-edging our relationship. It makes me wonder if Gideon did his growly asshole thing and warned them all to be okay with it.

Meh. It works out for me either way, and I know if it was genuinely a problem, Percy would have said something. He's been busy lately, smoothing a lot of ruffled feathers in the community. The information on the raids got out, but it's been carefully filtered, because the last thing we need is anyone thinking there's some shit-hot fertility treatment in the works and trying to restart the research. So there are holes in a lot of our stories, and it's pretty much only the fact that many, many community couples were abducted and subsequently found at CCA compounds that's preventing widespread outrage. On the plus side, we located Dr. Tish's personal data store at the secondary compound where I was taken. It's actually where most of the experimentation was done in the past and seems to have been his primary residence and lab. At least we can console ourselves with the knowledge that he has to find a new place to hole up. And his notes on the project are incredibly detailed, so we know now what the CCA has been working toward —not domination or even annihilation of humans on the physical plane, but enslavement. That definitely goes to show that people can be asshats no matter what species they are. What makes it even more shocking and downright stupid is that physical species is not eternal, so if the CCA had succeeded, they could very well have returned to the physical plane as humans in their next incarnation and been enslaved by the system they established.

Talk about short-sighted.

Anyway, Tish, the two other sorcerers who helped him develop the weaves, and another senior researcher got away, with the asshole who helped kidnap me apparently driving the escape vehicle. Our people have tracked them halfway across the country already, and I'm confident we'll get them eventually. There aren't many places that are safe for them anymore, since we've been using the information we found in the raids to shut down all CCA strongholds and hideouts. Noah was surprisingly helpful with this, as he'd overheard a lot of conversations while he was sneaking around the underground base that helped us narrow down locations.

Once we finished debriefing Noah and Percy confirmed that his intentions were definitely good, we set him up with an apartment and asked what he wanted to do next. His life was basically a shambles, after all—his parents weren't really his parents and upon handing him over to the CCA had taken their cash and fled; he'd been out of contact with all his friends from his old life for nearly two years and in that time had experienced things that made him unsure he could connect with them again; and—most importantly for Noah—he'd lost his college placement offers. Part of him wants to get back to the life he'd been building for himself, and that includes a degree, but he's now unsure if that life would still fit.

So he's weaseled his way into an internship at CSG and is educating himself on the community while he considers his next steps. I've kind of taken him under my wing. After all, it wasn't that long ago that I was a human educating myself on the community. And fuck knows I have experience with leaving everything in my life behind, including parents who turned out not to be.

Speaking of… in Dr. Tish's research files were the names of my biological parents. My mother was a human hired to take part in the project. She was murdered by the CCA shortly after my birth—everybody who knew about the project and had been to one of the compounds was. I'm not sure how big a loss it is not to have known her, though—she was hired to seduce my father and get pregnant, then give me up. It's literally in the contract she signed. She was assigned my father as a target and initiated—Tish's word, not mine —a relationship with him. They lived together for months before she got pregnant with me and bailed back to the CCA.

My father, on the other hand… Aidan did some checking for me, and he's apparently a decent guy. Tish targeted him because his family line has a reliable genetic history of being able to partially shift, which definitely bred true in me and is now one of my favorite things to do, second only to licking Gideon's abs. He was single back then, but about ten years ago, he got married. I'm not sure if I want to meet him or not. I don't even know if he knows I exist—Tish's records show that my mother left without telling him, but I recently learned in a very embarrassing experience that I will never forget that pregnancy is something that can be scented very early on. So he might have known and been waiting for her to mention it. I can't know if he was upset about her leaving or if he looked for her unless I ask him, although Gideon and the others have offered to do some low-profile digging.

I guess I'm just not ready to know.

On the plus side, I've got time to think about it. My life is a lot longer now than I ever thought it would be.

"Sam, you ready?"

I snap out of my deep thoughts and force a smile for David. "Sure, coming."

In the meeting room, Percy passes around manila folders that have the profiles of the shortlisted candidates in them. "We'll go through these in order first—a quick rundown, any questions you want to ask—and then at the end we'll discuss who would fit better."

I'm only half listening, though, because I already started shuffling through the profiles, and the third one stopped me in my tracks. "Um, excuse me, who nominated Alistair?" I look around the table.

"I did," David says, just as Andrew wiggles his fingers in my direction and Elinor says, "Me."

"Actually, Sam, everyone did except you. I was surprised by that." Percy raises an eyebrow.

"You didn't nominate him?" Gideon asks, draping his arm over the back of my chair.

"You *did*? Why didn't you tell me?" I'd thought about it—wanted to, because Alistair has the experience and it would be great to work with him again—but in the end it didn't seem right to nominate my best friend.

Speaking of... I turn my ire on Elinor. "Isn't there a rule about you nominating your cousin?"

She shrugs. "Not really. We all have to agree, in the end, and he was just one of the candidates I picked. He made it through Percy's screening, and we're not going to pick someone who can't pull their weight, so why would we have a rule about it?"

There's something not right about that, but I can't quite figure out what it is, so I just glare at her.

"What's the problem here, Sam?" Gideon takes my hand and squeezes it, studying me closely.

Ugh. I shrug. "There's no problem. It just... it feels

weird now. I have to try and be impartial when I really just want to vote for my best friend."

"And on that note," Percy cuts in, "why don't we start reviewing these candidates so Sam can get this dilemma over with?"

Sometimes I really hate being the youngest and newest member of the team *and* having been the product of genetic experimentation. Everyone likes to tease me. I hate being teased.

Under the table, Gideon runs his hand along my thigh.

Well, I guess there's one kind of teasing I'm okay with.

———

THE DECISION IS MUCH TOUGHER than any of us thought it would be, and that's not even taking into consideration the emotional toll of only needing to do this because we lost Lily. The top six candidates are all exceptional, and we spend literally hours weighing them up. In the end, Alistair is our selection. It's actually because of his existing ties with us that we choose him—there was a three-way tie between him and two others. They're all equally qualified in different ways and all have a great track record. The only variable, the thing that put Alistair above the others, is his connection to me and Elinor and the fact that he worked directly with the team when they rescued me.

So we pick Alistair and hope he wants the job, because if he declines, we need to pick between the other two. I'm pretty sure he'll take it, though. It's a great promotion and he likes us. Plus, it will mean he won't have to cower before Vivienne every day. Harold knew what he was doing when he asked her to be their admin.

"Let's just tell him now," Andrew says, eyeing the papers covered in pro/con lists with disgust. "Get it over with, and if he says no, we'll just stay here until it's done."

"He's not going to say no," Elinor tells him. "But I vote for telling him now, too."

Percy pulls out his phone and glances around the table. "Any opposed?"

"No," David says, and Gideon shakes his head as I shrug.

"Then let's take a bathroom break while I call and get him up here."

Alistair, when he arrives and hears our offer, isn't offbeat, flirty, funny Alistair, my best friend, but rather professional investigator Alistair—sharp, questioning, and definitely a good fit for the job. As we expected, he says yes.

"Welcome aboard." Percy's smile is broad but at the same time a little sad. It's hard not to think that we're only doing this because of Lily's death.

"I'm surprised you asked me," he admits. "Thrilled, of course, and honored, but still surprised. I thought with Ellie being on the team already, you wouldn't want another hellhound."

I groan, because for some reason that just never occurred to me.

"We'll be keeping a strict eye on you both," David warns jokingly, but I can tell from the way he's gone pale that he didn't think of it either.

"We'll be good," Elinor promises. "Mostly, anyway.

And Sam's an expert at keeping unruly hellhounds in line."

"Even if he is a cat," Alistair agrees, then ducks when I throw a pen at him, just like he used to when I was admin for my old team.

Looks like the good old days and the exciting future are coming together. It's either going to be fun or leave me in need of a tankerful of brew.

———

As WE LEAVE the office hours later, I slip my hand into Gideon's and lean against him. Maybe he's not the only one in this relationship who's touchy-feely. "Where to tonight, your place or mine?"

My first visit to Gideon's house came right after we left the bunker lab complex. He refused to take me home, saying it was technically a crime scene that hadn't been fully processed, would contain bad memories for me, and wasn't as secure as his place. I let him get away with it because I was too tired and upset to really care that much, and I was curious about his home. It would have to be super organized, right, what with his chronic need to alphabetize cupboards to aid in thinking.

Wrong.

At home, Gideon thinks by constructing Lego sets. He has literally hundreds and a room just for them. He no longer organizes his own belongings, and so his kitchen cabinets are a mess, with things stacked and piled in no apparent order at all, and his wardrobe is not only *not* color coordinated, it's basically just a pile of clothes on a chair and shoved willy-nilly into the dresser. How he doesn't look wrinkled all the time is something

I'm in the process of trying to work out. The lead theory is that he growls and scowls at his clothes until the creases fall out in fear.

Overall, though, his place is bigger than mine, nicer than mine, and even closer to work than mine, which is pretty shocking considering how close I am. We split our time between the two—after Gideon insisted on over-seeing the cleanup and security installation at mine and then approved it as fit to live in again.

"Mine," he murmurs, leaning close so his breath brushes my skin and makes me shiver uncontrollably. I'm still going through my second puberty, and Gideon *loves* how sensitive it makes me. He takes every opportunity to rile me up in the most "innocent" ways. "There's something I want to show you."

"Yeah. I'll bet there is."

His laugh is loud and startles the people waiting for the elevator with us. Several of them edge away, while two step up as though preparing to shield the others. Gideon doesn't laugh a lot at the office, as you can no doubt tell.

"It's fine," I assure them. "He's just remembering that time he ripped the fingers off a suspect." I pat his chest with my free hand. "It amuses him to recall the screams."

Half of them suddenly decide to take the stairs.

"Was that really necessary?" he chides. "You're the one who's been trying to get me to be nicer to people."

"I know, and I feel really bad about it. But this way, we'll get more space in the elevator. It's okay for you, but I'm at armpit level with you and your giant brethren, and I'd rather not have my nose shoved in one because the elevator's crowded."

He's still chuckling over that when we make it out onto the street. It's a nice evening, and I love that we can walk home. It gives us a layer of separation between work and home that doesn't include traffic or being crammed into a bus or train—because armpits, remember? And now that I'm a shifter, there's a whole range of new experiences for me to enjoy while walking. Did you know that you can differentiate between the scent of car exhausts? Aidan taught me before he went back to Ireland, and Alistair has been coaching me since. I can reliably pick the make of most cars now, but still struggle a lot with the model. My olfactory sense and my ability to filter and identify what I'm smelling are getting a lot better. Aidan set me up with some simple exercises—cars being one of them—until he can come back and help me some more. We talked about me spending some time with the local clans and letting them help, but I'm not ready for that yet. After all, I'm a freak—an adult cat who'd never shifted until recently. Who has very little idea about customs within the clan, and is still learning what my body is capable of.

Aidan and Alistair both assured me that it was fine to take things slow. It's probably the only time they've ever agreed. Alistair still holds a grudge over the compelled shift, even though I've reminded him a million times that it was done to me with my explicit consent.

I stop to admire the planter boxes on the steps leading up to Gideon's townhouse. I once asked him how he managed to get the flowers so big and healthy, and he said "by paying an expert gardener."

He gets the front door open, and I leave the flowers to follow him inside.

"Want a drink?" I offer, heading toward the kitchen. "I was thinking pasta for dinner, so I could open a bottle of red wine if you don't want brew."

"In a minute," he says, catching my elbow and towing me in the opposite direction. "I want you to see something."

"Oh, really?" I can't say I'm not up for that. Second puberty, remember? And it's been nearly ten hours since I had my hands all over him. But at the top of the stairs, he turns right. "Wait…" I furrow my brow as he leads me away from the master bedroom. "Do you actually have something to show me? That's not a sexy-times line?" I can't decide if I'm disappointed or curious.

Both.

We walk past the main bathroom and the second bedroom, otherwise known as the Lego Lair, and stop in front of bedroom number three. As far as I know, this is used as a combination guest room and storage room, since there's a small home office downstairs and a proper guest suite on the third floor.

Yep. Three floors. Told you his place was bigger.

He throws open the door, and I gasp, because inside, he's pretty much recreated my living room, albeit a bit cramped.

My eyes narrow. "Gideon, did you *move my stuff?*" He sometimes forgets that life has boundaries. Being born to privilege, then turning out to be hot, intelligent, and a total badass has meant that he pretty much gets his way whenever he wants it—except with me.

"Yes, but I'll move it back. It's just here for illustrative purposes."

I'm getting a headache. Only Gideon could have

movers transport the contents of my living room to his house to illustrate a point. "Okay…?"

"You should move in with me."

Bam.

I knew this was coming, of course. It makes sense—we're together all the time anyway. There's no way on this plane or the next that I'm ever letting him go, and I know he feels the same. Really, there's no point in maintaining separate homes.

Yet, it's still a shock.

"This could be your space. You can do whatever you want with it, but when I piss you off or you need some quiet time, it's here. Yours. Sacrosanct. I hate it when you go home, even if it's just for a few hours. I want you here all the time. Or if you don't want to live here, we can find somewhere else—we could even try living at your place." The doubt in his voice makes me laugh. He smiles too, but his gaze is intent on me.

Finally, I sigh and stretch up to kiss him. "Convince me," I murmur, and the smile changes from cautious to devilish. He backs me up until we reach the couch—my couch, the one we've made out on many times—and pushes me down on it, but when I sprawl sideways and reach for him, he shakes his head.

"Sit up." He sinks to his knees.

Ooohhh. My cock goes rock-hard just at the sight. Gideon is wicked fucking awesome at giving head. I sit up and undo my pants, wriggling free of them and my underwear with an eagerness that I don't give a shit about hiding. Gideon chuckles, then grabs my hips and positions me how he wants me.

The first swipe of his tongue is all it takes for me to be "convinced," but there's no way I'm interrupting while he's so focused. His hot, wet mouth is heaven, and the way he looks up at me while he swallows me down is enough to start every nerve ending in my body tingling. I suck in a deep breath and try thinking about dead bugs and moldy cheese, but it's no use—Gideon's mouth is just that good. Plus, I can't look away from him and the sexiest fucking sight ever.

But I'm not coming without him.

Swallowing back a moan as he flicks his tongue against that sensitive spot just below the head, I release the death grip I had on the couch cushions and stroke his horns.

He jerks slightly. He had to know this was coming—it's my favorite thing to do while we're having sex—but he still reacts the same way every time. I might as well be stroking his dick.

Our competitive natures come into play as we each race to make the other come first—him with his incredible mouth and tongue on my cock, and me rubbing his horns. It's not really a coincidence that we both give in at the same time, muscle-tightening, hot-flushing release washing through us.

When my brain comes back online, I'm sprawled across Gideon on the couch. He must have put me there, because I have no memory of it. His hand is sliding lightly up and down my back, one of those idle, casual touches that's so intimate.

There's nowhere I'd rather be than here.

"I think moving in sounds great," I murmur, kissing his chest.

His hand stills. "Oh, yeah?"

I rise up to hover over him. His normal resting bitch expression is softer when we're alone like this, even if he's not actually smiling. It's also so incredibly dear to me. I love that grumpy, scowly face.

"I love you." I've never said it to anyone before, but it's the most natural thing in the world.

A smile so beautiful that I want to take a photo of it breaks over his face, and in the next second, he's sitting up, almost knocking me to the floor. His big arms come around me, and he buries his face against the side of my neck.

"Love you so much."

Nothing ever felt so amazing as this momen—

"Hey, Sam? Gideon? You guys home?"

Gideon pulls back, his scowl firmly back in place. "I'm going to kill him."

Sighing, I kiss him once more, then detangle myself and get up. "Give us a minute, Alistair!" I yell, then add to Gideon, "You can't kill my best friend. That's my job. We also need to get the security weaves upgraded now that you've got a shifter friend. The ones that hold back people with bad intentions don't work on people who genuinely like you and are generally welcome to visit."

As I straighten my clothes, Gideon flops back on the couch and stares at the ceiling. "Life was better when my friends were people who would never dream of walking in uninvited. I blame you for this."

Heading for the door, I blow him a kiss over my shoulder. As annoying as my friends can be, having them is something I'll gladly accept blame for.

Want to read a Sam and Gideon bonus scene? There are two ways to grab it:

Subscribe to my monthly newsletter
(bit.ly/LouisaMBonus)
OR
Join my Facebook group, RoMMance with Becca &
Louisa (look for the pinned post).

And the mayhem at CSG continues with Andrew and
Noah in *One Bite With A Vampire*.

ALSO BY LOUISA MASTERS

Here Be Dragons
Dragon Ever After
The Professor's Dragon

Hidden Species
Demons Do It Better
One Bite With A Vampire
Hijinks With A Hellhound
Sorcerers Always Satisfy

Met His Match
Charming Him
Offside Rules
Between the Covers (M/F)

Joy Universe
I've Got This
Follow My Lead
In Your Hands
Take Us There

Novellas
Fake It 'Til You Make It (permafree)
Out of the Office

After the Blaze

ABOUT THE AUTHOR

Louisa Masters started reading romance much earlier than her mother thought she should. While other teenagers were sneaking out of the house, Louisa was sneaking romance novels in and working out how to read them without being discovered. As an adult, she feeds her addiction in every spare second. She spent years trying to build a "sensible" career, working in bookstores, recruitment, resource management, administration, and as a travel agent, before finally conceding defeat and devoting herself to the world of romance novels.

Louisa has a long list of places first discovered in books that she wants to visit, and every so often she overcomes her loathing of jet lag and takes a trip that charges her imagination. She lives in Melbourne, Australia, where she whines about the weather for most of the year while secretly admitting she'll probably never move.

http://www.louisamasters.com

Printed in Great Britain
by Amazon